11 2012

SMOKE ALARM

A Selection of Recent Titles from Priscilla Masters

The Martha Gunn Mystery Series

RIVER DEEP
SLIP KNOT
FROZEN CHARLOTTE *
SMOKE ALARM *

The Joanna Piercy Mysteries

WINDING UP THE SERPENT
CATCH THE FALLEN SPARROW
A WREATH FOR MY SISTER
AND NONE SHALL SLEEP
SCARING CROWS
EMBROIDERING SHROUDS
ENDANGERING INNOCENTS
WINGS OVER THE WATCHER
GRAVE STONES
A VELVET SCREAM *

available from Severn House

SMOKE ALARM

A Martha Gunn Mystery

Priscilla Masters

This first world edition published 2012
in Great Britain and in the USA by
SEVERN HOUSE PUBLISHERS LTD of
9–15 High Street, Sutton, Surrey, England, SM1 1DF.

British Library Cataloguing in Publication Data

Masters, Priscilla.
  Smoke alarm.
  1. Gunn, Martha (Fictitious character)–Fiction.
  2. Shrewsbury (England)–Fiction. 3. Detective and mystery
  stories.
  I. Title
  823.9'2-dc23

ISBN-13: 978-0-7278-8199-1 (cased)

Typeset by Palimpsest Book Production Ltd.,
Falkirk, Stirlingshire, Scotland.
Printed and bound in Great Britain by
MPG Books Ltd., Bodmin, Cornwall.

With thanks to Mel, Ruth and Debbie – a very profitable lunch at the Royal Shrewsbury Hospital. Thanks for the idea, the inspiration and ultimately – the book. You've earned your free copies! And also to Rosie Morris, whose informative book brought events to life.

PROLOGUE

24 February, 1968

The end of the day was worst, when the nurses locked the door and she was shut in with all the others. Incarcerated. There were so many steps she must go through properly or she would not sleep and instead spend the night shouting and screaming like all the others, begging to be allowed to go through the necessary ritual again to find the elusive Sandman, the one her mother had told her about, who ensured oblivion right through the night. If she could find Him there would be no nightmares or screaming fits, no visitations or bed-wetting. Nothing. Simply nothing. These nights all she wanted was for the black velvet curtain to hang in front of her eyes and block out the terrifying visions; the visions which were shared in one form or another with the other occupants crammed like cattle into the ward. She moved her eyes to look, keeping her head and neck rigidly still. None of them liked to feel they were being watched. And yet they were – all of the time. There was no privacy. It was a poor illusion. Around her she heard the others shuffling through their own personal rituals, each one muttering to herself, reminding her of the order of things. They all wished for oblivion. It was their happiest state. Their only happy state. But though she found it difficult to be quiet, screaming didn't help. Instead of indulging her and letting her try again to find the perfect sequence that looped towards that special, hidden place, the nurses would tell her she was too noisy and disturbing the others, and then they held her down to give her an extra injection. It made her swim into a dreadful and uncertain place full of mists and spirits. It was a black, squelching quagmire into which she sank, drowning in the thick sludge. It was the worst place, a sucking, vampire place from where she could not escape, a place where she knew all around her was awfully wrong but was powerless to do anything to right it; she could only snivel and cower from her fear. So she made sure not to break the ritual but to keep quiet and still. And hope that the welcome black velvet curtain would drop across the stage.

Soon after arriving (how long ago was that? She didn't know), she had worked out a system of perfect ritual. The first step towards tranquillity, or karma, was to enter her bed area with her arms straight down by her side as though glued to her thighs. This ensured that the fibrous membrane which protected her from the others was not pierced. It was equally important that she entered her magic space still wearing all her clothes. *All* her clothes, mind, coat too. Sometimes a hat, even gloves, if it was winter and she had worn them throughout the day. No matter how much the others laughed at her *they* were on the outside, *she* on the inside. Now she was safely alone, in her protected environment, as long as *no other patient* crossed that invisible line which marked out *her* space. As long as no one pierced the bubble. Step one completed. But she couldn't relax. Not yet. Once inside things could still go wrong.

She slipped out of her cardigan, sliding it down her arms very, very slowly, making sure none of it touched the floor because that would contaminate it and mean she would not be able to wear it tomorrow. Safely.

She only had the one cardigan so if she couldn't wear it she would be cold. Still, if it touched the floor at all it would have to be washed. Twice. By her. The nurses would not wash it for her. They would refuse to indulge what they saw as an 'illness'.

So she had worked out a way to be absolutely sure that the cardigan was not contaminated. It was not allowed to go any nearer than two inches from the floor. Two inches which she measured herself with her eyes.

Tonight she managed it all very well and was pleased with herself, allowing herself a mental pat on the shoulder, glad that Nurse Gowan had cleaned the black plaster marks off. They would insist on sticking a plaster on when she had had one of the blood tests to check the levels of drugs in her body were not too high. And removing the plaster left an unsightly black mark which she was conscious of. But the mark had been removed. She would sleep tonight, she was sure. She hung the cardigan on the coat hanger and looped it over the hook on the wall before slipping her feet out of her shoes and placing them, side by side, heels to the back, only the tips of their toes peeping out from underneath her chair.

So far so good. She heaved a sigh of relief.

Although the ward was overcrowded with patients' beds along the walls, top to toe as well as down the middle, she was barely conscious of the others around her, all completing their own nightly dance, except to be aware that this was a very quiet night.

Her nightdress lay on her pillow, carefully folded, its short sleeves splayed out so they would not crease, the pillow with its open end facing the wall. That, too, was important. And again it had something to do with the Sandman. It kept her good dreams inside it and stopped nightmares from entering, firstly through the pillow and after that, climbing her hair and knocking on her skull. Finding a way, somehow, along the roots through her scalp, into her head and infecting her brain with more awful terrors. To try and lock out this train of thought she started breathing more deeply, more slowly, as the doctor had shown her. In, hold, out. In, hold, out. She smiled, again rather pleased with herself. It did help. He was right. She would tell him so – tomorrow. It did help her gain control. She removed her blouse and folded it symmetrically so the buttons were dead centre, three buttons done up and exposed and the cuffs folded up – just a little. Not too much. She performed the next task very, very quickly, removing her vest and brassiere and tucking them underneath the dream pillow, out of sight but ready for the morning when she awoke.

The look of worry never quite left her face. It always looked strained and unhappy because she was always waiting for the next thing to go wrong. And there were many things that could go wrong. Too many. But all this anxiety had left its mark. She was a thin, stooped woman, prematurely aged, with a permanent, deep frown line, straight, greying hair and small, anxious eyes which never really looked at anything. What she always prayed for was to be invisible, to blend in so perfectly with her background that no one actually saw her. She wanted to be a wraith. Insubstantial.

Around her the other women were shuffling into their beds,

lying end to end because of the overcrowding. But there was no contact between them. No words spoken, no gesture – friendly or hostile. They were all beings separated by their perception of the world around them. And yet they were too near for any of their strange comfort. Some reacted badly to this forced convergence by screaming or kicking the nurses. Some chattered to themselves – nonsense, mainly. Others, like her, were watchful and silent, locked in with their own fears.

She slipped her nightdress over her head then unbuttoned her skirt and slid that down her thighs in perfect time with the nightdress descending, so no sliver of flesh was exposed. She stepped quickly out of it. She had not wanted it to touch the floor and had tried pulling it over her head, but that didn't work either. Her body felt too vulnerable. Naked. When the skirt was folded she sat on the side of her bed to remove her tights, which must then be tucked underneath her skirt, out of sight. It was all right for her outer clothes to be on show but not her undergarments. This was important. *Everything* was important.

She stood up so she could fold the sheets back in a tidy, triangular shape, then sat down on the edge of the bed, swivelled round and pulled the sheets and blankets up to her shoulders in one skilled sweep. Then she was ready to sink back against the pillow and hope that tonight would be one of the good nights.

When she first lay down the lights were still on so she did not dare close her eyes but kept them wide open and fixed on a small mark on the ceiling. A mark which could also indicate whether she would have a peaceful night because it could change, looking one minute like a fish or a hound, a bloodstain or a cloud, or anything else, sometimes changing every second. After the lights were turned off she continued to fix on the spot where the mark was. The lights were supposed to be turned off at nine o'clock precisely. It upset her very much if the lights were extinguished either earlier or later than this formally agreed time but tonight was a good night, the nurses punctual in switching them off.

So far so good, she thought again. At her head she heard another patient breathing slowly, practising the same relaxation techniques that the doctor had shown *her*. It annoyed her that he shared her therapies with others. They should be only for her.

A personal plan. At her feet was another woman, already snoring noisily after her medication. She lay against the pillow, relieved that tonight she had got it all so right and wondering what shape the mark would assume in the dark.

Hopefully an angel. An angel of sleep.

ONE

The smell of smoke seeped into her dream, teasing around in the air, swirling like mist over water. Still in her dream she sniffed and smelled and wondered what could be burning. In dreams we use and translate our senses, adding little pieces of fiction to rationalize it all. And so it was with her. She sniffed and seemed to smell wood smoke, even seeing the flames, crackling and spitting at her like a fire-tongued cobra. Still in her sleep, she smiled. It reminded her of something pleasant. A barbecue on a summer's evening. Roasting pork. Now her dreams took flight across the oceans and deposited her elsewhere, somewhere equally pleasant, to a South Sea island, waving coconut palms fringing a sparkling sea. In her dream, Christie Beech fumbled at the connection until she remembered, while still the charcoal burned. She had read, somewhere, that the scent of human flesh cooking smells just like that – roasting pork. Cannibals from the South Seas, she mused dreamily, called edible man Long Pig. She smiled into her pillow. Long Pig.

At some point the smoke drifted into her conscious mind, so she felt alarm in that last second before waking. She sat up. And began to cough. Then she heard the noise. Crackling, roaring, glass breaking and a terrified scream.

And finally she was properly awake, knowing that this was no dream but reality. If she didn't get out of here she would soon be Long Pig.

She choked on the smoke of her own home which was being destroyed. She had to find the door. Get out.

Where was the door?

The light didn't work – she hadn't really expected it to. She put her hand out, tapping for something familiar to anchor her bearings, picturing the layout of her bedroom. She was sliding out of bed to the floor. Smoke rose, didn't it? So she must creep along the floor underneath the smoke. She crawled around her bed. Now the door should be in front of her. Her eyes were smarting as she tried to peer through the smoke. If only she could see something familiar: the mirror, a picture. Feel something solid: wall, window, door. Help!

The noises were increasing now. Glass cracking, flames devouring. Someone screaming. Not her.

It was that that galvanized her into desperation. 'Addie!' she screamed over the noise. 'Addie.' She could not call again. She was coughing too much. Something terrible tugged at her mind. 'Father?'

But her brain, like her room, was filling up too quickly with smoke. If she did not escape now she would die.

Long Pig.

Die along with her family? Jude, Addie, Father? All Long Pigs? It was enough to send her, on her hands and knees, to where she thought the door was. But when her hands reached out they touched not a door handle but the feet of the chest of drawers. 'Wrong place,' she spluttered, angry with herself. 'Wrong place. Try again.' She coughed again, only this time she heard her lungs dragging the smoke in, her breath rasping noisily. She tried to wipe her eyes, tears of frustration bathing them. Oh, if only she could see. But rubbing only irritated them so she could not keep them open. They streamed. She wiped her nose with the back of her hand and tried to fight off the rising panic, tried to think. Rationally. There were two chests of drawers in her bedroom, both along the back wall, one either side of the bed which she believed she had rounded. If she had touched the one near the door it should be . . . here. She groped around for it. If it was the other then in her confusion she had got out of the wrong side of the bed and was nearer the window. Too high to jump out. She would have to skirt round the bottom of the bed again to reach the door. But where was she? Near the door or the window? One meant possible life; the other probable death. It wasn't a great choice, was it, to leap or burn?

She could smell the pork. Choking now she groped around with her left hand and touched . . . nothing. Her right hand. The bed. So she would have to manoeuvre round the foot of the bed to reach the door. And safety?

She had little time to work it out.

Even in the dark she could see the smoke swirling around, feel it. Taste it. She pressed her face to the floor, struggling to breathe air. Every breath now was more difficult, but she must breathe or she would die. She must get out. There were the others. She must save them. The others. She coughed and already seemed to hear a death rattle in it.

She could feel the heat rising.

Had anyone raised the alarm? Was anyone going to help her and her family?

She heard wood splintering. Help? A fireman with an axe?

She crawled around the foot of the bed. She thought she had her bearings now, helped by the mental image she had pinned in her mind. Think. Think bed. Think window. Think door. Door. She had reached it. She groped upwards for the handle. Thank God,' she breathed. 'Thank you, God.' She depressed the handle. Pushed. It was locked. She fumbled around. Where was the key?

She was lost. Her daughter, her son and her father-in-law. All lost. Long Pig.

She screamed.

And a finger dialled triple nine.

In all the years that Colin had heard the alarm sounding in the station and they set off through the streets, blue light strobing, siren screaming, he wondered what would be at the end of it. Most of the time not a lot. A bit of burnt toast that had set the smoke alarm off, and before anyone bothered to investigate someone panicked and dialled 999. Of course, he thought as he took his place on the seat and strapped himself in, he might be a bit more lucky tonight. It might be something a bit more dramatic: a car accident where the victim had to be cut from the wreck. Personally he rather enjoyed those jobs, slicing through the doors of a beloved vehicle like a can of baked beans, particularly if the vehicle was a Mercedes or a Porsche or a Lexus. Once he'd sliced through the door of a Jaguar XJS to find a quivering octogenarian inside. That had given him a certain buzz. But too often there was a complete and utter lack of drama. People got stuck, didn't they? Kids with fingers down plugholes, fat people in bathrooms, their backsides jammed solid into the toilet seat. Nothing but embarrassment there. And no kudos for the rescue team. And then there was the fireman's best friend, the old chestnut of cats in trees. So Colin's heart had almost stopped racing when he was summoned to the scene. Almost.

This was a house fire.

As they rounded the corner, siren shrieking out its message, *Out of the way, out of the way, we stop for no one and nothing*, he knew that this was the real thing. The real McCoy. The event they had been trained for. A proper, lethal, blazing fire. Smoke and flames streaming through blackened and cracked windows. People trapped inside. A chance to be a hero. Adrenaline pumped into his bloodstream. Even as they pulled up and started to assess the scene a window smashed and flames burst out gloriously, licking the walls with beautiful ferocity like a fiery, victorious tongue, and even though the hour was late and the house detached and in its own grounds it was watched with *oohs* and *aahs* by an awed bevy of bystanders, as though it was a fireworks party. But Colin knew different.

This was no party.

The boy stood on the burning deck.

His favourite poem since he'd been a child.

'Good grief,' Tyler, the station chief, exclaimed. 'Good friggin' grief. I just hope no one's in that inferno. Better get some back-up, Agnew. We've no chance of sorting this one out on our own.' He grinned and quoted the famous Jaws movie line about needing a bigger boat with a poor attempt at a Yankee accent.

Colin was already connecting the hose to the fire hydrant and left Carol Jenkins, a junior fire officer, to make the call appealing for reinforcements.

The minute she was off the line he shouted to her, jerking his head towards the bystanders. 'Try to find out, will you, from that lot over there, whether anyone's inside. And let's get some barriers up, keep 'em away. Don't want no heroics.'

Carol addressed the entire crowd. 'Anyone in there?' she shouted. 'Does anyone know if someone's in that house?'

She had to recruit every decibel available to her normally soft voice to be heard over the deafening noise of jets of water, sirens, the yells of police and firemen and, worst of all, the crackle of the greedy God Vulcan as he consumed what must have been until a little while ago a lovely period house in a very desirable Shropshire village, Melverley, whose usual drama was flooding from its two rivers, the Vyrnwy and the Severn. As he aimed the jet of water through a broken upstairs window it struck Colin that Melverley Grange was a beautiful place. Victorian, Gothic, huge. It must have been someone's treasured home, their pride and joy. Probably. Not now. Would it ever be again? His mind battled with the sums, the thousands and thousands of pounds of mortgage repayments, the years of hard work. All going up in smoke.

The cost of restoration would be enormous. He just hoped they were insured.

It was cruel to witness the destruction of such a beautiful place. It was the worst fire he'd ever attended. Just for a moment he almost wished that the call-out had been a cat up a tree.

Even from here the heat from the inferno was intense enough to singe his eyebrows. It was a scene right out of hell. The demonic figures were his own colleagues dancing in their High Viz suits. He glanced to his left. Carol was talking to a man in a black anorak. Even under the stress of the moment, Colin smiled. In her uniform and yellow hard hat with sturdy boots you'd never have known Carol was a woman, let alone a petite size eight beauty. Though he knew her well, apart from her height even he wouldn't have been able to pick her out from the figures silhouetted against the fire, trying to put it out, make sense of it all. Restore order. Ah, well.

He wondered what the man in the black anorak was saying as Carol pointed at the property, entirely ablaze now. They were losing the battle with Vulcan. The God of Fire was winning.

If anyone had been inside Colin knew it would be hopeless trying to save them. The best they could hope for would be the recovery of bodies, probably charred by now. As if to underline his point at that very moment the first floor caved in spectacularly and the flames leapt, triumphantly, out of the windows.

A police car hurtled around the corner. PC Gethin Roberts had already had more than his fair share of drama. His career, though brief, had been eventful. One could say he'd been lucky – or

unlucky, depending on one's point of view. As he caught sight
of the scene ahead of him Roberts squared his shoulders, stuck
out his pointed chin and trusted he looked proficient, professional
and just a little older than his twenty-six years. As he gulped
and swallowed his Adam's apple bobbed in his neck, giving him
the look of a nervous chicken. He pulled the squad car up next
to the second fire engine. Let the others do the crowd control
bit, he thought, as he threaded his long legs out through the car
door. He wanted a bit of the action.

'"Scuse me.' Elbowing the fire officer in front of him out of
the way, he addressed a stout, middle-aged female spectator who
appeared transfixed by the sight of the sizzling flames, tilting her
face upwards towards them – in worship, it appeared.

Roberts cleared his throat noisily. 'Do you know the people
who live here?'

She didn't take her eyes off the burning building to look at
him but continued to stare ahead as she nodded slowly. He could
see the flames dancing gleefully reflected in her eyes.

It was one of the fire officers who shouted him the answer.
'A family lives here,' he said. 'A whole bloody family.'

Roberts felt his face tighten as a window exploded. It looked
as though the entire property would be completely destroyed,
reduced to ashes even with the efforts of the fire service. He was
no fireman but he could tell there wasn't any chance of saving
this unfortunate family now. 'Were they in?' he asked.

Neither the woman with the mad eyes nor the fire officer could
answer truthfully so both simply nodded. 'We think so,' the fire
officer he had unceremoniously pushed aside said.

'Oh, shit.'

Roberts had never quite given up the idea of heroics. He was
so keen to impress his girlfriend, Flora, with tales of adventure
and heroism that she had a distorted, dramatic view of life in
the Shrewsbury police force as a constable. But the trouble with
this fantasy was that PC Gethin Roberts had to sustain this drama
to retain his girlfriend's admiration, or so he thought. And it was
getting rather difficult. His stories, in truth, were becoming more
and more far-fetched and unbelievable. When fire officer Colin
Agnew saw the lanky policeman stride purposefully towards him
he read his intention quite clearly. 'Not a chance, mate,' he said,

holding his hand up like a traffic officer so there could be no mistake about his message. 'Anyone in there will be dead by now. No point risking your own life for roast corpses, Constable.'

Roberts made a face. Still, he thought, Flora wouldn't know what *actually* happened, would she?

He so wanted to be a hero. He grabbed a fire blanket and darted round the back of the house, smashed the window and threw open the door. Someone or something staggered towards him, hands held out. He threw the blanket on top of it and dragged it outside.

TWO

Friday, 25 February, 9 a.m.
The coroner's office. Bayston Hill, Shrewsbury.

Jericho had that look about him, Martha observed as she entered her office. She could read the expression perfectly – a certain smugness that her assistant habitually wore when he knew something she did not. Yet.

She refused to rise to the bait. 'Good morning, Jericho,' she said briskly and waited, knowing he would soon crack.

And crack he did. Starting with a rasping clear of his throat. 'Ahem.'

She waited.

'Inspector Randall's been on the phone, ma'am.'

She teased him. He liked nothing better than for her to look keen – and curious – then dangle her on a string. 'Really,' she exclaimed, her face deliberately bland, 'so early? I wonder what that can be about.'

'There's bin a fire in the village,' he announced grandly. 'A house fire.'

'Oh, dear.' Martha's thought was inevitable – that as she was a coroner this house fire must have proved fatal to someone. Jericho's next words confirmed her suspicion.

'People's missin',' he continued, shaking his straggly grey locks.

'Burnt? In the house fire? How many?'

'They don't know yet. It's still too hot in there and unsafe.' Jericho couldn't resist embellishing the tale. 'Beams fallin' in around their heads. Broken glass. Poisonous gasses and the like.' He paused, allowing the graphic description to sink in before adding in something of an anticlimax, 'Inspector Randall said he'd be over some time this morning to discuss it with you. He wonders if you'll be wantin' to visit the scene of the dreadful fire.'

'Yes, yes, of course,' Martha responded quickly. She felt vaguely ashamed now of having treated Jericho with such levity when the news was so grim. She couldn't rid herself of the image of a twisted, blackened corpse. There was something about the destruction of a person by fire that conjured up images of screaming, burning martyrs. She shivered. She wondered sometimes where this image, so physically painful, clear and visual, had come from.

Then she remembered.

'Coffee *and* chocolate biscuits are on your desk, Mrs Gunn.'

She looked at Jericho curiously. Did he know she had this particular horror of fire? Chocolate biscuits were usually the portent of a particularly trying day. And this one had barely begun. 'Thank you, Jericho.'

DI Alex Randall arrived at a minute past eleven, when she was on her second cup of coffee, but had resisted the biscuits even though they were *white* chocolate – her *absolute* favourite. Jericho announced the detective over the internal phone, his voice holding a tinge of resentment. He considered Martha his responsibility – no one else's. Nevertheless, if someone had to intrude the inner sanctum of the coroner's office, he grudgingly told his friends, 'it may as well be Detective Randall as anyone else'.

Jericho stood in the doorway peering nosily behind the inspector, who greeted Martha with a grim smile. 'Morning, Martha. Sorry to be the bringer of such dismal news.'

'Hello, Alex,' Martha replied, looking up from the pile of letters she was checking very carefully, correcting and signing. Her new typist was, she suspected, dyslexic and adept at ignoring spellcheck. 'Come in. Close the door behind you.' She could see her assistant's inquisitive face peering round, almost until the door clicked shut.

Alex Randall crossed the room in three long strides, a tall, spare figure in his early forties with irregular, craggy features, a large hooked nose and piercing hazel eyes beneath thick eyebrows, which were now almost meeting in the middle as he frowned. He was a valued colleague who was fast becoming almost a personal friend. Almost. He kept himself very private.

'Sit down, Alex,' she invited. 'You'd better fill me in. Jericho tells me there's been a house fire and I assume it was fatal or you wouldn't be here.'

The detective gave a terse nod but remained standing. 'A neighbour sounded the alarm at a little after eleven thirty last night,' he said, beginning slowly, but his eyes looked troubled.

'Go on.'

'It's a family home in Melverley. Melverley Grange.'

Why was he finding it so difficult? Martha wondered. He was a detective inspector – no stranger to violent death and tragedy. She watched him, puzzled.

'Christie and Nigel Barton, a well-known couple in their early forties, lived there with two teenage children. And Nigel Barton's elderly father, William, lived with them. He had Alzheimer's.'

She waited for him to continue.

'Some time late last night fire broke out in the two front rooms downstairs, quickly spreading to the upstairs bedrooms.'

'Two front rooms?'

'You miss nothing.'

'It's a big property?'

Alex Randall nodded. 'A lovely old house. As you can imagine the scene is awful this morning, in broad daylight.' He folded his long frame into the wing armchair and kept his eye on Martha. 'There's something about fires,' he mused. 'In the night they're dramatic, exciting, all flashing blue lights and activity.'

'Careful, Alex,' she said, smiling. 'You're beginning to sound like an arsonist.'

Alex grimaced and continued. 'But in the daylight you see the home it once was so completely destroyed. Blackened timbers, soot-stained curtains, broken windows, wrecked furniture.' He met her eyes. 'All the damage in its ugly starkness.'

She stayed silent. He had seen this. She had not.

DI Randall leaned right back in the chair and half-closed his eyes. 'Baldly, Martha,' he must have realized she was watching him because he gave her the ghost of a smile, 'the facts are this: the emergency services took the call at 11.38 p.m. from a Mrs Lissimore, a neighbour, who was returning home after a night at Theatre Severn. The play ended at eleven p.m. and she had driven home. As she turned into the road she saw smoke and flames coming out of a downstairs window. She dialled nine-nine-nine from her mobile phone. By the time the fire services arrived, four minutes later, the blaze had taken hold, engulfing the property. They were able to gain access but only to the rear without risk to life.' Another ghost of a smile. 'At least, the *firemen* didn't gain access. They were too well trained and sensible. It was one of our PCs. Gethin Roberts, everybody's hero.'

Martha looked at him warmly. 'I seem to have heard that name before, Alex.'

'He does seem to have a habit of stumbling right into things.' Alex returned her smile before continuing. 'As I said, a family lives – lived – there. Nigel Barton and his wife, Christie, their fifteen-year-old daughter, Adelaide, their son, Jude, aged fourteen and Nigel Barton's father, William. Mr William Barton was in his late eighties and has Alzheimer's.' Alex hesitated, as though he was on the point of saying something. Martha waited but Randall didn't enlarge. It could wait, she decided, knowing Alex's habit of holding information back until he was certain it was true. He disliked conjecture.

'Nigel Barton was away from home, in York. He supplies shops with window advertising. He's worth quite a lot of money. The house is – was – lovely.'

She felt like prompting him again. She wanted him to tell her quickly. Get it over with. Who had died? Had anyone survived? Which of these unfortunate people had been burnt alive? But she held her tongue and waited. And got her answer.

'Mrs Barton, William Barton and Adelaide are all unaccounted for.'

'And the son, Jude?'

'Gethin Roberts,' DI Randall couldn't quite suppress a shadow of amusement, 'quite against any advice, broke in through the back door and found him in the kitchen near the door. Jude

Barton has ten per cent burns, mainly on his hands and arms.'
He met her eyes. 'It's always puzzled me,' he said. 'How do they
calculate the percentage?'

'It's the rule of nines,' she supplied, almost absently.

'That doesn't take me much further,' Alex responded with a
tinge of another smile.

'They divide the body into eleven areas, head, right arm, left
arm and so on. Each one represents nine per cent. That's how
they calculate the percentage of burns.'

'Oh,' he said, looking a little disappointed. 'Simple when you
know how.'

She gave a short laugh. 'Then I shouldn't have explained.'

Randall returned to his story. 'The fire services haven't been
able to do a thorough search of the house yet,' he said. 'It isn't
safe. So we can't confirm exactly what happened but it already
appears,' he said carefully, 'that there are troubling features.' His
frown deepened so his eyes seemed to sink further into his face.
Then he gathered himself together. 'Basically,' he said, and she
could almost anticipate his next words, 'accelerants were used.'

'Poured in through the letterbox?'

His frown deepened. 'No. You'd have to look at the house to
understand. It has a huge hall with little furniture and stone walls.
Any accelerant poured through the letterbox might well have had
little effect.'

'I see.'

'One of the downstairs windows had been forced. We think
that the arsonist entered the house through the window. It appears
that petrol was poured in a number of places but the fire started
in the downstairs lounge. Jude Barton has drawn us a plan of
the house. The seat of the fire was right beneath Mrs Barton's
bedroom.'

Without allowing her any time to absorb this he continued:
'The old man had a bedroom and a bathroom on the first floor,
as did the daughter, Adelaide, and Christie herself. All three, it
would appear, died in the fire. Jude, the son, had rooms on the
top floor.'

Martha narrowed her eyes. 'And he survived?'

Randall nodded.

'How?'

'Naturally he's shocked and sedated and very upset but he claims he was awake and smelt the smoke. He says he tried to get down the staircase but the smoke and flames made it impassable. Their cleaner, a lady called June Morrison, rang this morning and has been very helpful with further information about both the house and the family. The top floor was originally the servants' quarters and had a separate staircase which is very narrow and has a stout pitch pine door which opens on to the first-floor landing and is usually kept closed. It was probably this that saved Jude's life – it kept the smoke out of his room. That and, because of the narrowness of the staircase, he says he kept a rope ladder in his bedroom. He climbed down the back of the building on this, anchored to a metal ring which was already attached to the wall.'

'So how did he get the burns?'

'He says he tried to get to his mother and sister, entering through the back door into the kitchen, but when he opened the door it was full of smoke. Roberts dragged him out.' His mouth twisted. 'I can't decide whether to discipline him or give him an award.'

Martha nodded. 'So it appears that the three people on the first floor all died, while Nigel Barton was away. And Jude? How is he?'

'He'll be OK. Shocked but the hospital have him stabilized on oxygen and a drip and say he'll be OK. They may transfer him later for surgery on his hands to one of the burns centres, probably Birmingham or Stoke, but for now he stays where he is at the Royal Shrewsbury Hospital. He's fully conscious, obviously able to give us a statement.'

Martha nodded. And again waited. Something else was troubling Alex Randall. But DI Randall was a cautious man who tended to check his concerns before he voiced them. She had come to realize that about him in the years they had worked together.

He drew in a deep breath, as though about to dive off a high board. 'One of the fire officers managed to gain preliminary access to the building this morning. Apparently, according to him, the doors to the rooms of Mrs Barton and Adelaide appeared to be locked. The body of a woman was found lying near the door of Mrs Barton's room. We're assuming this is Mrs Christie

Barton. Another body was found, again behind a locked door, underneath the bedclothes. It appears that both died from smoke inhalation. Of course we'll have to wait for the post-mortem but we can be fairly sure that these are the bodies of Christie and Adelaide.'

Martha felt a shiver. 'Why were there locks on the bedroom doors?'

'According to Jude his family were very security conscious. All the internal doors had locks and when the house was empty the rooms were locked in case anyone broke in through a bedroom window.' He leaned forward. 'The two main downstairs rooms both had bay windows which did not extend to the first floor. That meant that there were small balconies outside the bedroom windows, though with flames shooting up from below this might not have been a possible escape route.'

Martha needed a few seconds to digest this information. 'Just a minute, Alex,' she said, 'are you telling me not only that this fire was *deliberately* started but also that three people were locked in their rooms to prevent their escape?'

Randall looked miserable. 'Two. The old man's body was found on the landing,' he said heavily, not meeting her eyes.

Again Martha did not quite digest the information. When she did she looked at him.

He read her gaze. 'We don't know yet.'

'But it's a murder enquiry.'

'It will be a major police investigation,' he finished. 'But . . .'

'But what? Do the family have any enemies?'

'Not that we know of yet.'

'There's something more that you don't like to say, Alex, even to me, isn't there?'

At last he met her eyes. 'Six months ago,' he said slowly, 'according to June Morrison, there was a fire at the Barton's house. It apparently started in the old man's room. He was confused, Martha. He said he'd been cold and set fire to some newspapers to get some warmth. Mrs Barton smelt the smoke and raised the alarm. On that occasion there wasn't a great deal of damage and the insurance company paid up. But the family were careful not to let him have lighters or matches. It is possible,' he continued, 'that he started this fire and possibly accidentally locked the doors. He may have thought he was helping. Who knows? He was very confused.'

'There's a great deal of difference between a confused old man starting a fire in his bedroom and deliberately igniting petrol and locking your daughter-in-law and granddaughter in their bedrooms to make sure they can't get out.'

'I know,' he said shortly. 'Mrs Morrison also said that on a couple of occasions Mr William Barton was violent towards his daughter-in-law.'

'And yet Nigel Barton not only continues to allow his father to live there but also goes away on a business trip, leaving his father with his wife and two children.'

'Mrs Morrison said William Barton "didn't mean it". It was all a "misunderstanding".'

'Does Mr Barton know yet what's happened?'

'He was contacted an hour ago. He's probably on his way back as we speak.'

Martha tapped her fingers on her desk as she thought. 'Don't let any of this leak out to the press, Alex. Not yet.' They were interrupted by Martha's phone ringing. «Simon» flashed up. She answered it. 'Hi, Simon. Can I call you back in . . .' Her eyes met Alex Randall's. 'Fifteen minutes. Yes.'

Randall couldn't pretend he hadn't heard the girlish, breathy tone in her voice. Who was this Simon? he wondered, before telling himself off. Whoever he was it was none of his business.

She was giving him a wide smile, almost as though she could read his thoughts and they amused her. 'I'm so sorry,' she said, eyes dropping to the mobile phone. 'Just a friend.'

Alex shrugged and returned to the topic of their conversation. 'It's very difficult to keep secrets here, Martha. Everyone in the village and the town will know someone who is personally involved in the Melverley tragedy – nurses, doctors, fire officers. There'll be plenty of tittle-tattle buzzing around before long. All we need is for one of the journalists to ask a perceptive question and the tongues will wag even more.'

'But these are merely suspicions. You don't know anything yet, do you?'

He shook his head but his face was guarded, his emotions tightly reined in.

'And the boy, Jude?'

'We have an officer with him. He's in a state of shock. He's put two and two together and realizes he's lost his mother, sister and grandfather. He needs his father with him before we can interview him.'

'Yes, of course.' She was silent for a moment before pursuing her own thoughts 'What do you think happened there last night, Alex?'

He gave a dry laugh. 'You know me, Martha: I'll wait until we have full access to the scene and some of the forensics back. And I suppose I should speak to Mr Barton, see what he thinks. It'll be hard.'

He stood up but didn't leave or say goodbye. 'Martha,' he said, hesitating awkwardly, 'I do appreciate being able to come here and talk to you like this. It is helpful, you know.' He gave the ghost of a smile. 'Thank you.'

She met his eyes and practically flinched at the pain in them. Her instinct was to ask him what was the matter, to stroke the brown hair streaked with grey, to iron out the creases of unhappiness that scored his face, even to touch his mouth and try to curve it into a smile but she had never crossed this line. So she did none of these things, instead saying briskly, 'My pleasure, Alex.' They shook hands formally and Alex Randall left.

Martha stood for a while, still conscious of the tall detective's presence. They had been involved in cases over a number of years but she still knew virtually nothing about him and this frustrated her. Was he married? Yes. Happily? No one knew. What was his wife like? Beautiful? Plain? Fat? Thin? Tall? Short? Blonde, red-haired or brunette? Again, no one knew. Children? Yet again, no one knew. Friends, private life, where he lived, what his hobbies were? She had never heard him talk about his wife or any children, or even hint at any hobbies: football, golf, running, cycling, eating out – any of the pursuits that men in their forties generally had. It was all a secret. He was an enigma. All she knew for certain were two things: that sometimes he looked awash with misery and unhappiness. And the second was that he was one of those rare men who are both ugly and attractive at the same time, highly masculine and completely unaware of their sexual attractiveness to the opposite sex.

She gave a little snort to herself. 'Oh, get on with the job,' she muttered, 'stop daydreaming.' She made a face at herself. She was no adolescent. Even so, she drew her handbag mirror out of her make-up bag, studied herself in the mirror, slicked some lipstick on and continued lecturing herself. 'This is a tragic case.' And no one could be more aware than she that if their worst fears were realized it would be a horrid headline grabber. She would have her work cut out. There was no time for distraction. Or dreams.

She picked up her mobile phone and rang Simon back.

THREE

Friday, 25 February, 2 p.m.

It was a little after two p.m. when firemen Colin Agnew and Will Tyler satisfied themselves that the property/crime scene was safe for a specialized incendiary forensic team to enter with two police representatives: Sergeant Paul Talith and the hero of the moment, PC Gethin Roberts. The firemen had given Roberts a hard hat and a stern talking to before patting him on the back and warning him that one day, if he wasn't more careful, he would be a dead hero. Roberts had simply smirked and pictured Flora's face when he related the embellished story to her. The headlines in the local papers had particularly pleased him – *Hero policeman saves boy's life from burning house.*

On his way to the station that morning PC Roberts had puffed his chest out and strutted past the newspaper hoarding, hoping and praying that someone would recognize and congratulate him.

No one had.

A crew had spent most of the morning propping up beams and putting in Acro jacks to support fragile timbers. As the major damage had been to the front of the house they had entered through the back door, the door through which Gethin Roberts had made his heroic gesture, earning himself the headline. He probably *had* saved Jude's life.

They trooped in through the kitchen, passing blackened walls, wall and floor units almost completely destroyed. The cooker was twisted metal. Other appliances could only be guessed at. A kettle? A microwave? Gas had exploded parts of the kitchen wall and scorched the cupboards. As a kitchen it was now practically unrecognizable. The flooring had melted into crests and troughs of plastic; the windows were cracked and blackened, the curtains charred rags which blew and teased in the morning breeze. The burnt furnishings plus the water from the firemen's hoses had left the house full of sooty pools, the materials soggy and heavy. Plastics had melted, electrical wires waving like sea snakes, the scene lit through windowpanes dirtily stained in vague patterns, like church windows only in monochrome, the only colour being soot black. The cold night had frosted some of the surfaces as though to relieve the depressing lack of colour. It was a little like the Snow Queen's Palace in Narnia – slightly surreal. Except that instead of the sparkling purity of snow all was overlaid by the unmistakable and sinister smell of smoke. As they stood in the kitchen and the photographer recorded the scene, Paul Talith was just beginning to piece together the events of last night. This, then, was where Jude Barton had been dragged out of the burning wreck by Gethin, and so escaped the fate of three members of his family.

Colin Agnew butted in. 'We think the door into the kitchen from the hall must have been open which is why it caught the damage so badly.'

Talith and Roberts simply gazed around them. Even without the death toll it was a scene of utter destruction.

They moved through the hall then, the team of specialists recording the scene, and stood in the doorway of the lounge, looking straight up through the joists into the bedroom. The breeze through the window caused the devastated curtains to flap narrow tendrils in the breeze as though the scraps of charred material themselves threw up their hands in horror. Talith continued looking around, slowly and very carefully. Now the initial revulsion was wearing off he was recording the scene to his memory. The sofa was still recognizable; the fabric was flame retardant but the metal frame had twisted and distorted, like Dali's melted watches. One of the forensic team sniffed suspiciously. Over the scent of the burning there lingered the unmistakable whiff of petrol. The team set to work, collecting samples, marking spots, taking photographs, video recording and making notes and measurements. The soot had covered the upper surfaces only, so when Colin Agnew moved a cushion on the sofa underneath the colour was still bright. A pretty orangey red but soggy now, heavy with saturated water. He replaced it. The fire hoses had splashed gallons and gallons of water into the place. Everywhere was drenched. And as the fire had streaked upwards the ceiling, too, had been damaged. Fire moves quickly, so beams and furniture had slipped from the first floor and now hung, drunkenly suspended, the risk of them falling blocking the officers' progress, though the health and safety team had secured them with ropes.

In every other downstairs room they were greeted by the same sight. Fire does not destroy as completely as it distorts so they were still able, in general, to identify everyday objects which made the scene even more horrible. Gethin Roberts stared, appalled by the sight. Perhaps the collection of wires and melted tubes had once been a television; maybe the shelves had held books rather than sheaves of charred and sodden paper? He thought about the modest home he shared with Flora and reflected how much there is in a house to burn or, to use the phrase they kept trotting out, 'combustible material'. Everything plastic, everything paper, everything wood and plenty besides.

They sloshed back into the lounge, a little spooked now because they knew they had to climb the stairs. They also knew, from the preliminary reports, what still lay up there. The staircase was charred but had been pronounced safe by the health and safety team as long as they ascended in single file. So they climbed, picking their way along the skeleton of beams and rafters black and exposed like ribs on a body, and paddling through soggy carpet that reminded Roberts, who was the most fanciful, of a paddy field. In parts the floor had collapsed so they had to take extra care. Halfway along the landing they came across the first body, his clothes partly fire-damaged. The two firemen stared down grimly. It was a timely reminder of the purpose of their job: to save life and preserve property.

'And still they don't change the batteries on their smoke alarms,' Agnew muttered to no one in particular but everyone in general. Talith pulled out his mobile phone and requested the presence of the police surgeon. It was pretty obvious there were no survivors here but death still had to be pronounced by a qualified doctor and permission granted by the coroner before a body could be moved. Gethin Roberts, too, glanced down briefly at the shrunken frame and the grey hair. 'Mr Barton senior, I presume,' he said, trying to keep the squeak out of his voice. It sounded so juvenile, panicky. Talith was more detached, able to observe the condition of the body without emotion. Ironically William Barton hadn't suffered such severe burns as his grandson. At a guess, Talith thought, smoke inhalation was probably what had killed him. His hair wasn't even singed, only his clothes. He lay, curled up in a foetal position, one arm extended, his mouth open, his skin tone grey, his eyes almost closed but not quite.

'Poor old guy,' Colin Agnew said sympathetically. 'Nasty way to die.'

'Yeah.' They were all agreed on that one.

Agnew, too, was trying to piece events together. 'I wonder why he was up here, what he was trying to do?' He glanced around at the charred doors and wondered which was the old man's bedroom and which were the two females.

They left William in the same position and turned their attention to the two doors in front of them, towards the front of the house, left and right. And now they could see where Fire Officer Ben Hardwick's axe had hacked open the doors of the front bedrooms. Ben was trained in gaining access to serious and hazardous fire scenes and it had been he who had made the initial reports back to the station. Police and fire personnel would now have to work closely to piece together events. These two front rooms had borne the brunt of the damage being directly over the seat of the fire and, according to Hardwick, this was where the bodies of the two women had been found. His job had been thorough, securing the scene without disturbing forensic evidence.

They entered the first room. Christie Barton was lying on her side just inside the door, wearing a black nylon nightdress which had partially melted on her legs. Her hands were balled into fists. It looked as though she had been beating against the door until she had been overcome by the smoke. Her mouth was open in a silent scream, her lips a dusky blue-grey. All of them stared down. Although they had been expecting this, the sight of her still shocked them. But Talith's mind was busy. He was registering everything so he would be able to report back to Detective Inspector Alex Randall, his superior and the senior officer investigating the fire and the resultant deaths of the three members of the Barton family. Talith could see Christie Barton's handprints on the paintwork, flat as she had slapped on the door, trying to escape or gain attention. But the door had remained locked, the key dropped to the floor. Access had finally been gained, too late, by Hardwick's axe. Now they were in the room with her all four of them felt the sheer hopelessness of her plight. The minute a room fills with smoke the victim becomes disorientated, uncertain where windows, doors and pieces of furniture are, unable to get their bearings however familiar the room. Ask any fireman. If she had been able to get out and reach the back of the house she might have stood a chance had she not been overcome first by the smoke like her father-in-law. Talith eyed the key and wondered. There was a bolt high up on the inside of the door that had been slid open.

They all looked around, their emotions remarkably similar though their observations were different. The room was very badly affected. The source of the fire had been directly beneath the bed and the flames had leapt upwards. It stood in the centre of the room, its headboard against the right hand wall, a pile of burned fabric now punctured by the unmistakable spiralling springs of a mattress. It helped the police and firemen to anchor the geography of the room. Either side of the bed stood a chest of drawers, the paint burned and blistered but still intact and recognizable as pieces of furniture. A wardrobe stood along the wall to their left, teetering on the weakened floorboards. Hardwick had secured it. The window was ahead, cracked, blackened – and closed. There was no electricity in the house. It had had to be switched off because of all the water. The day was dull and chilly so spotlights had been rigged up using a generator. It made the damaged bedroom look like a stage set, their actions a scene from a macabre play. Roberts and Talith stared uneasily at each other.

They left the scene to the scrutiny of the firemen and forensics team who were carrying on with their work and entered the second bedroom, the one across the hall, adjacent to the main bedroom, again accessed through a locked door splintered by an axe. And yet again the lock was shot across, the key dropped to the floor and the bolt inside the bedroom open. Talith frowned as he stepped through. He could put two and two together. Locking her in? Deliberately? To die? It was as cruel as . . . He was at a loss. Then he realized. As cruel as the Holocaust. Or as cruel as the burning of martyrs. His mind kept busy. Was it possible that the old man on the landing had been making an attempt to reach his daughter-in-law and granddaughter, without realizing that the landing would have been smoke-filled and he would quickly be overcome? Or was it possible that he had locked the doors from the outside in a misguided effort to keep the women safe? He heaved a big sigh. In the end there had been no escape for any of them – except the boy, Jude. Talith and Roberts stepped forward. Adelaide Barton was lying in her bed, underneath a duvet discoloured by the smoke but still recognizable as patterned with pink cupcakes. The duvet was drawn over her head, her body a small, slim shape beneath the smoky bedclothes. And again Talith tried to fit together the evidence with a plausible theory. Why had Adelaide hidden underneath the duvet? Had she been trying to protect herself from the smoke? Or had sheer terror forced her to seek refuge in a familiar place where she felt, ironically, safe? Who knew? An insinuating wind blew in through the window as though trying to whisper something chilling in his ear. Talith knew one thing at least: both women had been aware of what their fate would be. He lifted the duvet.

The girl was dead, her face, like her mother's dusky and discoloured but, unlike her mother's, Adelaide's features were peaceful as though she was merely asleep. 'Poor thing,' he muttered. 'Poor . . . little . . . thing.'

This room, too, had been badly affected by the smoke, but not quite as badly as her mother's. Smoke damage rather than the fire was what had discoloured the walls, ceiling, furniture. Everything was covered in a layer of oily smoke. The windows had cracked and the fire hoses done their work through broken panes. But it was obvious that without the fire service this house would have been nothing but a blackened shell, the three bodies buried beneath rubble and the task of the police to find the perpetrators would have been that much harder. It was lucky that Mrs Lissimore had been returning from Theatre Severn, noticed the fire and raised the alarm. Melverley was a quiet village. It was quite feasible that the fire would have gone unnoticed and *four* members might have died last night. It was a terrible thought and for once even Gethin Roberts was not focusing on what he would say to his beloved Flora about the fire but reflecting on the sheer tragedy of the situation, a beautiful house ruined, three lives lost, a family torn apart by tragedy. He heaved out a great big sigh.

Talith glanced at him. 'You all right there, Roberts?'

Gethin managed a half grin. 'Yeah.'

Talith clapped him on the shoulder and said nothing more.

Now there were the formalities, form filling and protocol and waiting for the police surgeon to confirm what they already knew without a medical degree between them: all three were dead. But until pronounced so they could not be moved to the mortuary for the post-mortems. So they waited.

Alex rang Martha at two forty-five. 'I've got Nigel Barton here, Martha,' he said, 'at the station. He got back an hour or so ago. Naturally he wants to go to his home but we're waiting for Delyth Fontaine to confirm death on his father, wife and daughter.' There was a brief pause. 'I don't want him to see his family like that. Not there. I want them moved before he sees it all. Tidied up. I've suggested he go straight to the hospital and comfort his son.'

'That seems like a good idea.' Correctly she read the request behind the words. 'Did you want me to come out to the house?'

'Would you? That'd be great. I could do with your perspective.' She could hear relief lighten his voice. 'I'll give you a lift,

Martha. Pick you up in twenty minutes?' He sounded almost jaunty.

She knew it was unusual, to say the least, for police and coroner to work quite so closely together but Martha and Alex had fallen into this way of tackling violent death. Shrewsbury was, in general, a peaceful town but all towns have their crimes and need their solutions. The dead deserve justice. It was Martha's mantra. So they both derived some benefit from these shared opinions.

She unhooked her coat from the door and went outside to tell Jericho that she was going to visit the scene of last night's fire. Needless to say, he pursed his lips, shook his iron-grey hair and looked disapproving, but wisely said nothing.

Twenty-five minutes later she was sitting in Alex's car.

As he drove the eleven miles west of Shrewsbury to the village of Melverley he filled her in on the details so far. 'We've found the three bodies.' He glanced at his watch. 'The two women in their bedrooms and William Barton outside on the landing near the top of the stairs. He was facing towards the women's rooms, whether to try and rescue them or what we can't tell yet. And we may never know.' He glanced at his watch. 'Delyth Fontaine should be on her way to confirm the deaths right now. Oh, and there is confirmed evidence of accelerant – petrol in both downstairs rooms and on the stairs.'

'A deliberate fire then, which killed three people – nearly four? Murder.'

Alex nodded.

'Tell me more about the Bartons.'

'Barton is a successful businessman; his wife teaches music in a few schools. Adelaide Barton is fifteen years old and was due to take her GCSEs this summer. Her brother, Jude, is fourteen. Come on, Martha . . .' He took his eyes off the road for a second to meet hers. 'What can this ordinary family possibly have done to warrant this?'

She met his gaze unflinchingly. 'You know the answer to that as well as I do, Alex. They were either the deliberate target or our arsonist chose Melverley Grange at random, perhaps because it is a lovely old house. Have there been other arson attacks in the town or the surrounds?'

Randall concentrated on the road again. 'There have been a bunch of moronic teenagers but their modus operandi is entirely different. Their fires are pretty half-hearted. They've only ever chosen targets in the town. And they tend to torch four or five properties in the same road. Besides, they've got the best alibi of all. They're banged up in Stoke Heath. No.' His frown was deep and troubled. 'It isn't them.' He turned right up the B road.

She was silent for a minute then asked, apparently innocently, 'How did Nigel Barton sound?'

Alex Randall took his eyes off the road again before giving her a grin. 'Nail on head, Martha?'

She gave a wry smile. 'Just think of it as a nasty, suspicious mind at work.'

'That's very nasty,' he said, frowning.

She looked out of the window at the country road, small cottages, peaceful green fields. 'Yes – well, fires are, aren't they? And my nasty and suspicious mind has had a lot of material to feed on over the years.'

Alex gave her a quick look but carried on driving without comment.

She continued. 'And Jude? How's he?'

Alex grimaced. 'In a lot of pain. They've had to give him morphine.'

'Right.'

They travelled the rest of the way in companionable silence, each mentally working through the drama. They were in the village of Melverley ten minutes later.

It was easy to pick out the property. Quite apart from the extensive damage and the blackened building, there were crowds of people simply looking and more cars parked along the verge than attend an average church bazaar. Martha climbed out of the car, her eyes fixed on what was left of the house. The destruction, even from the outside, was terrible – quite apart from the knowledge that three people had died inside. She frowned, her mind already trying to piece the drama together, to make sense of it all and find a logical explanation. She had some experience of house fires but the inquests she had conducted on the victims had, in general, been accidental fires in terraced houses with dodgy heating equipment where exits were limited to front door, back door and windows. This was a large, Victorian detached property with plenty of nice big windows and multiple exits for escape. Only they hadn't.

She had conducted the inquest on a case only three years ago when a business man had deliberately set fire to his house after murdering his wife and daughter. The incident had scarred the people of North Shropshire and she had never thought she would have to conduct another inquest as traumatic as that. But here it was. Again.

Randall was eyeing her. 'Penny for them,' he said softly but Martha shook her head at him.

'My thoughts aren't for sharing – at least not yet, Alex,' she said with a returning smile, though he could easily have guessed at them. They were, after all, predictable.

Melverley Grange might have been a lovely house once but now it was a sorry sight. Like a woman who had once been beautiful the contrast of the present to the past made the tragedy all the more poignant. As though to underline their sentiments as they regarded the wreck a woman stepped forward, added a bunch of flowers to the tributes at the gates, looked up at the house, shook her head slowly and wiped away a tear with the sleeve of her anorak. Then she turned and walked away. She said nothing to either Martha or Alex, and her silence was more eloquent than any words she could possibly have said. The air of gloom and depression enveloped the entire scene. The flowers the woman had laid joined the others on the grassy bank outside the gates with various notes, the word *Why?* written on many of them, together with expressions of love and loss. Martha and DI Randall threaded under the Do Not Cross tape, walked up the drive together and left the bunches of flowers and sentiment behind. They had a job to do.

They met Delyth Fontaine, the police surgeon, at the back door, just stripping off her forensic suit. She pulled off her over shoes and greeted Martha warmly. 'Hello, Martha.'

Martha's response was equally warm. She liked Delyth, a large, untidy woman who cared a lot less for her own appearance than her beloved herd of Torddu mountain sheep. 'So what have we got, Delyth?'

'Elderly male and two females. Probably all died of smoke inhalation. They weren't burnt to death, that's for sure.' Delyth's voice was matter-of-fact, almost cheerful. 'The older woman – almost certainly Christie Barton – suffered the worst injuries: burns to her legs caused by her nylon night clothes melting. According to the forensic team the women appeared to have been locked in their rooms, which makes the incident worse. Much worse.' Her voice remained unemotional, uninvolved. 'Are you happy for me to move the bodies to the mortuary, Martha?'

Martha nodded. 'And perhaps you'll have a word with the pathologist, Mark Sullivan – see when he can do the post-mortems?'

'Will do.' The police surgeon's job over, she left and Martha and Alex threaded their way into the house.

Martha had visited crime scenes before – even fire-damaged crime scenes – but the destruction of what must have been such a beautiful and luxurious home was beyond her experience. She could only look around in pity and shock as she, too, slid into a forensic suit and overshoes. It certainly wouldn't do for the *coroner* to sully a crime scene. She and Alex paddled into the kitchen, Martha looking around her, trying to imagine family life here. But it was difficult in the smoky, blackened remains.

Alex led her into the sitting room and pointed out the window. 'This was where the petrol was introduced, according to the forensic team, and Talith and Roberts are in agreement.'

She turned to him. 'I thought you said the window was forced.'

He nodded.

'It looks more to me as though it was raised,' she observed. 'Look.'

DI Randall moved closer. It was a sash window that had splintered and virtually been destroyed.

'The weight and then the window itself would have dropped,' Martha said, 'when the sash cord was burnt through. I think it was pushed open and the fire caused the glass to crack. Besides,' she looked across at him, 'surely the firemen would have broken this window anyway to get their hoses through?'

DI Randall nodded without making comment. But he was

frowning as he slipped a glove on and fingered the scorched wood. 'It's got a window lock on the inside,' he said. 'And as far as I can tell it's undone.'

They both tried to work out the implication of this.

'Melverley's a peaceful little village,' Martha pointed out, 'hardly a major crime hotbed. I think it very possible that the Bartons would close their windows at night but not necessarily bother to lock them.'

'OK,' Alex agreed slowly. 'Here's my theory: someone breaks the window with this rock.' He indicated a large stone on the floor.

'And where did the rock come from?'

'There's a wall outside,' Randall said. 'The stones are quite loose. Then he climbs the stairs, locks the two women in their rooms. Doesn't bother about the old man who wanders, confused, on to the landing. Our arsonist then splashes petrol down the stairs and in both downstairs front rooms, sets fire to the place and escapes again through the window.'

'Possibly,' she said.

DI Randall gave her a sharp glance but said nothing.

They heard a noise coming from upstairs and Sergeant Paul Talith appeared at the doorway. 'Sir,' he said. 'Mrs Gunn? Hughes has found something. Upstairs.'

They climbed up to the first floor and picked their way towards Roddie Hughes, the crime scene investigator coordinating all the evidence. Efficient and meticulous at his job, he was an Essex boy who had come to Shrewsbury for a holiday and never quite made it home. He was universally liked in the force.

Hughes was holding up a plastic evidence bag. They both peered at it. Inside was a small piece of metal.

Martha frowned. 'What is it?'

'It looks very much like part of a cigarette lighter,' Hughes said. 'One of those disposable ones.'

'Where did you find it?' Randall's voice was sharp and gravelly.

'It was in the old man's dressing gown pocket,' Hughes said.

Martha's heart sank.

FOUR

Alex and Martha stepped past the body of William Barton, taking a swift glance at the body of the frail, elderly man. 'Not much of an end to a life,' Martha observed, noting his foetal position and reflecting how strange it was that the majority of people lie like this within the womb and die in the same position. 'I wonder where he was heading.' Her glance drifted towards the two splintered bedroom doors.

Alex's face tightened. 'More like: what was he up to?'

'He could have been trying to let the women out, thinking they might have been overcome by smoke.'

Randall looked unconvinced.

Martha spoke again. 'I wonder if he was a smoker.'

Randall looked at her. 'You're trying to find an innocent explanation for the fact that he had a lighter in his pocket. Where's that suspicious mind you're so proud of?' he teased.

But Martha's expression was sober. 'William Barton is unable to defend himself. I don't want him taking the blame if he's innocent.'

Randall was already two steps ahead, anxious to examine the other two bedrooms for himself. He went first to Christie's room. A blanket covered her body now and the arc lights had been dimmed so the room had less of the atmosphere of a lit stage than an empty theatre when the show's over and the audience gone. The scene was clearly marked out, the story easy to read, helped by forensic markers, chalk lines and fingerprint dust – the smoke-blackened walls and furniture, the bodies of the mother and, in the other bedroom, her fifteen-year-old daughter. Each was covered with a sheet, the illumination through cracked and blackened windows making the atmosphere dingy, and everywhere there was this pervasive stink of smoke, a smell that seemed to epitomize destruction. Even as they were inspecting Adelaide Barton's room the mortuary van arrived outside and backed up to the front door.

The three bodies were zipped efficiently into body bags and taken away, the attendants descending the stairs in careful steps. Martha watched the van take its cargo down the drive, heading for the mortuary where the post-mortems would be performed. She stood back, looking through the window for minutes after the van had turned left on to the B road that led back to Shrewsbury. Years ago she'd thought she had learned to detach herself from scenes like these, to forget the human story of suffering and pain and concentrate instead on the science and facts of the case – the job, or so she told herself. But every now and then cases caught her out, usually because of some common ground in her home life. In this instance Sukey, her daughter, and Adelaide Barton were about the same age. Presumably they would have had the same expectations of their lives. Exams, exams, exams, university, probably more exams, possibly marriage, a home, children. Not anymore. Adelaide's future had finished cowering under bedclothes locked in a smoke-filled room. It was unbearably cruel.

Martha was vaguely aware of Detective Inspector Alex Randall at her side, watching her with curiosity though he did not speak, clear his throat, move or remind her in any way of his presence. Yet she was well aware of the tendrils of empathy which reached out from him, the sympathy warming those perceptive hazel eyes, and almost of the bony hand touching her own. She did not dare look at him in case she was wrong; she didn't want him to read her vulnerability. So she analysed silently as she emerged back on to the landing, observing the patch of paler carpet which marked the spot where William Barton had recently lain. The case was this: two women, locked inside their rooms and an old man whom, in spite of her defence, she was already picturing as crazy and demonic, spilling petrol and setting fire to the house.

Yet, as she studied the shape on the carpet, she knew that something about that theory wasn't working. She scanned the landing, pictured the old man's body stretched out, in his dressing gown and slippers and apparently with a cigarette lighter in his pocket. Her eyes were drawn to another door at her side. 'And the second floor?'

'Up here.' Paul Talith had climbed the stairs to join his boss.

He pushed open the door and led the way. The stairs were boxed in with wooden planks behind the thick, pitch pine door. Badly scorched and blistered on the outside but intact. And while the inside also showed signs of fire damage it had held back the fire. Pitch pine contains a great deal of sweet sap and the heat had made this trickle down the wooden panels before cooking it as hard and black as basalt. Reaching out, Martha could still feel the heat retained in the wood. It was now more than fifteen hours since the fire at Melverley Grange had been extinguished and the surfaces still felt warm. But the door had done its job, acted as a firebreak and this, and the rope ladder, had saved Jude's life. Martha frowned. But having escaped he had then returned to the house to try and rescue his family? She was curious and wondered what he was like, this heroic teenager. She touched the door again. If the fire had reached beyond it and Jude Barton had not had the foresight to keep a rope ladder in his room he would have had no route of escape and would have died with the rest of his family. The staircase would quickly have become impassable and the sheer height of the house made it too high to jump without sustaining serious or fatal injury. Jude Barton had had a very lucky escape, which led Martha to wonder about the rope ladder. It seemed odd for him to have one. Had the boy half expected something like this? She filed the question away with all the others. In time she would ask them all. And get answers.

'Shall we climb?' Alex invited then stood back politely, allowing her to walk up the narrow stairs ahead of him, their footsteps making a hollow sound. There was no stair carpet, only the painted wood of the treads.

There were five rooms on the top floor, two to the right and two to the left either side of a central bathroom. The two rooms on the right were patently only used for storage, suitcases, boxes of books and unwanted furniture, while Jude had occupied the two rooms on the left. Apart from the lingering smell of the smoke there was no evidence of the fire that had raged in the floors below leaving devastating carnage. Up here was relatively normal. The rooms on the left were much as you would expect a teenage boy's room to be: untidy, clothes and belongings everywhere, a computer, Xbox, an unmade bed, posters on the wall of robotic super heroes. The bathroom was the same. Spicy deodorant still scented the room, overlying the smoke, but the towels were on the floor, the shower tray lime-scaled, hairs blocking the plughole. It was an all too familiar sight to Martha. Sam, her son, had much the same attitude to bathroom hygiene. '*What's the point, Mum, it soon gets messy again,*' and '*it can't be* really *dirty – I only wash in it.*'

Inwardly she smiled and Randall picked up on it. His own eyes twinkled as he looked at her. 'Are all teenage boys the same, do you think, Martha?'

She laughed but ill-advisedly used the opportunity to probe. 'Yes,' she said with a chuckle, adding light-heartedly, 'Don't you have any children, Alex?'

She regretted the question in the same instant that the words were out of her mouth. His face froze, shoulders stiffened and he looked away quickly, though not quickly enough. She had seen a look of intense pain cross his face, like a quick, black cloud over the sun. Silently she chided herself. *Big mistake, Martha.*

'No.' He answered the question shortly. 'Not anymore.'

It was an odd answer. Martha took a surreptitious look at him but he kept his eyes away and volunteered nothing further. It underlined the fact that while her friendship with the tall detective might have grown it was still primarily a professional relationship which might develop into a closer friendship using slippery stepping stones to find a way to cross a deep river. It would be only too easy to fall in. And the water was ice-cold. Quite inhospitable. She did not want to fall in. So she concentrated on the job in hand, examining the boy's rope ladder, noting the steel ring screwed into the wall. It was a professional job. She tugged at it. There was no give. It was firmly anchored. This, then, had kept the boy alive although, she supposed, it was just about possible that the door at the bottom of the stairs would have kept the inferno away long enough for the firemen to effect a rescue. Fire engine, tall ladder, dramatic rescue. A Boy's Own dream. But instead Jude Barton had descended a rope ladder. Equally dramatic. She must find out the circumstances of his descent. She took a last look around his room before following the others back downstairs.

When they had finally returned to the hall Alex asked her: 'Seen enough, Martha?' She noted a stiffness in his manner now, a distance in his voice and she sensed his resentment that she had stolen an unauthorized peep into the life he so zealously protected from outside view.

She retreated into formality. 'Almost, Alex, thank you. I'd just like to have a quick word with one of the firemen and then I really should get back to the office.'

He obviously felt constrained too. 'I'll get one of the officers to drive you,' he offered. 'I need to do some more work here.' He was avoiding her eyes, she noticed. She wanted to apologize for storming his castle but knew it was best to say nothing more. What was it her mother was always saying? Least said soonest mended. Her Irish mother had a phrase for all occasions. But even though the phrase was a cliché Martha was well aware that words would not heal the rift that had opened between them. Better then to stay quiet than make any attempt to smooth it over with words.

She found Colin Agnew outside the property, inspecting the damage around one of the downstairs windows. Martha introduced herself and regarded the devastation alongside him. 'How long do you think the fire had been burning before the alarm was raised?'

'Well over half an hour,' Agnew responded. 'It had really taken hold.' He looked at her. 'It took us two hours to get it under control. There were six fire engines all pouring water into the place. And one of the clocks on the mantelpiece of the downstairs sitting room had stopped at just after eleven.'

Martha almost burst out laughing. 'Oh, don't give me that old mushroom,' she teased. '"The clock stopped at −" It's always a fake.'

'Well, it would fit in with the damage and everything else,' Agnew said, standing his ground.

'OK.' Martha turned to go then stopped. 'Oh, and the rope ladder?'

The fireman nodded. 'Still attached to the wall.'

Alex had moved behind her, watching her very carefully indeed. So hard that one would have thought he was trying to divine her thoughts, poach them and take them for his own, but in reality he was probably wondering where her line of reasoning would take her.

Her mobile phone rang then. It was Mark Sullivan, the pathologist. 'Hello, Martha,' he said. 'Sorry to call your mobile. I did try the office but Jericho said you were out.' He chuckled. 'Naturally he wouldn't tell me *where* you were. He protects your privacy with admirable zeal. Where *are* you?'

'At the scene of the fire,' she answered. 'I thought I should take a look.'

'I was wondering about the post-mortems,' he said. 'Will you want to attend?'

'It depends, Mark. When were you thinking of doing them?'

'Tomorrow morning?'

'Then, no. Sorry, Mark, I can't make it. Prior engagement. Perhaps you'd drop by my office on Monday morning and run through your findings?'

'Sure. See you then.' And he ended the call.

PC Gethin Roberts drove her back to her office. She couldn't resist asking him about his dramatic rescue. 'Are you all right, Constable?'

'Slight burns to my hands,' he said, indicating a bulky dressing on one of them. 'Apart from that I'm fine.' His eyes slid across to her. 'Bit shaken up, to be honest.'

'It was very brave of you.' She hesitated. 'Jude, the boy, he escaped using his rope ladder. How come he went back in to the house?'

'He wanted to try and rescue his mum and sister.'

'And grandfather?'

'He only said his mum and sister. But then he was in shock. His clothes were alight. He was hysterical. He must have been in a lot of pain. He was babbling on about his mum and sister but didn't mention his grandfather. Mind you, there was so much noise, shouting and confusion that he might have done and I just didn't hear him.'

They'd reached her office. 'Thank you, Gethin.'

The PC blushed.

'I hope your hand isn't too painful?'

He shook his head.

'And that it gets better soon.'

'Thank you, ma'am.'

She closed the door.

Martha spent the rest of the afternoon doing paperwork, dictating letters and signing forms, but her mind kept drifting back to that smoke-blackened house, the sad sight of the three bodies, the destruction of the rooms in which the two women had been locked, the thought of Adelaide cowering underneath her bedclothes, her mother desperately trying to escape. And the boy, Jude, shimmying down the rope ladder like a superhero. The rope ladder itself, which he had thought to acquire as his escape route. Why?

And when her mind drifted from this it was to relive the mortifying embarrassment she had felt when DI Alex Randall felt obliged to answer her probing and intrusive question. Even now she felt hot with embarrassment at the thought and wished her brain would erase that particular memory.

Eventually, although the rest of the day dragged, like all Friday afternoons, she finished her work and was ready to leave.

Saturday, 26 February, 9.30 a.m.

This Saturday was Martha's morning for the dreaded visit to Vernon Grubb, who had a hairdressing salon in the centre of town, along a narrow street bordered with ancient and crooked black and white buildings. She parked in the Raven Meadows multi-storey car park and walked out into Pride Hill. The salon was also black and white but that was where history ended and contemporary art began. Inside Vernon Grubb's salon was more like a space station, white shiny surfaces and stainless steel, plenty of electronic devices that bleeped and alarmed. Vernon Grubb greeted her with a disapproving 'tsh tsh' at her hair, throwing a black nylon cape over her shoulders and leading her straight to the mirror to confront herself. He was nothing like the cliché of a mincing, slightly effeminate male hairdresser: tattoos, gold jewellery and polo-necked shirts, but had the bulging biceps, meaty thighs and general bulk of a rugby prop forward. One day, Martha had long ago decided, she would pluck up the courage to ask how a man who would have looked more at home in the front of a rugby scrum had taken up – of all professions – *hairdressing*. However, so far, she had not dared to risk it. Grubb could be quite outspoken and very unpredictable. So she was left to puzzle as he lifted tress after tress, strand after strand of her thick and unruly red-gold hair, tutting and scolding at the way she managed it. Or according to him, mismanaged it. True, she could never quite dry it as neatly or silkily as Vernon himself, but she bought pounds' worth of conditioners, serums and sprays from him, and expected at least some allowance for that.

It made it worse that Vernon Grubb was a broad Geordie. 'It's time you took your hair more seriously, Martha, pet,' he scolded her. 'It's your crownin' glory, you know. People'd kill to have such a red.'

'People would kill,' she remarked acidly, half turning her head to his increased disapproval, '*not* to have hair this colour and so naturally untidy. Especially in my job.' She eyed him in the mirror balefully. 'Can't you *do* something, Vernon? Dye it or something? Black, maybe? I'd love to have black hair.' She looked at her reflection and pictured herself with black, straight, shining Cleopatra hair, but was dragged back to reality by Grubb.

'You should be ashamed of yourself, Martha Gunn. Black hair? You'd look like the witch of Endor.'

'Well, at least tone it down.'

'There is such a thing as a criminal offence,' he said severely, folding his arms and scowling, 'even in the hairdressing world.' But his good humour had returned. He was smiling again as he talked, displaying the gap between his front teeth. 'And to start messing around with your hair would be one of them.' His lips pressed together in a Presbyterian grimace and he folded his arms, scissors poking out of one hand, comb from the other. 'I'll not do it. And that's that. So you can just stop asking.'

He'd subdued her very brief and weak rebellion. She tucked the cape tighter round her shoulders, settled back with a sigh and said, 'Oh, do what you like then. You always do anyway.'

'Thank you, Mrs Gunn.' Vernon looked smug. 'Now then, just let me tuck this towel around you. Good. Now, lean back.'

Expert hands took over then, shampooing, massaging the scalp, a dripping walk back to the chair and the scissors snipped their way into action. At the end of it Martha looked at herself in the mirror and approved, even giving herself a slightly smug smile. 'Why can *I* never get it like this myself?' she asked.

Vernon looked even more smug. He whipped the wrap away. 'Going anywhere nice tonight then, Mrs Gunn?'

She eyed herself in the mirror and caught the light dancing in her eyes. 'Certainly am,' she said.

'And are you going to tell me where?'

She shook her head.

'Or who with?'

Another shake of the head. She stood up, said goodbye to both reflections in the mirror, the fantasy lady with black tresses and a slightly excited middle-aged woman.

Monday, 28 February, 8.45 a.m.

Monday, as always, came around far too fast but the day brought its compensations. Today felt like the first real day of spring. Already the trees were beginning to burst through their winter drabness. They were *almost* green. One felt convinced that spring really was 'just around the corner'. Bulbs were poking up through the soil to be greeted by a jolly sun beaming benevolently down on them. Anticipation, Martha thought as she drove round the ring road towards Bayston Hill, was so often better than arrival. How many summers were a disappointment? But spring? Never.

She parked in her usual spot and pushed open the front door. Jericho was waiting to ambush her in the hall. 'Nice weekend, Jerry?'

'Very nice, ma'am,' he answered in his slow, Shropshire burr. 'Quiet, just with Mrs Palfreyman and myself, but very pleasant for all that.' He could hardly avoid adding the nicety, 'And you, Mrs Gunn?'

'Very good, thank you.' She could have said so much more now that Sam, her son, had moved back in with them: that he was on loan from Liverpool to play for Stoke City and her Sunday had been spent watching him play and cheering on his side. That almost as soon as Sam had walked in through the door, Agnetha, the au pair, had tearfully left, returning to her home land of Sweden to be married in a couple of months' time and that she, Martha, had finally, finally given up her grieving for Martin's death from cancer when the twins had been only three years old, and that she had finally dumped her normally sensible, practical, middle-aged 'mumsy' role to go out on a date. A proper, romantic, dinner date. She could still feel her toes tingling with the remembered anticipation. The only problem had been that the 'date' had been with her old friend – or rather, the widower of her late friend – Simon Pendlebury. And although the evening had been pleasant – very pleasant, Simon being an urbane, amusing and polite character – it had not been the toe-tingling, breathless experience of her early dates with Martin. When she had got home on Saturday night she had undressed and felt numb and a little depressed as she climbed into bed. It wasn't the same.

Dr Mark Sullivan had made an appointment through Jericho, the guardian of her gate, and appeared at 10 a.m. He'd brought with him the notes and pictures of the three post-mortems he had had to perform on Saturday. He walked in, a man of medium height and unremarkable appearance, blue eyes behind glasses, hair brown. He was a few years younger than her. 'Basically,' he said, 'they all died of smoke inhalation with varying degrees of burns. As you'd expect seeing as her bedroom was directly over the seat of the fire, Mrs Christie Barton had the most severe burns, most sustained post-mortem. There is very little inflammation around the sites which were basically hands, forearms, and legs. She was otherwise healthy as was her daughter, Adelaide. The old man had some heart disease and a little underlying fibrosis of the lung but he too died of smoke inhalation. He also had some ischaemic changes in his brain. I understand he had a diagnosis of Alzheimer's. I'm waiting for the results of a brain scan he had about a year ago.'

'That's right.' Martha looked sharply at the pathologist. 'No other wounds, Mark?'

'No.' He shook his head.

'OK.' She looked at him and marvelled at the change the last twelve months had wrought in him. Mark Sullivan, a brilliant pathologist, had had a serious and fairly obvious drink problem as well as a reputedly wretched marriage. But now he was a different man. Not half drunk most of the time, with shaking hands and bloodshot eyes but clear-eyed, steady-handed and best of all sober. 'You've changed,' she commented.

Surprisingly Mark Sullivan took this as an invitation to sit down, smiling, and confide. 'I had to,' he said bluntly. 'Otherwise . . .' He didn't enlarge but stayed sat down, still smiling at her.

'Well, I've noticed,' she said. 'And it's a welcome sight, I can tell you, in a doctor with your talent.'

'It was a big change,' he said. 'I was drinking too much.'

She deliberately didn't respond but now Mark Sullivan had begun to open up he seemed anxious to continue.

'Like most people I was drinking for a reason.'

Again she made no response but watched him.

Sullivan ploughed on. 'My wife and I – we're divorced.' He smiled now. 'Take away the reason why you're drinking too much and everything else falls into place.'

'Well, I'm glad of it,' she said. 'You're a good pathologist, Mark; it would have been such a waste.'

He stood up then. 'Thanks,' he said, grinning at her, and left.

FIVE

Tuesday, 1 March, 7.30 a.m.

Martha opened her eyes and remembered why today felt special. It was the first of March, not only in her mind the first day of spring but also St David's Day, patron saint of Wales. She made a mental note to ring her dad this evening and wish him happy St David's Day, knowing he would be noisily celebrating at the pub, wearing either a leek or a daffodil, (the emblems of Wales), and watching the St David's day concert broadcast live on the large-screen TV from Cardiff's Millennium Centre. The weather was bright and cold and she was still smiling as she drove round the ring road towards her office in Bayston Hill. Today the weather displayed the best of early spring, the time when a young man's thoughts turn to love. Martha pulled in outside her office, switched the engine off and sat still for a minute, contemplating. And a woman fast approaching middle-age? What do her thoughts turn to in the early spring? She pushed the thought aside and opened the door. Jericho was waiting for her. 'Any news about the fire?' She tried to make the question sound casual but Jericho wasn't fooled for a minute.

He shook his head solemnly. 'Not so far as I've heard,' he said. 'In the *Shropshire Star* last night it said that they was looking for an arsonist.' His Shropshire burr was always more pronounced when he got overexcited. He paused, his eyes as round as saucers. 'I can't think how anyone would do such a terrible thing.'

'No word from Detective Inspector Randall, then?'

'Not this morning, Mrs Gunn.' Jericho Palfreyman spoke firmly, eyeing her with bright-eyed curiosity. It was time to drop the subject. She moved towards her office door. 'Coffee's already waitin' on your desk, Mrs Gunn,' he called after her.

That was another thing about Jericho. He had to have the last word.

She walked into her office and closed the door behind her. Quite apart from the scent of fresh coffee that steamed from the mug on her desk, she simply loved the room. High-ceilinged, unmistakably Victorian but with oak-panelled walls, it had an air of substance, dignity and a reassuring permanence. It was a good place to interview grieving and sometimes angry relatives. It lent gravitas to the situation. But the best feature of the room, in her opinion, was the bay window, floor to ceiling, which gave her a bird's-eye view of the town. Bayston Hill was, as its name suggested, on an elevation to the south of Shrewsbury. Shrewsbury town itself was on a small hill in an oxbow of the River Severn. This had protected the English town, wealthy from the proceeds of Welsh wool, from the attentions of the hostile and sometimes aggressive Welsh. The geography of Shrewsbury was also the reason why it used to be cut off when the rains washed down heavily from the Welsh mountains, raising the level of the river and making the town, in effect, a fortified island. Shrewsbury (or Scrobbes-byrig, which was its Anglo Saxon name – the Fortress of Scrob) had been susceptible to floods for hundreds of years – right up until the council had installed flood defences. These now protected the town and sent the unwelcome waters shooting downstream. Elsewhere.

The window gave her a fine view of the town, familiar landmarks fixing its points: the spire of St Mary's (tragic witness to the first hang gliding fatality), the English Bridge with its elegant Georgian buildings, and the cross at the top of the domed church of St Chad's with its distinctive round shape. Martha warmed her hands around her coffee mug and still smiled. How many times had she played a trick on friends and relatives? Taken them into the quiet graveyard of St Chad's and watched them read the tombstone of Ebenezer Scrooge? They always fell for it. 'He's a real person, then?' they'd ask until, laughing, she had to tell them that the town of Shrewsbury had been the setting for the 1984 film of Charles Dickens's *A Christmas Carol* and that this stone was merely part of a film set which had not been removed when the shooting was over, left to become yet another tourist attraction.

She looked over the town, feeling a certain pride and affection for it then, reluctantly, turned back to her work. She was not paid to dream around spires but to try and make some sense, truth, logic and justice out of death. She was haunted by the image of Christie Barton fumbling with a locked door, trying to escape the bedroom, her lungs gradually filling with smoke, finally suffocating while the fire raged. And Adelaide Barton, cowering underneath her bedclothes. They were truly awful images. She was not smiling now but frowning. And the old man, she wondered. What part had he played in the drama? Perpetrator? Muddled interferer? Who could know? Would they ever know the full truth?

Once she had settled down to work the images receded and she quickly lost track of time. She was absorbed in reading reports, checking statistics and taking phone calls, one or two from hospital doctors. Periodically Jericho came in with coffee, sometimes biscuits, and at lunchtime a sandwich nicely set out on a plate with a glass of fruit juice.

But the back of her mind was still tracking around the fire, considering it from a different angle now. She was thinking about the living, wondering how Jude was and how his father was responding to the tragedy. What was his view on the events of Friday night? she wondered. How was he reacting? Once or twice she glanced at her phone, tempted to ring Alex Randall and ask him how the enquiry was progressing but she resisted the temptation – with difficulty. It was a relief when Jericho buzzed her at four o'clock to say that Detective Inspector Alex Randall was on the phone and had asked to speak to her.

Randall was brisk. He sounded as though he was having a very busy day. 'Sorry to interrupt your work, Martha.' He spoke quickly. 'I thought you might like to be kept up to date with the investigation into the Melverley fire.'

'That's very thoughtful of you, Alex. Thank you. I was wondering if you'd found anything out.'

'Well, not a lot so far,' he confessed. 'That's why I didn't ring earlier. I've been at the hospital.'

'How is Jude?'

'*Physically* the doctors say he'll be OK,' he began.

Martha picked up on the implication. 'But mentally?'

'He's devastated. Got real survivor complex, feeling guilty he didn't wake and raise the alarm – that he saved himself, but left them in the burning house and failed to rescue them.'

'Poor boy.'

Alex continued: 'I don't think we'd quite realized how traumatic his descent on the ladder was. He was terrified the rope would burn and he'd fall. It must have been dreadful.'

'Yes,' she agreed.

'And that's on top of the burns to his hands. The doctors have told me he may need skin grafts but they haven't told him yet. His father knows.'

'Has Mr Dalton been able to throw any light on the arson?'

'He's given us one or two leads but they seemed pretty feeble – business associates, a boy that Adelaide was involved with who came from a fairly unsavoury family, stuff like that. Nothing that really grabbed me.'

'Did you run the idea past Nigel that his father might have started the fire? Did you tell him you'd found a lighter in William's dressing-gown pocket?'

'No, I didn't tell him about the lighter. I thought he had more than enough to take in. I did mention the previous fire to him. He insists it was just an accident. And he definitely doesn't see his father as some sort of avenging arsonist.'

'And how did he respond when you told him that his wife and daughter had been locked into their rooms?'

'He absolutely insisted it must have been an accident.' Randall paused. 'He couldn't believe anyone would do such a thing deliberately, let alone his father. He said his father could be quite confused. He ventured the explanation that when his father woke to the fire he might have been trying to help the women out of their rooms and accidentally locked them in instead.'

'I could maybe swallow that one if only one door had been locked. But not both.'

'Well, he describes him as nicely muddled.'

'Two locked doors,' Martha said. 'That's not muddled coincidence. It's deliberate.'

'Mmm.' Randall's response was non-committal.

'And how did Mr Barton respond to his son descending by a rope ladder?'

'He couldn't keep the admiration out of his voice. He's very proud of Jude – and the fact that he tried to save the rest of the family. He thinks the boy's a hero.'

'Which I suppose he is,' Martha said slowly. Then she added, 'What was your impression of the dynamics of the family?'

Alex didn't answer straight away. It took him a minute or two to come up with a response so the line was quiet. 'It's hard to say, Martha, with such a tragedy. I mean, I've never met Barton senior, Christie or Adelaide. But there's no doubt of the affection between father and son.' He paused, frowning before finishing. 'Perhaps by spending time with Jude and his father I might learn a bit more about the rest of the family.'

'What's your instinct, Alex?' She couldn't resist pressing him.

On the other end of the line, Alex laughed. 'I had the feeling you were going to spring something like that on me. I don't know,' he said. 'I really don't know. It's early days yet. So far I'm a bit flummoxed. Initially I believed it was a random arson attack. For no particular reason Melverley Grange was picked on, maybe because it is such a grand and beautiful old house. But if it was a random attack it doesn't explain why the women were locked in their rooms. I've wondered about the old man. He started a fire before but no one has described him as demonic or crazy.'

'Alzheimer's isn't that sort of crazy, Alex. It isn't clever and it isn't calculating. As his son has said, William was nicely muddled, occasionally unhappily confused but not calculatingly deliberate or cunning. Where would he have got the petrol from? I take it he doesn't drive?'

'No.'

'Well, that'd take some planning. And if he had started the fire why didn't he escape when he could have?'

'Overcome by smoke?'

'Perhaps.' Martha continued: 'Believe me, Alex, this just isn't the sort of thing people with Alzheimer's do – lock people in their rooms, set fire to a house then climb the stairs and perish with the rest. Did you consider that? If he was the one who started the fire downstairs he must have climbed the stairs afterwards. That doesn't make any sense.'

'Unless he was trying to save his granddaughter and daughter-in-law.'

'I wonder.'

'But,' Alex pointed out, 'remember, he was found with a lighter in his pocket.'

'I still don't care,' she said stubbornly. 'William Barton was a victim too. As much a victim as his daughter-in-law and granddaughter and very nearly his grandson as well if Jude hadn't been quite so resourceful and forward thinking. Worse than that, Alex, if Barton senior is *wrongly* blamed for the fire he is the fall guy. The scapegoat, which would mean that the real villain goes free. Someone wanted us to believe that this old man committed this horrible and deliberately cruel act. An elderly man whom his son fondly describes as nicely muddled. How do we know he was crazy, anyway?'

'Mark Sullivan told us there were clear signs of Alzheimer's on a scan done a year ago of Mr Barton's head.'

'Well, maybe you should just check up on that. See if he's had a proper psychiatric assessment.' She waited a while before putting another thought into his head. 'Well, you've told me you have possible leads through Nigel Barton.' Martha pressed on. 'And one via Adelaide. Is there no one else in the frame?'

'No one, just the three business leads Nigel Barton gave us

and Adelaide's boyfriend. We will check them out, of course, but I'm not hopeful that it'll be that easy or that obvious.'

'Have there been other similar arson attacks?'

'Not in Shropshire.'

'Elsewhere?'

'Not unsolved.'

'So are we looking at an inside job? Something personal?'

She knew by his silence that Alex Randall was uncomfortable. His tightly uttered, 'It would appear so,' was practically forced out of him.

'What about Jude? Does he have any enemies?'

'A fourteen-year-old boy?'

'Yes, a fourteen-year-old boy.'

'We've yet to question him along those lines.'

'And Mrs Christie Barton. What about her? Is she Caesar's wife, above suspicion?'

'I do wonder if she had –' Randall sounded angry with himself. 'Oh, it's such a cliché. I wonder if she did have a secret life.'

Martha responded with an arch, 'Don't we all?'

But Randall's silence on the other end of the line told her that he was confused by her riposte. Then it must have dawned on him that she was teasing. He chuckled but she noticed he did not pursue the comment. Instead he said slowly, 'Martha, do you suspect everyone in this case?'

She answered calmly but with conviction. 'Yes, I do, Alex. Looking at it plainly, this was a case of arson which resulted in three deaths. Nearly four. This was no serial gang of silly boys playing up and down the street with a box of matches to disastrous results. This was a house deliberately chosen. Selected, if you like. Someone deliberately entered that house, locked Christie and Adelaide in their bedrooms, then set fire to the house. I think William Barton was trying to effect some sort of rescue. Maybe I'm wrong but I believe it was deliberate murder, not an accident. No one else in the entire village was targeted, were they?'

'No.'

'Have there been other cases of arson in Melverley in, say, the last five years?'

'No.'

'And did anyone see strangers wandering around the village that night?'

'Not that we've picked up on so far.'

'I take it there's no CCTV in the village?'

His silence affirmed her assumption.

'OK, so all I have is a great long list of questions that need answering. Why did this happen? What was the intent? To murder two women, or was the old man the target? Was it Jude they were really after – and failed? Why *did* he have a rope ladder installed? It seems an odd thing to me. Or was Nigel Barton the real target and our arsonist was unaware that he was not at home that night? Is there some vengeful woman behind this? Did Nigel Barton have a mistress who might wish his family harm? Why lock Adelaide and Christie in their rooms? Also, isn't it unusual for an arsonist to actually enter the property to splash the petrol around? It wasn't even ridiculously late. The family could have still been awake. Have your forensic people found any sign of him – or her?'

'Whoa, there.' Randall chuckled. 'Slow down. I can't keep up.' Then he added, 'I've said this before: you're wasted being a coroner.'

'Am I?' The question was not asked to provoke flattery or invite compliments but as a genuine query. And DI Randall responded in kind.

'Well, no. Not really. You aren't wasted as a coroner.' He cleared his throat in embarrassment. 'What I mean is you'd have made a bloody good cop.'

She laughed. 'Thank you very much, Inspector. Praise indeed.'

'You're welcome.'

They both sensed that the conversation was over, said their goodbyes and hung up.

And somehow the exchange with DI Randall had made St David's Day doubly special. The awkwardness was over, the intrusion forgotten or at least forgiven.

Both a leek *and* a daffodil.

SIX

Tuesday, 1 March, 6 p.m.

Alex conducted the briefing, his eyes roaming around the room speculatively. They'd taken over the church hall in Melverley as their operations headquarters. The place had a gentle feel in spite of the whiteboards, graphic photographs and rows of chairs holding police personnel. As an environment it wasn't hugely conducive to crime solving but it served its purpose and at least it was near the burnt-out house.

As Randall wrote on the board he was well aware that the lines of enquiry he was outlining coincided with Martha's ideas.

At the top he wrote a list of these potential lines, underlining the categories heavily. <u>Business associates of Nigel Barton.</u>

Next he wrote the name, <u>William Barton,</u> underneath detailing questions:

What exactly was his mental state?

Is he a serious suspect?

Is it possible he deliberately started the fire and locked the women in their rooms?

What was he doing on the landing?

Why did he have a lighter in his pocket?

Randall stood for a moment, staring out over the faces of his force. The two people best placed to answer these questions were the old man's son and grandson. Could he rely on them to be honest in their responses? One had to hope so.

Next he wrote: Did William Barton smoke?

A minor question, surely easy enough to obtain a truthful answer? A simple yes or no. Randall would soon learn that this case would not be simple from any angle. There would be no simple yeses or nos.

Next he wrote <u>Jude</u> followed by a question mark – nothing else.

Then the 'unsavoury man' – probably a boy who had had some sort of relationship with Adelaide.

And lastly he wrote Nigel Barton.

Underneath:

Money concerns?

Another relationship?

Business associates?

It was a simple matter of checking out the man's alibi, surely. If he had been miles away at the time of the fire – whatever his personal life – he couldn't have had anything to do with it. But Randall was a realist. Nigel Barton couldn't have had anything to do with it unless, he added mentally, someone had done the dirty work for him.

But at the back of Randall's mind was the fear that none of these lines of enquiry would lead them to their arsonist, that this was not a personal, planned attack but a random selection. In which case, as they had no local leads, they were in trouble. It threw the entire investigation wide open. It could have been anyone who poured the petrol, anyone who locked the doors, anyone who threw the fatal match. He didn't want to explore this particular avenue even in his mind.

He threw more questions out into the room for the officers to consider. 'Who was the intended target? The obvious answer is the women. They were the ones who died, after all. But . . .' He eyed Talith and Roberts, knowing they would mentally wrestle with every problem he threw their way plus a few more, 'one could question whether they were the intended victims. Fires are an unpredictable method of murder. People do die but sometimes they do not.' He turned back to the board and studied it for a while without speaking.

The name Jude seemed to pop out at him. He frowned. This was the boy who had had the foresight to keep a rope ladder in his bedroom, as though anticipating a catastrophe. The boy who managed to escape the inferno alone, with no more than minor injuries and those mainly to his hands sustained, presumably, in the rescue attempt. Suddenly he was very curious about Jude. Leaving the officers to pursue the lines of enquiry he'd suggested, he singled out Gethin Roberts.

'Can you just run through what happened last Thursday evening?'

Roberts cleared his throat, wondering whether he was about to get a ticking off or praise. Scanning his superior's face, he still wasn't sure. 'When I got to the house,' he began, 'it was obvious that the entire front was going up in flames. They were shooting out of the bedroom windows. The noise was terrific. Glass breaking and this whooshing noise – it was like the fire was alive.' He decided to risk levity. 'I can see where the ideas of dragons came from. You'd swear—'

'Carry on,' Randall said curtly.

'It was hot, too. I couldn't believe that anyone could be alive in there.' Nervously he cleared his throat again. 'But when I went round the back of the house it didn't look too bad. I just wondered if maybe someone just might have managed to get downstairs so I thought I'd go in. The back door . . .'

DI Randall interrupted. 'Was it open or closed?'

'Closed,' Roberts said.

'Locked or unlocked?'

'I don't know, sir. I smashed the glass and shoved it.' Roberts frowned. 'It all happened so quickly,' he said. 'The boy, Jude, was running towards me. His clothes were on fire. I pulled him out and threw him on to the ground. He was screaming. Then some firemen and the ambulance crew arrived and they took over.'

'How bad was the fire in the kitchen?'

'Right after we'd got out there was an explosion. Gas, I'd expect.'

Some of Roberts's colleagues were listening in with incredulity. Roberts paused for a moment. Flora, his girlfriend, had given him a right telling off about risking his life yet again for the job. But she had also made it plain that she was very proud of him too. It didn't hurt to be the partner of a hero. Roberts was allowing his mind to drift. He would be nominated for a police bravery award. A night out at the Dorchester!

What Gethin Roberts omitted to say was that when he'd heard the explosion his knees had buckled and he too had sunk to the ground, to be yanked away from the burning house by a couple of burly fire officers who had railed against him for being an 'idiot'. That was the word they had used and it still stung. And his hearing was still muffled.

Randall's hazel eyes rested on the young constable with a degree of perception. So when the young constable looked at him he felt he had been stripped bare and that the inspector knew exactly what had happened that night, both earlier and later.

Actually, DI Randall thoughts had already moved on from the young constable's actions that night and were taking on a new thought. He needed to talk some more to Jude Barton. 'Tell me one more thing,' he said, ideas forming an incomplete patchwork inside his head.

'Sir?' Roberts was all attention.

'Did you actually see Jude Barton descending the ladder?'

'No, sir.'

'OK. That's all – for now.'

Roberts was dismissed.

Wednesday, 2 March, 10 a.m.

Nigel Barton was at his son's bedside, going over events, and not for the first time.

'Did you hear Addy or your mother screaming?'

Jude Barton eyed his father. 'I'm not sure,' he said. 'Sometimes I don't know what I heard that night. I don't know if I'm remembering something real or if I'm just having another bad dream.' One bandaged hand moved towards his father. 'And Gramps,' he said. 'Why did he do it, Dad? Why did he lock them in? They could probably have got out otherwise.'

Nigel Barton regarded his son. Then opened his mouth. 'We don't know that it was gramps who did that, do we?'

The boy sat very still.

'You didn't actually see him lock the doors, did you?'

Jude pressed his lips together.

His father was silent too for a minute or two, then, 'Jude?'

'Yes, Dad?'

'I want you to promise—'

Nigel Barton's mobile phone interrupted. Nigel cursed then answered. 'Barton,' he said curtly.

'I need to speak to you.' Even Jude could make out the words and pick up on the anger.

Nigel answered tersely. 'I'm at the hospital, with my son.'

The same female voice came back again. 'I said I need to speak to you.'

Jude watched his father's lips tighten and anger burn in his eyes.

'The Armoury,' he finally said. 'Three o'clock this afternoon.' 'Don't be late.'

Nigel Barton ended the call and put his phone back in the breast pocket of his suit. He offered his son no explanation and Jude did not enquire. When his father finally did look at him he realized he was not angry with him anymore. He was frightened now and worried.

Nigel Barton leaned over the bed. 'I have to know. Did you hear them?' He didn't need to finish the sentence or elaborate.

His son shook his head. 'It was noisy, Dad, really noisy.'

His father hugged him then in a rare display of affection. 'Why, oh why on earth did you go back in?'

'I thought I could let them out,' Jude muttered.

His father hugged him even tighter. 'Thank God you're all right,' he said. 'I could have lost you as well.'

When it was time to go his father patted him on the shoulder. 'Everything's going to be all right, Jude,' he said awkwardly. 'I don't want you to worry.'

But instead of being reassured Jude's eyes filled with alarm and panic. His bandaged hand moved towards his father.

Nigel walked towards the door. 'Be brave, son, be brave. I have to go to the police station now and make yet another statement. But I don't want you to worry. It isn't your fault. You understand that?'

Jude eyed his father uneasily.

'It isn't your fault,' Nigel repeated. The words were emphasized with great deliberation. Jude stared as the door closed behind his father.

Wednesday, 2 March, 12 p.m.

'Thank you for coming in so promptly.' Alex Randall rose to greet Nigel Barton. 'Again, I'd like to say that I'm sorry for your loss, sir.'

Barton still looked haggard, as one would expect of a man who had had such a tragedy. But there was more. Randall caught the distinct whiff of concern. This man grieved for the recent past but he was also apprehensive for the future. This was a very worried man. He took stock. Nigel Barton was around five foot nine, slim, in a rumpled suit which he had patently worn for the last few days. He looked pale and shocked. There were dark rings around his eyes. He looked up and stared straight into Randall's face. 'Thank you,' he said softly.

By the time the bereaved man had sat down Randall had formed his opinion of him. The DI looked at all people in the same way and tried to find one word in the English language to size them up. Nigel Barton was . . . frightened. Martha Gunn was . . . warm. His wife was . . . but here one word was not enough. He needed two.

He turned his attention back to Barton. He was of average height. Neat, short grey hair, neither thin nor fat. His features were small and regular, his teeth unremarkable. Nigel Barton would never stand out in a crowd because he was neat and average and yet Randall sensed there was some aspect of his character which was neither neat nor average. But Barton kept this facet of his personality deeply hidden. DI Randall would need to use every ounce of his talents to unearth this irregularity. Again, he said, 'I'm sorry for your loss. It's an . . .' Words failed him. *Appalling tragedy* seemed inadequate.

'Thank you, Inspector,' Barton said formally. 'But I know you haven't asked me to come down here to offer prolonged, though doubtless sincere condolences.'

Randall met his eyes but had no clue whether this was mockery, cynicism, the aftermath of shock or politeness. He continued: 'At the moment our investigations waver between this being a random arson attack which your household was unlucky to have sustained or . . .' He let the sentence hang in the air.

'A random arson attack hardly explains why my wife and daughter were locked into their rooms so they were unable to escape the fire,' Barton said, a look of pure torture twisting his face.

'You must have formed your own idea of what happened?'

Barton stared back. 'I believe that's your job,' he said tightly.

'Well, it is, but we're always happy to accept any help from the victims and their families.'

'I have no idea.'

Randall appraised him. Nigel Barton was no fool. He must have some ideas. He challenged his eyes. But, perhaps wisely, said nothing more. He knew that whatever Barton's theories might be he was not going to make this easy for the police. Perhaps he was concerned he might point the finger of accusation in the wrong direction. Randall cleared his throat noisily. 'You understand there are some set questions I need to ask.'

Barton nodded.

'I hope you don't mind if I record this interview?'

After the briefest of pauses Barton nodded again. Randall switched the machine on.

'Can you think of anyone who might bear you a grudge?'

'I've already answered this in part to your sergeant,' Barton said curtly. 'I had a Turkish fellow working for me until fairly recently. I discovered he was setting up a rival business and networking my clients. I fired him on the spot.'

'His name?'

'Yusuf Karoglan. He's from Marmaris, I understand.'

'And now?'

'He has a business in Chester. I don't know how well it's doing.' His lips tightened. 'It doesn't seem to be having any impact on my business so I assume not particularly well.'

Randall nodded. 'And?'

'Ben Hatton. Ben was a really good worker. Nice guy. I had thought of taking him on as a partner but business got slack and I had to let him go. He was very bitter about it. Tried to black-mail me.'

Randall's ears pricked up.

Barton looked uncomfortable. 'I have a certain way of organizing my products,' he said testily. 'It's not patented but it works.

Hatton threatened to leak the secret. Even said he'd take the patent out himself. He couldn't have done that but business isn't so good I could afford to use up money fighting something through the courts.' He stopped and Randall looked at him enquiringly. 'There is something else,' Barton said. 'Hatton was married to a girl called Julie. Beautiful thing. He was absolutely obsessed with her. But she was a very high-maintenance lady. Liked expensive clothes. Big diamonds, flashy cars. Plenty of beauty treatments, long-haul holidays, five-star hotels.' He gave Randall an amused look. 'You get the picture. When Hatton lost his job he lost her too and I have heard he turned to drink. I have also heard that he blames me for everything.'

Randall regarded the man. There was not the faintest hint of guilt or regret. 'Is he right to?'

Barton leaned forward. 'Sorry?' Even in that one word there was a threat.

'Is he right to blame you?'

Barton settled back in his chair. 'I thought that was what you said. No, he was not right to blame me.' He tried his hand at a touch of humour. 'As they said in *The Godfather*, it's not a personal thing. I couldn't afford to keep him on. He was going to cost me. I couldn't trust him.'

'And has he found another job?'

Barton shrugged. 'I don't know.'

'Is there anyone else?'

Barton's face looked vaguely distasteful. 'A little pipsqueak called Pinfold whom I caught fiddling expenses. Said he was staying in hotels and really sleeping on friends' floors, buying all the drinks and even, I suspect, snorting a bit of coke. A despicable character.'

'Despicable enough to torch your house?'

Although they had been working towards this very question it pulled Barton up short. He opened his mouth, gaped, tried to speak. Then inserted his finger round his collar as though it was choking him. Then he frowned. 'No,' he protested. 'No. At least, I don't think so. He's bad, but he's not that bad.' His face froze. 'But . . .' he said and his voice trailed away.

Mentally Randall marked the word. Barton was beginning to think. 'Anyone else?'

His face grim, Barton shook his head again.

And Randall continued: 'Do you have contact details for the three business associates?'

'I do – they may be out of date since Hatton's marriage broke up. Karoglan you'll be able to track via the Internet. He advertises quite robustly. As for Pinfold, last I heard he was living with his mother who has a cottage here in the village. Made life quite embarrassing for me, I can tell you. Without giving away all the boy's secrets I couldn't tell her why I'd sacked him which made her very resentful. I haven't seen him around lately though.'

'Right. I understand.' Alex began to square up his papers then picked up the subject again. 'If you had to bet which of these three men would be most likely to torch your house – and make a mistake because you weren't even at home – which would you think most likely?'

Barton's face froze as he thought before answering. Then he said, 'I can't believe any of these three would do such a terrible thing but oddly enough there are different reasons for all three. Karoglan is hot-headed and cruel. If he had set the fire it's possible he might have locked my wife and daughter in their rooms and taken malicious delight in doing so.

'Hatton was obsessed with Julie. In some ways it made him unbalanced. She was very, *very* beautiful. There was something feline about her. Big green eyes. She had a wonderful figure, lovely teeth, shiny hair.' He looked across at Alex. 'She was really gorgeous. A head-turner. When he lost her he became extremely bitter and angry. If he blamed me for the loss of the love of his life – well, who could know what he'd do?'

'And Pinfold?'

'He was just a wanker,' Barton said disparagingly. 'And when he was high on coke he would have done anything. His mother spoiled him rotten. And it's not just him. His mother was so protective of him even she might have wanted to wreak revenge.' He looked at Randall. 'It's a terrible thought that I might somehow have indirectly caused the deaths of three members of my family.'

Randall wanted to point out the anomaly in the statement but instead he pressed on. 'As far as you know do any of these four people have a criminal record?'

Barton shook his head. 'Not as far as I know,' he said then gave a weak smile. 'I expect you can check it all via your police computers.'

Randall nodded and cleared his throat before continuing. 'I understand that your daughter had a boyfriend of whom you disapproved?'

Barton pursed his lips. 'My daughter was fifteen years old,' he said brokenly. 'She was an intelligent girl with a potentially very bright future. She'd talked about going in for Law. She was certainly capable of it. Sean Trotter hadn't a patch on her intellect. He was a sporty boy without a brain. All brawn.'

Alex demurred. 'Surely that's a bit of a cliché?'

Barton blinked. 'In this case no. He was a thick boy with superficial good looks and plenty of muscle. He didn't have a brain.'

'I see. And where does he live?'

'In the village somewhere.'

Randall waited.

'They were in the same school.'

'Thank you.' Randall paused, knowing his next question would be sensitive.

'I understand your father set fire to his bedroom last year some time.'

'It was an accident.'

'Did your father smoke?'

'He smoked a pipe. After last year's incident we tried to stop him smoking in his bedroom but we'd catch the occasional waft of tobacco smoke drifting across the landing.'

'We found a cigarette lighter in his dressing-gown pocket.'

Barton dropped his face into his hands and gave a loud sigh.

'One more question, Mr Barton.'

Barton looked up warily, his eyes fixing on the detective as he waited.

'Your wife, daughter and father. Were their lives insured?'

Barton went slightly pale, recovered himself and spoke steadily. 'They were, as a matter of fact.'

Alex waited.

'My wife's life was insured for half a million,' Barton began. 'My daughter . . .' Raw emotion crossed his face. 'My daughter and my father also had life insurance for a quarter of a million each if their deaths were not due to natural causes.' His eyes challenged Randall's. 'Naturally sickness was particularly excluded in the case of my father.'

'I see.' Alex let out a slow, thoughtful breath.

Wednesday, 2 March, 2.30 p.m.

Two hours later he was relating the result of the interview to Martha, in detail, knowing she would be frustrated that she hadn't met Nigel Barton yet and anxious to hear Randall's opinion. 'So what did you make of him?'

Randall didn't answer her straight away but frowned into the distance. 'Difficult to judge after such extreme trauma,' he said. 'I don't think he can really comprehend what's happened. I think he was too stunned to form any opinion of who set the fire.'

'But he gave you some names of people who might have felt animosity towards him and his family?'

'Yes,' Randall said.

'So what's your next step?'

He stood up. 'Jude.'

This was the second time Alex Randall had met Jude Barton. The first time had not been helpful. The boy had been sedated and still very traumatized by his experience. It had felt cruel to press him for details. Jude Barton looked like a poet, with pale skin and very dark hair that flopped over his eyebrow. He had long, fringed eyelashes and thin, sensitive fingers, also long. Randall wondered if he had an aspiration to become an actor. He certainly had the looks for it.

He settled down in the chair at the side of the bed and studied the boy. Jude's eyes were almost closed as though it was too much effort to keep the lids open. He looked weary. Both hands were still swathed in thick bandages. Randall wondered whether he would need the skin grafts the doctors had mentioned. After a minute's silence he realized that Jude was waiting for him to speak. 'First of all, Jude,' Alex said, adopting a friendly tone, 'I want you to know we're all very glad that you survived.'

The boy's attempt at a smile was heart-rending. Tears squeezed out of his eyes. He made no attempt to brush them away but let them roll down his cheeks.

'And I'm really sorry about the rest of your family,' Randall continued.

'Thanks,' the boy muttered, looking away.

'Tell me a bit about the evening of the fire. Anything you remember about earlier on.'

'It was just ordinary,' Jude said, his gaze wandering away from Randall towards the blank wall. He gave a cynical snort. 'So very ordinary.' He turned his head back so his eyes stared straight into Randall's. 'Mum made tea around seven.' He couldn't stop his mouth from curving into a smile. 'Cottage pie. She was always making that.' His mouth twisted again into a look of obvious pain. 'I went back into my room. I had some homework to do. Addy was in her room, listening to some music, I think. Mum and Grandad were watching TV downstairs. I went back down for a hot chocolate and some biscuits around ten. Addy was still in her room. I shouted goodnight to her but I don't think she heard me. She was probably listening to her MP3 player. Grandad was in bed too.' Another grin. 'I could hear him snoring.'

Randall interrupted. 'So your grandfather was asleep then?'

The boy read nothing into this. 'Yeah, he sort of catnaps half the time then wakes up in the middle of the night all confused, not knowing where he is. He sort of wanders around. Once or twice he's even wandered up the stairs and into my room in the early hours. Gives me a right shock. He looks like a ghost and hasn't a clue where he is. Whoever finds him just takes him back to bed.' Jude grinned. 'Like a sleepwalking child. He's quite obedient. It's not a problem,' he added finally and defensively.

He seemed to have forgotten the fact that his grandfather was now dead and there was the question whether he had been the one who had set the fire. But at this point in the investigation it would have been unkind to remind Jude of this fact.

'Go on. Finish telling me about the evening.' Randall wasn't sure how or even whether this glimpse into the Barton's family life would help but it was worth a try.

'Mum was just coming upstairs with a mug of tea.' Again his eyes clouded as he remembered, probably realizing that this had been the last time he had seen his mother, wished his sister goodnight and heard his grandfather breathing. Randall didn't want to remind him, but had to prompt, 'Ye-es?'

'I went up to my room. I had my headphones on.' He hesitated. Swallowed with a noisy gulp. 'I can't hear a thing when I've got them on.' A look of mischief lightened his expression. 'Drives Mum mad.'

'And a thousand other mothers, I expect.' Randall joined in. 'Then?'

'I must have dropped off to sleep.' He paused. Frowned. '*Something* must have woken me but I'm a long way off all the others. I opened my door and I could smell smoke.' He looked away. 'I panicked, Detective Randall. I didn't know what to do. I thought Grandad must have . . .' His voice trailed away miserably but Randall knew what he had thought: that his grandfather had started another fire.

'I made a plan. I shut the door. Then I thought I'd take my keys down with me and climb down the rope ladder.' There was another brief spark of mischief. 'I'd tried out my rope ladder before. I knew it was safe. I thought I'd climb down,' he said again, 'and see what was happening. When I got down I went round the front of the house. Then I could see it was worse. Much worse than I'd thought. It was terrifying. There were flames and smoke bursting out of the front windows. The bedrooms, too, where Mum and Addy sleep. I got in through the back door. But it was hopeless.' He buried his face in his hands and groaned.

Alex interrupted. 'Was the back door closed or open, locked or unlocked?'

The boy looked at him with respect, as though he had just realized that DI Alex Randall was a real policeman. 'As far as I remember,' he said carefully, 'it was unlocked but closed. I might be wrong but I don't remember having to use my key. I think it's probably still in my pyjama pocket.' Jude Barton's pyjamas were currently in forensics. He looked anxious. 'I closed the door behind me to stop the draught making the fire worse.'

'Did you decide which key you needed?'

'I had both,' Jude said carefully. 'Front and back. But when I'd looked out of my window I could see that the fire was worst at the front. I could either hang the ladder from a hook at the front or at the back but I could never have climbed down the front of the house or got in through the front door so I went round the back. I got into the kitchen but not much further. It was like hell.'

'Could you hear anything else?' He meant the women screaming, the grandfather calling, but he didn't labour the point.

The boy closed his eyes wearily. 'I don't know. There was so much . . . drama . . . and noise going on. I don't know what I heard or what I thought I heard. I might even have been screaming. There were sirens and . . .' Again he paused. 'I've thought and tried to remember if I did hear Mum or Addy or Grandad but I don't really know. Not for sure. I don't know what was in my head and what was real. When I close my eyes I seem to hear them screaming but I still don't know whether it was my imagination or what.' Again he covered his face with his hands. 'I don't know what's real any more. And then I saw the policeman coming for me and my clothes were on fire. My hands felt hot. I couldn't find the door because the smoke was thick. I *think* I was shouting for Mum and Addy but I don't know. The screaming might all have been inside my head. I just don't know.' His mood shifted slightly. 'And what good will it do? It won't bring them back whatever I remember. Then the policeman dragged me out.' The dark eyes met his. 'I'd have died in there if it hadn't been for him. I would have died with Mum, Grandad and Addy.' He leaned back on the pillows, exhausted, before adding softly, 'Maybe I should have done.'

Alex allowed him his silence before asking very softly, 'Who do you think started the fire, Jude?'

The boy shook his head. 'I can't think of anyone,' he began then stopped abruptly. 'I don't know anybody that horrible.' His eyes closed. 'That wicked,' he said. There was another brief silence before he finally said a firm, 'No.'

'Did you hear anyone else in the house that night, other than your family?'

Jude shook his head.

'Your father tells me that your sister had a boyfriend.'

For the first time during the interview the boy grinned. 'Oh, you mean Hotter Trotter.'

Randall smiled along with him.

'It wasn't anything like Dad thought,' Jude said. 'Dad thought it was really serious and Addy was going to drop out of studying.' He grinned again. 'To go off with that spudhead? I don't think so, Inspector Randall. It was just Dad.'

'You mean your father didn't want Adelaide to have a boyfriend?'

'He couldn't have cared less,' Jude said, 'as long as it didn't interfere with her going to uni.'

For the first time, Alex reflected, as he left the hospital minutes later, he could perceive a crack in what had appeared such a perfect family. He could almost hear Martha snort that there was no such thing – except when it was long dead and gone, and retrieved from an inaccurate and fantasy-producing memory.

SEVEN

Wednesday, 2 March, 3 p.m.
The Armoury

The Armoury was an eighteenth-century building to the north-east of the town. A neat Georgian building, it had the atmosphere and décor of a London wine bar, the walls lined with bookshelves, scrubbed tables and high windows which overlooked the Welsh Bridge and the River Severn. It was a popular meeting place with a warm and friendly ambience but there were dark corners too, hidden from the public gaze, where acquaintances could meet surreptitiously, or so they might think. Shrewsbury is not really a big enough town to hide in.

Nigel Barton tried his best to sidle in, arouse no attention, find one of these corners and wait. But he was fully aware that anyone who happened to glance in could and probably would see him. And that was just what he didn't want.

Not right now.

Wednesday, 2 March, 3.30 p.m.

Detective Inspector Alex Randall knew that the investigation needed to start somewhere. It was no use floundering around like headless chickens. They had to begin by eliminating suspects. He had made the decision to start with the three business associates of Nigel Barton but he wasn't overly optimistic. Already he had the feeling that this would be a long and tortuous case. They had no real leads but Alex Randall was as determined and tenacious as a python, enveloping people in its coils before tightening.

So the first step had been to send DS Paul Talith to speak to Yusuf Karoglan.

As Barton had told them, Karoglan had set up a rival business in Chester, just outside the town walls. It was a smart-looking place overlooking the racecourse, modern in contrast to the ancient city, with bright advertising and neat parking spaces at the front. Outside stood a silver grey Lexus ISF. Roughly £60,000's worth of car. Talith wasted a few minutes admiring it, wishing he had one of these instead of the eminently practical Ford Focus which he and his wife shared. Then he turned away. Ah, well.

He knocked on the door and it was opened by a secretary wearing an expensive-looking and well-fitting black suit, very, very high heels, black, straight, shining hair and scarlet lipstick. Talith stared at her, taken aback. She reminded him of Morticia Adams. There was a vampirish, almost predatory air about her which the DS wasn't quite comfortable with. For the second time in as many minutes his mouth dropped open and he stood and stared, then remembered his manners and flashed his ID card, mumbling that he wished to speak to Mr Karoglan.

'Then I invite you in, Sergeant,' she said with a flirtatious curve of those very red lips. 'Although I don't suppose I have any choice, do I?'

Talith had recovered himself. His response was a bland smile of his own. 'Is Mr Karoglan in?'

'Yes.'

'Can I speak to him?'

Her response was arch as she moved behind her shiny desk. 'Does *he* have a choice?'

His reply was blunt. 'Not really.'

'Right, then. Do I get to know what it's about?'

Talith had a sudden fantastic urge to leap over the desk, kiss those red lips and ask her what business it was of hers? Tell her that secretaries don't have the right to know *everything* about their bosses. Instead he gave a goofy grin and watched as she pressed a button on her keypad and told Karoglan, presumably, that Detective Sergeant Paul Talith of Shrewsbury police wished to speak to him.

Karoglan was no surprise. Oily, handsome, dressed in a silky continental suit, he appeared in the doorway, his hand already held out and a smile pasted across his face. 'Hello,' he said in a Mancunian accent, 'how are you doin?' Without waiting for a response he continued with the traditional, 'And how can I help you?' When Talith didn't respond straightaway he followed this with an eagle glance and a perceptive, 'I suppose it'd be better if we went in my office. Eh?'

'Thanks.'

The office was predictably Spartan in its furnishings with a small table in front of the window, two black leather chairs and a desk whose top was bare apart from a computer screen. On the table was the sole ornament in the room, a rectangular, blue glass dish decorated with an orange fish swimming across its middle. The wall reflected the minimalist taste of the room with one huge painting, a Turkish street scene of a man with curving slippers sitting in the foreground smoking a hubble-bubble pipe. It looked an original rather than a print. Talith's eyes swept around the room and returned to Karoglan, who was grinning at him. He jerked his head towards the painting. 'Yeah, well,' Karoglan said with a self-effacing grin, 'had to remind myself of the old country.'

The old country, Talith thought. Judging by his accent he'd probably never even been to Turkey, except maybe on a two-week package deal. Karoglan motioned Talith to sit and looked alert. Alert, Talith reflected, not wary. He dived straight in.

'You've heard about the house fire at Melverley?'

Karoglan frowned. 'Yeah. Awful. I heard Mrs Barton and her daughter died.'

'How did you find out?'

'A guy I used to work with.'

Talith hazarded a guess. 'Pinfold?'

'Yeah. That's right. He rang me up and told me. Awful.'
Karoglan's frown deepened. 'How did it happen?'

'We don't know.' Talith paused, his lids hooding his eyes.
Karoglan was an intelligent man. He'd know why he was here.
He decided to approach his questions obliquely and made his
voice deliberately pally. 'What was Pinfold's take on it?'

'Shocked. That's about it. Such a horrible thing to happen.
Was it an accident, do you know?'

Talith said nothing and after a hard stare Karoglan leaned
forward across his desk, his elbows flat. 'You're not telling me
it was deliberate?'

'It's possible.'

'Oh, sweet Jesus.'

He must have caught the surprise in Talith's face. He grinned.
'There are such things as Turkish Christians, you know.'

Talith laughed too. Against his better judgement he rather liked
the fellow. But he was not here to make friends. 'I have to ask
you – do you know anything about the fire?'

'No.' There was just the hint that Karoglan might be about to
take offence.

'And, just for the record, where were you last Wednesday night
between the hours of ten p.m. and two a.m.?'

Karoglan chuckled and gave a meaningful glance at the door,
'I'll give you one guess,' he said, playfully assuming a Jack-the-lad
expression.

Talith kept his face deliberately wooden. 'And can anyone
corroborate your story, sir?'

Karoglan got to his feet in one agile movement. 'Teresa, love,
can you come in here a minute?'

She was an elegant creature, Talith reflected, as Teresa entered
the room, tossing her black hair behind her like a chiffon scarf.
'Yusuf?'

'Just tell the Sergeant here where I was last Thursday evening,
there's a darlin,' he drawled lazily.

Talith was a weenie bit jealous of the careless, easy way Karoglan
had with Teresa. If he'd had a girlfriend like that he'd have treated
her like porcelain, not like some cheap, ordinary woman.

But Teresa didn't seem to mind. She aimed a friendly smile

in the sergeant's direction. 'I think I cooked for you that night, didn't I, darlin'? And then we watched a spot of telly and then . . .' The scarlet lips curved and she looked straight at Talith. 'I wouldn't be a bit surprised if we went off to bed.' She gave Talith a mocking look. 'That do you, Sergeant?'

Talith's response remained wooden. 'Are you absolutely sure that's how you spent last Thursday evening?'

She nodded, not smiling at all now and actually not looking quite so pretty either, but even more vampirish.

Talith persevered. 'And you wouldn't mind signing a statement to that effect, miss?'

'Holloway,' she supplied, then shrugged as though the whole thing was of no interest to her. 'Not at all – if that's what you want.' She looked back at Karoglan. 'That all?'

Neither man moved and she took the initiative, her high heels clopping on the parquet floor like a horse's hooves. Both men watched her go. Behind her she left an aura of femininity and predation.

'See,' Karoglan's voice was chummy now, conspiratorial. 'If you think about it, it's obvious. I had no axe to grind with Barton or his family. If anything he'd have had the quarrel with me.' He gave a nasty smile. 'I'm the one who's sucking his business bone dry. And . . .'

He didn't need to mention either the secretary or the Lexus parked outside. Talith was perfectly aware of both and Karoglan knew it. He was a man who would always underplay his cards. And yet the alibi could so easily have been arranged. And Talith was perfectly aware that Karoglan would be a ruthless and cruel opponent.

At the same time as Talith's encounter with Karoglan, PC Gethin Roberts had tracked Ben Hatton down to a small printer's in Slough. It didn't look a particularly prosperous business but rather seedy from the outside with a corner of the window boarded up and the chipboard plastered with graffiti. Hatton himself opened the door, bloodshot eyes and a day's stubble on his chin. He smelt stale and eyed Roberts warily.

Gethin Roberts swallowed hard, his Adam's apple bobbing nervously in his neck. 'I'm from the Shrewsbury police,' he managed. 'We're investigating a fatal house fire in the village of—' He got no further.

Hatton glared at him furiously. 'So what are you coming here for?'

Roberts stood his ground. 'We believe you . . . knew . . . the family,' he said bravely.

'I knew them all right,' Hatton said grumpily. 'I knew them all.' He stood quite still for a moment, as though he'd forgotten the police officer was there. Then he gathered himself. 'I suppose you may as well come in,' he said grudgingly.

The shop inside was, if anything, even seedier than the outside. It smelt of tobacco smoke and sour milk and the carpet was badly stained, the counter made of thin, bendy hardboard. Even the machines looked ancient with sun-bleached plastic, wires and plugs everywhere.

Hatton sank down into one of the two chairs. 'So what are you doing here?' he asked. 'I left Barton's firm nearly three years ago. I've had nothing to do with him since then.'

Roberts felt very nervous now. 'I have to ask you,' he squeaked, 'where you were last Wednesday between the hours of ten p.m. and midnight?'

Hatton looked incredulous. 'You mean, you think I had something to do with it, that I drove all the way up to Shropshire just to set fire to Barton's house with his family inside? That's ridiculous.'

'Just answer the question,' Roberts said, 'please.' He wished he didn't sound quite so desperate.

'Look,' Hatton said. 'It's all water under the bridge. Me and Julie, me and Barton. It's all behind me now. I've moved on.'

Roberts wished he had the confidence to point out that it didn't look much to him as though he had moved on. If he'd had to put a judgement on the situation he would have said that Hatton had not so much stagnated as slid backwards. He had plenty of reason to hate Barton and his family. He decided to go out on a limb just a bit. 'How did you come to leave the firm?'

Hatton looked at him. 'I was sacked,' he said. 'I'd discovered a new way of doing things. Dear old Nigel really liked it. So much so that he took it on board himself. Took all the credit and all the profit. Bastard,' he muttered under his breath.

*   *   *

WPC Lara Tinsley tracked down Felicity Pinfold and found her defensive of her son and very bitter about 'the way he was treated'.

'Trumped-up charges,' she said angrily. 'That's what they were. Trumped-up charges. Dear old Nigel just wanted to get rid of Stuart.'

'And where is he now?'

'He's working in a bar in Holland.' This was a surprise.

'Does he come home much?'

'Now and then. I go over there mostly. Fond of the country, I am. It's civilized.' Her sharp little eyes missed nothing.

'Was Stuart home last week?'

She shook her head. 'He hasn't been back here since Christmas. He rings me a couple of times a week though. And I ring him if I've got any news.'

'Did you ring him about the fire?' Tinsley asked.

Mrs Pinfold's mouth worked as though wondering what to say and Tinsley waited.

Finally she got her answer. Felicity Pinfold gave a jerky nod. Lara wondered what her son's reaction had been. But there was no point asking Stuart's mother.

She wouldn't have told her anyway.

Randall, meanwhile, had decided that he would speak to Sean Trotter, the boy who had been Adelaide Barton's boyfriend. Though he didn't believe for a minute that the sixteen-year-old had set the fire at Melverley Grange and locked both his girlfriend and her mother in their rooms to die, he felt he must check out all available leads. If anything, he reasoned as he drove through the town, Trotter would have felt vengeful towards *Nigel* Barton – not Adelaide's mother, grandfather or brother. And certainly not Adelaide herself. As he drove out towards Melverley he passed the burnt-out wreck which had once been the Barton family home, and couldn't help the feeling of sadness which swamped him.

Trotter and his family lived in a very modest semi, probably once a farmworker's cottage. Randall knocked on the door and waited. Trotter opened the door to him. He was, as everyone had told him, built like an American football player, with huge shoulders and thighs. He was dressed in a Chicago Bears sweater and loose-fitting jeans. Trotter knew instantly who Randall was and why he was there. 'In case you're wonderin',' he said, 'I didn't go to school today. I couldn't face it. I haven't been in since—' He broke off then added, 'You *are* the police, aren't you?'

Randall nodded and briefly flashed his ID card. Nigel Barton and his son had mocked Sean Trotter as an 'all brawn and no brains' sort of guy but Randall's initial impression of the teenager was that he was blunt and honest, without guile, rather than stupid.

'Mum's not here and Dad's at work,' the boy said. 'Do you want a cup of tea or something?'

'Yes.' Randall reflected how very normal this appeared. Quite civilized. Sean reappeared a couple of minutes later with two mugs of tea. 'Didn't know if you wanted sugar,' he said. Randall declined.

They both sat down on a squeaky brown leather sofa.

'Tell me about Adelaide,' Randall invited.

Sean drew in a deep, brave breath and shrugged. 'She was just a really nice girl,' he said. 'Natural, fun. Just nice. We weren't in love or anything and she'd have gone off to university anyway.' He gave a great shudder. 'Not now,' he said quickly. 'She won't go now.'

Randall had to steer the subject round very gently indeed. 'Did you mind the fact that she would be leaving here?'

Sean simply shook his head. ''Course not,' he said. ''Course not. I was hoping to get a place at the sports college anyway. It's kind of built in to the way of things now. You have a relationship and then you both move on. I wasn't upset.' He dropped his head. 'But I am when I think of what happened to her.' His face paled. 'I keep picturing her screaming in there, burning. Going black. It's horrible.'

'She died from smoke inhalation,' Randall said, wanting to alleviate the boy's obvious pain. 'She didn't burn to death. She suffocated. She might not even have known what was happening.' But the picture he had in his own mind was of a frightened girl hiding underneath her duvet.

And Trotter didn't seem to be much reassured either. He closed his eyes and looked as though he was about to faint.

'Just for the book,' Randall said casually, 'I need to know where you were on the night of the fire.'

Trotter looked at him with his honest brown eyes and looked shocked. 'You suspect me?'

'Not really. It's just for the record.'

'Football practice till eight. Then I came home for tea and did my homework. I didn't go out.'

'And your parents?'

'They were both here.'

'Right.' Randall paused. 'Do you have any idea who might have done this?'

The boy shook his head. 'I can't think of anybody,' he said. 'As far as I was concerned they were just a family.' He was frowning. 'It doesn't make any sense.'

Randall couldn't see much point in continuing this conversation. It appeared that Sean Trotter had nothing more to add.

He returned to the station in a gloomy mood.

The briefing that evening was typical of the early stage of an investigation. Plenty of trivia to report but none that would move the case any further on. They hadn't really been able to exclude any of Barton's business associates. Yusuf's "alibi" was patently thin. Frustratingly they still had no idea why the arson attack had taken place, who had set the fire or even whether murder had been the ultimate motive.

EIGHT

Friday, 4 March, 10 a.m.

Martha waited for two days before she contacted Alex Randall again. She had had a busy couple of days – there had been a death on the operating table at the hospital and the relatives were naturally distraught. Spending time with them had distracted her from the Melverley fire, but now she wanted to know how the investigation was proceeding.

She'd hoped they would have made some headway but Randall sounded downcast on the phone. 'We're a bit short of lines of enquiry, Martha,' he said. 'None of the house-to-house calls has borne fruit. No one saw or heard anything.'

She tried to reassure him. 'It's early days yet, Alex.'

'I just can't seem to find a motive.' He paused. 'Unless you count the life insurances Nigel Barton had on his family.'

'That sounds promising.'

'Amounts to a million on the three family members who died.'

'And did he have a similar life insurance on Jude?'

'I don't know. I must ask him.'

'Was he in financial trouble?'

'It appears not. The house is paid for. And that must be worth a million easily. He has plenty of savings. His business is small enough to be healthy but necessary enough to keep going even in these tricky times and his wife had a well-paid job. He doesn't appear to need money.'

'Where's he living at the moment? I take it the house is uninhabitable.'

'Absolutely – quite apart from it still being sealed up as it's a crime scene. He's staying at The Lord Hill. Naturally the insurance company are footing the bill.'

'Of course.' Martha thought for a minute then made her decision. 'Maybe it's time I met Mr Barton, Alex. I thought I'd invite him here this afternoon. I need to explain some of the procedures to him anyway.' She felt she needed to defend her involvement. 'It's normal practice in a case like this.'

'I'll be interested to hear your impression of him.'

She smiled at the formal politeness in his tone. 'You know as well as I do, Alex, that an impression formed, particularly in such a strained situation, can be very misleading.'

'No one knows that better than you, Martha Gunn.' There was mockery in his voice now. He was gently teasing her. 'I'm trusting that you can slice through the grief and come out with some sort of valid impression at the end of it?'

She couldn't resist a smirk and caught sight of herself in the mirror looking decidedly coy. 'And what about young Jude? Is he still in hospital?'

'He went back to his father yesterday. He has to go in to the burns clinic for daily dressings but he appears on the mend.' Randall paused and she knew he was puzzling over something. 'I don't think his injuries are as bad as they first thought. There's been no more mention of skin grafts anyway.'

'Well – that's good news.'

'Ye-es.'

'Has he remembered anything else about the night of the fire?'

'Not so far.'

'Alex,' she hesitated. 'It isn't my intention to teach you your job but I think you need to go public on this.'

'You mean an appeal on the television?'

'I think it would be a good idea. Throw your net wider and ever wider.'

Randall chuckled. 'I think I might just do that, Martha. Thank you for the advice.'

'You're welcome. Any time.'

'Is there any particular reason why you think I should cast my net wider?'

'As there appears no obvious motive for the attack I was wondering whether this involves someone or something *outside* the family. What about Barton's business associates?'

'We're working on that line of investigation.'

'My impression is that this isn't quite such a domestic affair as it would appear.'

'Not an inside job then, Martha? You're still discounting Barton senior?'

'Oh, I don't know. I simply have the feeling that to blame the fire and what is basically murder on a confused old man is a very easy option and an excellent way of diverting you from looking elsewhere for a killer.'

'Mmm. Profound.'

Martha frowned – and again caught sight of herself in the mirror that topped a mahogany sideboard. This time the image was not quite so pleasant. She was frowning. She concentrated again on the phone. 'It isn't profound, Alex. It's an instinct.' She hesitated. 'Sometimes I fear I must have a criminal mind. I'm so good at thinking up nasty plots.'

On the other end of the line, Randall chuckled.

'And now I must get Jericho to track Nigel Barton down. I'll be in touch.'

Jericho soon contacted Nigel Barton over his mobile phone then put the call through to Martha. She was brisk and business like but, underneath, curious. The man had had a terrible loss. How would he be? she wondered. Traumatized? Still shocked?

'Mr Barton,' she began, 'it's Martha Gunn here. I'm the coroner for this area and as such will shortly be holding the inquests on the deaths of your father, wife and daughter. May I begin by expressing my sympathy? I am so very sorry. You must feel dreadful.'

Barton responded stiffly. 'I do.'

'It would be a good idea for you to come in to my office so we can sort out some of the details. It'll be easier. You understand there will have to be an inquest?'

Barton gave no response so Martha continued. 'I know this is distressing for you and I don't want to make it worse but in cases like this I obviously have to work very closely with the police.'

Barton simply grunted which Martha took as an assent. But then he began speaking in a peevish, irritable tone. 'Well, as you've probably realized, Mrs Gunn, my house is currently a crime scene so I do not have access to it except with a policeman present. It will also have to be assessed by my insurance company so for now I am staying partly in my office and partly in the Lord Hill Hotel. Do you want me to come to your office?'

'That would be a good idea.'

'This afternoon?' He spoke in a *let's get it over with* voice that again Martha found off-putting. But sometimes grieving relatives were like this – unpredictable in their responses. So she kept her cool. 'No, Friday.'

He sounded defeated. 'Three o'clock?'

'I'll instruct my assistant to expect you. Do you know how to find my office? It's in Bayston Hill.'

'No, actually.' And again the peevish tone was back. 'I've never had anything to do with a coroner's office before.'

'I'll put you back to my assistant. He'll give you directions. I'll see you on Friday, Mr Barton.'

It wasn't until she'd put the phone down that she realized why the peevish tone. Nigel Barton was simply sorry for himself, wondering why he had been singled out for such cruel treatment. People like this never failed to fascinate her, the ones who only saw dramatic, tragic events as they impacted on their own lives. If disaster did not touch them personally then it did not exist. World affairs, tragedies in far off countries, economic crises. It was as simple as that – to someone who was completely and utterly self-centred they were unimportant, the victims of such events as insignificant as ants.

Interesting, she thought. She was already beginning to form an opinion about Nigel Barton – even before she'd met him.

In the meantime Alex Randall had followed Martha's advice. In such a dramatic case it was not difficult to involve the TV and local radio stations who were always anxious to help the police with cases which were proving difficult to crack. He, too, had contacted Nigel Barton to ask him if he wanted to be present at the interviews or if he had anything specific he wanted to say, but Barton had declined. Randall hadn't asked him whether he minded the case 'going public'. It was up to him as the SIO to decide how best to tackle the case, not a bereaved relative. He didn't mind tiptoeing round the man but in his sights was an answer – a solution and a final prosecution for murder. He would do all he could to reach that point.

By lunchtime the drive of Melverley Hall was packed with press and TV and the usual public who magically appeared at the sight of such drama.

Randall began by outlining the case, telling the wider world that the fire had been started deliberately, using petrol, that the two women had been locked into their rooms, that Jude had had a lucky escape and that Willliam Barton had suffered from Alzheimer's disease and had also died in the fire. He left out the fact that Barton senior had caused a previous fire. But he did toss into the fray the fact that Nigel Barton had been away on business on the night of the fire. He left this to fester in the suspicious minds of the ladies and gentlemen of the media as he appealed for information, knowing that someone would pick up on this fact and ask a relevant question. Sure enough, a tall, blonde woman whom he'd encountered on many a previous occasion opened the interrogation. 'DI Randall.'

He inclined his head toward her.

'Jennifer Purloin, *Daily Metro*. Are you assuming that it was coincidence that Mr Barton junior was away on the night of the fire?'

Randall met her gaze unflinchingly. 'I don't know is the true answer.' He decided to take a step outside his usual stick-to-the-truth method. 'But my instinct tells me that if our fire-raiser was inside the house and able to lock the two women in their rooms he or she would also have been likely to know that Mr Barton junior was away from home for the night.'

The next question came from a very skinny guy with a tattoo on his neck. 'You say that . . .' He glanced down at his pad, 'Jude Barton was injured?'

'That's correct,' Randall said testily. He knew he was walking over uneven ground here.

'Are you able to tell us how Jude Barton managed to escape the fire?'

Randall replied tersely, uncomfortable with the story, and told him that the boy had secured a rope ladder outside his bedroom which he had escaped down, that he had re-entered the house in the hope of saving his family but had been beaten back by the ferocity of the blaze. Even as he said the words he had an uneasy feeling, as though he was relating a script. The story of heroism. He frowned, wound up the press interview and sneaked a glance at his watch. One o'clock. Just in time for the lunchtime news.

Nice timing.

Friday, 4 March, 1.15 p.m.

In a modest house in Sundorne, Shrewsbury, Monica Deverill was ironing while also watching the lunchtime news. As the detective made his appeal she stopped for a moment, the iron in her hand. Barton. William Barton. She stood still, remembering. Fire Officer Barton. She remembered that terrible encounter, recalled his voice, so different on the second occasion from the first.

He had said, *'It isn't safe here. Now come along, Mrs'* . . . She stopped. What was the woman's name?

She remembered her impatience on that night, her irritability
with the woman's slowness, with the little sequence of formalities
that had to be taken before she would climb into bed along with
all the others before she could switch the lights off. It was a rule.
Everyone had to be in their beds before the lights were switched
off. But she would not be hurried. The sleeves of her garments
had to be turned round the right way, the slippers peeping out from
under the bed. As she had waited she had thought she would die
of boredom and irritability.

It had been her job to check the day room, make sure all was
safe. But that night she had been too impatient, in a hurry, her
actions careless. This was her last night shift. Tomorrow she'd
had a date with the love of her life – Bill Deverill. Her mind
had been fixed on that.

What was the woman's name he'd been trying to rescue? As
she recalled the events of that night she remembered the more
recent occurrence and started breathing fast. William Barton? Oh
my word. Her hand smothered her mouth. *She'd just remembered
the name.*

The horror, the embarrassment, his accusations. Mad. He must
have been mad. But the feeling of guilt and nausea made her
sink into the nearest chair. As the contact number flashed across
the screen she rushed into the next room and found a pen and
pad, repeating the number over and over again so she would not
forget it. But she didn't dial straight away. She sat and thought
and planned, feeling a creeping sense of horror. '0800 . . .' She
copied the number down carefully then went back to her ironing.
She needed time to think.

At three o'clock precisely Nigel Barton arrived. Martha took
stock of him as he sat down opposite her. Considering the tragic
circumstances of the last few days there was little outward
evidence of the grief he must surely be feeling. He simply looked
tired. No – more than tired. Exhausted. Even when she invited
him to sit he dropped into the chair as though glad to be taking
the weight off his legs. Yet he was a spare man, his shoulders
bent as though he was years older. Even lifting his eyes to meet
hers appeared to be an effort. But he held himself in check. He
was neatly and soberly dressed, with fish-pale skin and green

eyes magnified by glasses with thick black rims, dark hair liberally streaked with grey. There was little to mark him out as the victim of such a tragedy besides the fact that his mouth seemed permanently down and this aura he had around him, that life itself was simply too exhausting. She introduced herself and then began to explain the machinations of the coroner's office.

'You are entitled to a copy of the post-mortem report,' she said smoothly, 'if you so wish, but I can assure you that all three died from smoke inhalation. I can't tell you whether their deaths were quick. There is evidence that your wife tried to get out of the bedroom. Her body was found just inside her bedroom door. The door itself was locked.'

'Yes, the police told me that.' A look of pain twisted his features.

Martha paused before adding, 'Your daughter was found in her bed, underneath the bedclothes.'

'Addy was asleep?' he asked eagerly, grabbing at this one straw.

Martha hesitated. She really did wish that she could spare the man this but she had a duty to tell him the truth. It would all spill out in the inquest anyway. 'She had pulled the bedclothes over her head, Mr Barton,' she said. 'The fire officer's opinion was that she had been too frightened to try and make her way to the door.' There was no need to torture the man by pointing out that even had she reached the door the attempt would have been futile. She simply added, 'I'm sorry.'

The man's resolve broke down then, but still in a quiet and contained way. He groaned and covered his face with his hands. Martha let him grieve. Her own belief was that grief is healthy. It is a tribute to the dead. It is *lack* of grief that chews you up and gnaws inside you like a rat in a box. But she noted that it was the description of his daughter's fate rather than the image of his wife desperately trying to escape that had finally cracked him.

Interestingly as soon as he had recovered his wife didn't feature in his next question either. He asked, in a tight voice, 'And my father?'

And Martha read a thousand accusations in that one, simple question. 'Your father also died of smoke inhalation,' she said. 'His body was found on the landing. It's possible . . .'

Barton cut her short then. 'Possible,' he said, opening his eyes. 'What's possible? That my muddled old father locked my wife and daughter in their bedrooms and then set fire deliberately to the house? Murdering them?'

Martha realized then that deep down Barton really was suffering, torturing himself with this scenario.

'We don't know that for sure, Mr Barton.' She felt she had better prepare him. 'We might not ever know for sure exactly what the sequence of events was. In the meantime, don't you think you should give your father the benefit of the doubt?'

Barton let out a heavy breath and said nothing.

Martha decided to do a little 'digging'. 'Tell me a little about your father? He caused a fire before, didn't he?'

'We were never quite sure,' Barton said slowly. 'Dad said he was just . . .' He stopped. 'It was hard to know sometimes what was in his mind. He'd talk about things that happened years ago as though they'd happened yesterday. And another time he'd forget whether he'd eaten a meal half an hour before. He'd ask the same questions over and over again. Watch kids' stuff on the TV.' His face was anguished as he looked at Martha then beyond her. 'It's my fault,' he said flatly. 'I was the one who persuaded Christie to keep Dad with us. She wasn't too keen – especially when once or twice he didn't seem to know her, and he could be quite aggressive.'

'Aggressive?'

Barton looked even more distraught. 'He got confused. He'd push her out of the way, argue with her, refuse to eat, wash. He was getting more difficult. He took a swing at her once or twice. Gave her a black eye. And another time he pushed her down the stairs.'

Violent would have been the adjective Martha might have used rather than *difficult* but she realized how important it was to let Barton choose his own words.

'That must have been very trying for your family,' Martha commented quietly. 'Not just your wife but also your son and daughter.'

Barton nodded.

'Was Jude able to enlighten you as to how his grandfather had been over the last few days?'

'He said he was all right. But, you know.' At last Nigel Barton's face lifted and he smiled. 'Dad and Jude, they were like this.' He twisted his middle finger around his index finger in the age-old gesture. Martha looked at his face and the fingers and sensed that he had just said something quite significant. But it was beyond her to work out what it was. She frowned and thought, *Time for another spot of digging?*

'When did you go away?'

'Wednesday morning. I was away for two nights. I had a meeting on Wednesday afternoon, another one on the Thursday and a third one planned for the Friday morning, early, all in the same area so it made sense to stop over rather than travel. I'd hoped to beat the traffic on Friday and get home just after lunch. I suppose,' he said, 'if I'd been there I might have smelt the smoke earlier and prevented the tragedy.'

'You might have died too.'

Barton bowed his head.

'Did you stay away often?'

'Once a month, rarely more.'

Martha digested this before asking, 'Was your father less aggressive with you than with your wife?'

'Marginally. I think he recognized me all right.'

'And Jude?'

'Yes – he seemed to always know us. And as I said – Jude and the old man were as close as peas in a pod. It was Christie and Addy that he was difficult with – the women.'

All of a sudden it was as though he realized he would never see 'the women' again. He sat still, rigidly staring ahead, awash with grief, then again dropped his face into his hands. 'I don't know what I'm going to do without them,' he said. 'I can't face going back to the Grange – not ever.'

'Time is a great healer,' Martha said gently. 'It is a cliché, I know, but like many clichés it exists because it is true. And I have personal experience of it.'

Barton lifted his head and, with a penetrating gaze, looked straight at her. 'Thank you for that,' he said. 'I believe you are sincere.'

And you? Martha wondered.

She ended the interview with the usual any questions, a promise to keep him informed when the date for the inquest was fixed and a card with the office contact details neatly printed. 'If you need further information you can contact my assistant, Jericho Palfreyman.' She paused for a moment before overstepping the mark and asking, 'Do you have any idea who might have done this?'

Barton stared at her. 'I can hardly bear to think it but I'm fearful it might be . . .' She waited but Barton didn't enlarge and, looking at the grief which scored his face, she knew he suspected his father.

It was almost six when Alex Randall rang the office. She had been about to leave but the interview with Nigel Barton had upset her and she'd decided to work a little later than usual. Jericho had already gone so she picked up the phone herself.

'Martha.'

'Alex?'

'It seems your idea might have borne fruit.' His voice held a small tinge – only that – of respect.

'How so? You've had lots of calls?'

'Quite a few. It'll take us weeks to follow them all up.'

'Any promising?'

'It's hard to tell, Martha, until you really speak to them. Some callers *sound* really promising but lead to nothing. Some are plainly cranks who just want a bit of attention and company or crave being in on the drama. Others sound like nothing, and they very often turn out to have that nugget of information that slots neatly into place. We'll have to see. We're all working on it. We'll start following them all up from tomorrow. I just thought I'd let you know that it was a helpful suggestion. I owe you one.'

Owe you one? A drink? Something to ponder on her drive home. 'Thank you,' she responded primly.

'How did you get on with Mr Barton?'

'Rather sad, really. He broke down a couple of times. He's convinced it was his father, you know? He says William was aggressive towards Christie and Adelaide. He blames himself; thinks maybe the old man should have been put in a nursing home where he'd have been taken care of. In the end Nigel Barton blames not his father, but himself for having foisted William on them and not having protected his family.'

'He's convinced it was his father?' Randall sounded very surprised.

'It would appear so.'

'You sound hesitant, Martha.'

'I always worry when the dead are blamed for something. They can't defend themselves. Besides, it doesn't really fit the facts, does it? If William had been fire-raising why break a window from the outside to divert suspicion away from him? Was he capable of being that cunning? Don't tell me someone with Alzheimer's is capable of complicated and future planning? It all seems a bit too neat, a bit too tidy, a bit too convenient. Don't you have any other leads? What about Barton's business associates?'

'Well, we have one, though whether it will lead anywhere I'm not sure.'

'What?'

'Stuart Pinfold paid a brief visit to the UK at the end of February from the twenty-third to the twenty-sixth.'

'How do you know?'

Randall chuckled. 'Good old mobile phones,' he said. 'Wonderful records.'

'So is he your hot suspect?'

'Put it like this, Martha: we're looking very carefully at him.'

She hesitated before asking her next question in a wheedling tone. 'Alex?'

'Ye-es?' His response was guarded.

'I'd like to go back to Melverley. Visit the scene again.'

The request didn't seem either to surprise him or to faze him. He answered smoothly. 'That can be arranged.' He paused. 'Looking for anything in particular?'

'I just want to get a clearer picture in my mind. In other words – oh, you know me, Alex. I'm just not convinced.'

He chuckled. 'I know you, indeed.'

'Thank you.' She wondered if she'd imagined the warmth in his voice and was misinterpreting his phrase, *I owe you one*. Probably not a drink or dinner or anything else. It was just a response.

'Will Monday morning be soon enough?'

'Yes. It'll be fine. See you Monday.' She felt almost gay. 'Have a good weekend.'

Randall did not reply.

NINE

Monday, 7 March, 9 a.m.

Alex rang Martha at nine, reminding her of her wish to return to Melverley Grange for a second look and arranging to pick her up at eleven.

Already, just over a week after the fire, Martha could see changes. A car and two vans were pulled up in the drive. Randall handed her a hard hat and put one on himself. Boards had been nailed over the broken windows and as they entered the hall a suited man approached them, holding out his hand. 'Saul Prendergast,' he said briskly. 'Insurance Assessor.'

Martha looked around her. 'Where on earth do you start?' she mused.

Prendergast followed her gaze. 'Start at the seat of the fire,' he said, 'look at structural necessities and decide what must be replaced and what is OK. Dreadful business.'

Alex and Martha agreed.

Two men passed them, carrying a Rolled Steel Joist. 'First things first,' Prendergast said. 'Make the place safe. Was there anything in particular, Inspector, Mrs Gunn?'

'Yes.' It was Martha who answered. 'Take me through the sequence of events, please.'

'Right.' Prendergast walked into the lounge. The furniture had all been removed as well as the charred carpet and some of the woodwork. There were boards across the ceiling so you could not now look straight up into the bedroom. Prendergast crossed to the window. 'As I see it,' he grinned, 'and I have seen quite a few burnt-out homes in my time, the glass was smashed, then the window was opened, either from the inside or the outside. It could have been left open when the house-holders went to bed or it could have been left unlocked and simply raised. As you can see, it is an old-fashioned sash window.'

Randall was listening intently, his craggy face absorbing the man's words.

'Petrol was splashed liberally around the room and in other parts of the house too but here and the other downstairs room was the seat of the fire. The stairs were much less badly damaged. I think the curtains, too, were soaked in petrol. The person left, again probably either through the window or possibly the back door. The front door was bolted on the inside. He possibly then threw a match through the open window. There was an explosion, blowing out the frame.'

Martha was studying the window as Prendergast was speaking.

Alex Randall was frowning. 'If that was how it happened,' he spoke slowly, dragging the words out reluctantly, 'the person who set the fire going could not have been William Barton, could he?'

'You mean the old man? Well, if it was him he must have returned via the back door after the fire was set, which seems unlikely.'

'And when were the bedroom doors locked?'

Prendergast shook his head. 'It must have been before the fire was lit.'

'Do you mean before the petrol was splashed all over the place?'

'Not necessarily.'

Martha was thinking. 'Can we go upstairs?'

'Yes, sure.'

They filed up the staircase which had Acro jacks propping up some of the treads. The smell of scorched wood was beginning to recede and a chilly breeze blew through the open door bringing in the cold scent of winter, fires, snow and pine needles. Outside was eerily quiet. Villages are empty on a weekday. Everyone is out at work.

Christie's bedroom was completely empty and dingy as a piece of wood had been nailed across the window. Access boards had been laid across the joists, a temporary replacement for the floorboards which had been burnt. It was a good-sized room, square and high-ceilinged. Martha looked around for a moment then left and crossed the landing to enter Adelaide's room.

This, too, had been stripped bare and the window boarded

across. The girl's room was slightly smaller than her mother's but it too faced the front of the house, overlooking the drive, and was badly damaged.

Martha turned to face Randall and Saul Prendergast. 'If someone had driven up the drive they would surely have heard the car? It wasn't very late, after all.'

Both men nodded. It was Alex who raised the objection, 'But if our fire-raiser did come by car all he had to do was to leave the vehicle just down the road and approach by foot.'

'Yes,' Martha agreed.

'And Jude said that Adelaide often wore her headphones so might not have heard anything.'

She was still looking around the bedroom.

'Seen enough, Martha?' Alex asked.

'Nearly. I wondered if I could take a peep at the kitchen and the rear entrance to the property?'

'Of course.' Prendergast was at his most helpful.

The kitchen hadn't quite been cleaned out as thoroughly as the bedrooms. Most of the appliances were still there. 'The damage is pretty bad, isn't it?' Martha commented. 'I'm surprised Jude Barton's injuries weren't worse.'

'He's lucky to be alive,' the fire assessor said. 'Very lucky indeed. There was a gas explosion and if he'd been in the kitchen a minute or two later the fire would have had a fourth victim. As it was he suffered some burns, I understand.'

As Martha and Alex left he gave her an amused expression. 'Well? Was that helpful? Has it thrown a light on events?'

'No.' She gave him a straight look. 'I don't even know whether that was helpful. All I can say is – possibly.'

He dropped her off outside her office and Martha returned to more mundane matters while DI Randall prepared for a long day doing desk work and a late evening briefing to analyse the public's statements.

Friday, 11 March, 11.58 p.m.

Another hand, another box of matches. A smile because petrol worked so well. Open the window. Quietly now. Don't want anyone to wake up, do we? People are sleeping; a car goes by.

A dog barks. Further along the street the lights go off. Even the late-night people have gone to bed now. They will sleep right through it.

Strike the match.

And then

Whoosh.

Stand back with satisfaction. Admire the artistry. The problem was always getting the fire started in the first place. More difficult than many supposed. Petrol was OK but volatile and dangerous to use. It could blow up in your face. To burn down a house is not as easy as people think. It takes a certain amount of skill. There can be a brief flash and then . . . nothing but disappointment. And even if the fire ignites properly there are sometimes, even on a freezing night in March, inquisitive people walking around or passing in cars. And everyone has a mobile phone to summon the emergency services, don't they?

But all it really needed, to the practised hand, was one small match, and significantly less than a gallon of petrol.

The briefing had gone on much later than any of them had expected and DI Randall needed to complete his report before he went. It was after midnight by the time he finally left the station. Good job he didn't have a wife who would worry at his lateness, he thought, twisting his mouth at the irony of the whole thing – marriage. Or at least his. As he turned out on to the main road through the town a fire engine passed him going at a fair old lick, as his grandmother would have said, lights flashing, siren blasting its presence. He watched it, mesmerized and still. Except to take his hand from the steering wheel and hold it up in mute appeal. Please, *not another one?* Not another house fire, not more fatalities. As though he was on autopilot the car glided in the wake of the blue light which blinked into the night.

'You got a feeling of déjà vu?' Agnew shouted at Carol Jenkins, trying to get heard over the din they were making.

'I most certainly do,' she shouted back. 'Another house fire. I just hope there aren't a couple of bodies inside this time.' They reached the blazing house and scrambled out.

Agnew trained his hose through the open window. 'Different sort of house, though, isn't it? We got any idea who lives here?'

'Retired nurse, the caller said,' Carol shouted back. 'Early sixties. Bit of an odd woman, by all accounts.'

'Well, I hope she's away staying with relatives or something because this is—' He was interrupted by a crash from inside. 'Beams,' he shouted. 'Stand back.'

That was when the roof finally caved in and the flames shot up in the night sky.

Against his better judgement Alex Randall had pulled up behind the engine, climbed out of the car and now stood, watching the fire, PC Gary Coleman standing at his side. Coleman had been on the beat in the town when the call had come through and he had been summoned to the fire in Sundorne. 'Sorry, sir,' he apologized. 'No heroics this time. I'm not as brave or foolhardy as Roberts.'

'Thank goodness for that,' Alex responded dryly. 'I suppose we'll have to wait to gain access to the property?'

'Yeah – it won't be safe until tomorrow.'

'I'll be off home then.' He took steps before turning back, eyeing the fire which spat and howled as though in a rage. 'Is anyone inside that?'

'We don't know, sir.'

'God,' Randall said. 'I sincerely hope not.'

'Yes, sir. I'll stay here a bit, sir, see what's what, do a bit of digging around the place.'

Alex patted his back. 'Good lad, Coleman,' he said. 'Good lad. Ring me if you have anything interesting to report.'

It was faint praise but it pleased the PC. DI Randall was not one to dole it out.

Saturday, 12 March, 8.30 a.m.

Randall had waited until 8.30 a.m. before ringing Martha. After apologizing for having woken her, (he knew he hadn't), he came straight to the point, as was his way. 'Martha, I wonder if I could pop over, just for a few minutes?'

Martha glanced at Sam, already packing up his football strip.

There was a practise session today in Stoke at the Britannia Stadium and she was the designated driver. Already her mind was beginning to work around it. Tom Dempsey, Sam's best friend and fellow player for Stoke City Academy, would be training too. If Dempsey's father could take the boys to the match she could pick them up – just before going out with Simon. Hey! Sorted. She gave herself a mental pat on the back.

And Sukey was going shopping to Telford with her best friends, Feodore, Rumilla and Sally. The gang of five were now four, thanks to Emma's parents having split up and moved away, much to everyone's disgust.

'OK, Alex,' she returned. 'I'll just have to do a spot of organizing. Come round in half an hour.'

A couple of phone calls, a bit of bargaining – an extra ten pounds in Sukey's purse for the fare to and from Telford and a promise to pick Sam and Tom up dead on five thirty from Stoke Under Eighteen's and she still had time for a quick make-up check, slip out of her jeans into a skirt and sweater and make a firm promise to Bobby, her Welsh Border collie, that his walk round the woods was not cancelled, merely deferred. He tilted his head on one side. If ever a dog could look disbelieving this was it.

Tom's father was round fifteen minutes later, a wiry, ruggedly handsome man who had once been a professional footballer himself. She thanked him and told him she'd deliver his son back after the training session. Sam had finally confessed to her months ago that he wasn't really happy living away from home even if it was with the hallowed Liverpool Academy but he still wanted to pursue his dream of being a professional footballer.

'See, Mum,' he'd said, without being at all abashed, 'to be *absolutely* honest,' (Sam always did this, emphasizing his words when he wanted something so very badly), 'I have already sort of worked it out. *Stoke* have a brilliant academy. I rang them up and they're keen on me. Better than that I could live at home with you and Suks and easily manage to go to school here *and* get to all the training sessions. Even better than all *that* Tom Dempsey is already there and absolutely *loves* it. He says it's *great*. Great atmosphere, good training, a really nice manager.'

His toffee-coloured eyes had locked on to hers with mute but compelling appeal. 'It's where I want to be, Mum. Here. Home, with you and Suks.'

Her heart had given a tiny little flutter of happiness that this teenage boy who had a gift for absolute honesty as well as football touchingly wanted to be at home with his mother and sister. Maybe she hadn't done such a bad job, after all?

'I don't know what to say, Sam.'

Sam grinned at her. 'Not a lot to say, is there, Mum? Just yes'll do.'

'I'll need to speak to them and . . .'

The look Sam had given her was a mixture of tolerance, a tinge of humour and more than a hint of pity. He knew she was beat; she knew it too. But from somewhere he had acquired the maturity not to rub it in.

She'd added weakly, 'But does Stoke have the same kudos as Liverpool?'

And he had his answer ready. 'They're an up-and-coming team, Mum, with a smashing stadium. Have you seen the Britannia?'

She had. Who could miss it driving in to Stoke along the D road? It stood, proud and pretty as a birthday cake, reminding her more of Frank Lloyd Wright's Guggenheim in New York than any football stadium she had ever noticed. She gave in then.

So here Sam was, resident again at The White House, with his twin sister and his mother, back in his own bedroom, which reflected his love of 'the beautiful game', pals all around him, settled at school and happier than she had ever known him. He almost seemed to burst, like the bulbs in spring, with joy, noise and colour and the truth was that she loved having him around. The house was different with a male. It smelt different, sounded different, looked different. Was different.

The White House had its beating heart back. Oh, yes, she loved having her son home again. She must do something to celebrate. Maybe paint the pretentiously named house a different colour and change its name to The Blue House, or The Yellow House. Certainly not The Black House.

Sukey, on the other hand, as her twin brother emerged as this joyous, happy teenager, was much more moody these days, perhaps a victim of her hormones. Martha had to acknowledge it: growing up was proving a real battle to her daughter. She suspected that Sukey missed Agnetha who had been their Swedish au pair for six years but had now returned home. Sukey was to go out to Sweden in the summer to attend Agnetha's wedding as a bridesmaid but over the years that they had been together the two had formed a close friendship which had been disrupted when Agnetha had left. Sukey was missing her buddy. Martha missed her too. Agnetha Halvorsen had been friendly and reliable. They had all been fond of her.

But life moves on. And so must her daughter.

The other thing that Sukey was finding difficult was the ambition she had recently formed to become 'an actress'. And Martha rather suspected that at least some of the moodiness and tantrums were because she thought these went with an actress's temperament. Martha wasn't absolutely convinced that at least some of the moods weren't simple affectation. Sukey Gunn was practising anger and pride, grief and arrogance and flashing tempers.

However, on that Saturday morning when she explained to her daughter why their plans were changing unpredictably, there was no hint of the prima donna. Sukey simply grinned and planted a kiss on her mother's cheek as she left to join her pals. Then, at the doorway, she gave Martha a backwards cheeky grin and winked at her. 'Have fun with your detective then, Mum.'

Martha reprimanded her. 'He is not *my* detective, young lady. He is, in fact, as you well know, a work colleague – also a married man and don't you forget it. This is purely a professional visit. Understand?'

'Oh, yeah,' Sukey managed in a voice laden with scepticism. The actress was, after all, emerging. 'And that's why he's coming round here to the house on a Saturday morning? What's so urgent, Mum, that it can't wait till Monday? Bye, then.' She just managed to get the words out before whisking through the door in sprayed-on jeans and a lovely fur gilet that Martha had bought her for Christmas.

Randall turned up forty minutes later and she knew the moment she saw his face that something was very wrong. His first words confirmed her suspicion, even as he climbed out of his car and approached her. 'It's not good news, I'm afraid, Martha.'

'Come in, Alex. Have a coffee and tell me what's going on.'

He stood for a moment, looking up at the façade of The White House, maybe thinking along the same lines that she had recently before following her inside to the kitchen. Without speaking he waited while she boiled the kettle and spooned the coffee into two mugs. They sat down at the kitchen table and Martha waited for him to speak.

'There's been another house fire.' His face was grim.

Even before her heart sunk she might have guessed it. 'Where?'

'In Sundorne.'

'Not Melverley, then?'

'No,' he said carefully, 'not in Melverley.'

'But you're connecting the two fires?'

He nodded. 'Same MO,' he said, 'according to the firemen who attended both scenes. It was started deliberately, again the front window was broken, accelerants used and someone is missing.'

'Who?'

'A retired nurse in her early sixties, named Monica Deverill.'

'Go on.'

'She lived alone – widowed some years ago.'

She waited.

'In good health.' He blinked and repeated, 'currently missing.'

'Oh, no?'

'We should have access to the house later today. The roof caved in not long after the firemen got there. It wouldn't have been safe to try any heroics last night.'

Martha felt a shudder of apprehension, trying to make sense of this latest grim news. 'Well, you can't blame William Barton this time, Alex.'

'No.'

'So are you thinking we have a serial arsonist here?'

He didn't answer but she caught a look of apprehension on his face that was surely mirrored in her own.

'Mrs Deverill has two sons,' Alex Randall continued, without answering her question. 'Both live locally. One in Wem, the other in Church Stretton.' He paused. 'And three grandchildren.'

Martha rubbed the centre of her forehead. 'Oh, dear,' she said. 'Of course we'll have to wait—'

'For access to the building and the forensic fire investigator.' He gave a wry look. 'He's having a busy time. We can't be sure yet that she was inside but—'

'But you *are* connecting the two fires.'

He nodded, his face grim.

'Then you know my next question, Alex. Is there any connection between the two families?'

'Hey,' he protested, a smile softening his craggy features. 'It's early days yet, Martha.'

Again, she waited for his response.

'Not that we know so far.'

'This retired nurse – did she have any enemies or was this a random attack?'

Alex's face creased with a grin. He was well used to Martha Gunn's ways. She might be coroner of Shrewsbury, mid and north Shropshire but he knew that she wasn't above a little sleuthing herself. A new perspective of 'helping the police with their enquiries'. He suppressed a smile. 'Again, too soon to say, Martha.'

'But I take it you've already spoken to her next of kin, the two sons?'

He nodded. 'They haven't seen her for a few days or spoken to her. That's not unusual, apparently. Since her retirement she's helped in the hospital shop. She also leads a very active social life and has been going on a number of cruises a year with various friends.'

'So she could be away?'

'If she is she hadn't told her family, which she normally would do, but she does have a wide circle of friends from her nursing days and sometimes pops over to visit them. Let's hope so. We're ringing round them now.'

'Have you tried her mobile?'

'It's not even ringing. Straight through to the answering service.'

'Boyfriends? Jilted lover?'

Randall laughed. 'She was in her early sixties, Martha.'

She decided to tease him a little. 'Come on, Alex, you think women hang up their hormones when they touch fifty? Goodness – I'd better get my skates on. That gives me less than ten years.'

She immediately regretted her levity. Alex Randall's flush rose slowly but unmistakably and very colourfully up his neck, reaching his chin before sliding up his cheeks and suffusing his forehead. He looked around the room in utter, sheer embarrassment with a touch of panic.

'I'm sorry, Alex,' she apologized. 'I was just teasing.'

It did little to relieve his confusion. 'Well, then.' Randall cleared his throat noisily. 'We don't know of any boyfriend or partner and neither do her sons, but it's early days yet.'

'And her computer will have been destroyed in the fire,' Martha mused, 'along with her emails. Car?'

'It isn't on the drive. There is a garage but when I last spoke they hadn't gained access.'

'Well, Alex, either Mrs Deverill is in there, dead, or she is alive somewhere else. If the fire was started deliberately, as you say, and she was inside, it will be another case of manslaughter. And again, like the Melverley fire, either a personal or a random attack. But I have to say Melverley is a small village some miles out of Shrewsbury. Sundorne, by way of contrast, is right on the edge of the town. The two sites don't appear to have much in common. If this retired nurse was deliberately targeted was it by the same arsonist who torched Melverley Grange? Why these two dissimilar properties? Pure chance? Or is there a reason why these two places, these particular people were selected? Is there any connection between the two families? Is there perhaps something in Mrs Deverill's past which will lead you to your arsonist? Is this the work of one arsonist or is it a gang? Or could this possibly be a copycat fire?'

'Phew. That's a lot to think about.'

'What's in your mind?'

'That we didn't release any details of the modus operandi of the fire at Melverley Grange.'

'Could this be coincidence then? In such a small area? Is it possible the nurse's house was selected purely at random? Maybe.

And if it was a random selection – well – we're all at risk.' She threw out her hands, relieved to see that Alex Randall's face had returned to its normal colour and expression. 'I've not come across any deaths in connection with arson over the last few years.'

'Luckily no one died in the recent arson attacks by those kids. They really are the only ones.'

'They got a custodial sentence? I thought the idea was to keep first offenders out?'

'They'd been cautioned before. They destroyed some school buildings. They'd stopped for a while – a matter of ten months or so – and then one night they did four houses along the row. In one of them there was a deaf old lady. Luckily for her she could just about pick up the smoke alarm and she'd had special flashing lights fitted by a deaf charity so she woke up. Otherwise she'd be dead. The other householders have been very much inconvenienced; they haven't been able to live in their own homes for over a year. The courts took a dim view of the whole thing, decided to make an example of them and sent them down.' He gave a sigh. 'Whether it'll teach them a lesson, who knows? Some of these youngsters can be surprisingly thick at learning lessons.'

Martha nodded. 'Quite,' she said, 'but it wasn't them either.' She smiled. 'Not unless Stoke Heath has suddenly become extremely lax in its security arrangements.' It was a 'safe' joke which Alex could join in. 'Absolutely not.' He grinned. 'Or unless Stoke Heath has a secret passage into Sundorne.'

'I very much doubt it,' Martha said.

'Did you have anything much planned this weekend?'

She was shocked at the question. She and the detective had never, ever explored their private lives. Their relationship had always been strictly business. She eyed him cautiously before answering. 'Apart from the usual ferrying Sam back from his football match, Sukey's ironing, catching up on domestic stuff and taking Bobby for a lovely long walk, you mean? Do any of those count as special?'

He regarded her without blinking, his head tilted to one side. Still asking the question, then.

'Well, yes, actually,' she said, 'I do have something special planned. On Saturday I have a date.'

'What?' It obviously wasn't what he had been expecting.

He began to bluster, to cover up his confusion, then said, 'Well, I suppose it's natural. You've been widowed for so long.'

She nodded her agreement.

Randall moistened his lips. 'So who's the lucky guy?'

'He was married to a very dear friend.' She knew she should be more honest with him. 'To be honest, Alex, it's more of a friendship than a romantic attachment. We both miss our partners. We're friends but I don't think it'll ever progress beyond that stage.'

'Why not?'

She searched his face and realized this was genuine curiosity. The very private detective was overcoming his natural reticence about private matters to interrogate her. She answered with blunt honesty. 'I don't know.'

'Was Martin *such* a hard act to follow?'

'I don't even know that, Alex,' she said frankly. 'It's more that the spark is missing.'

Randall grinned at her so she knew he had moved away from the serious questions and was teasing her now. 'Maybe that's just an age thing?'

'Maybe,' she agreed. 'Maybe, but you know, Alex, it would be strange to embark on a relationship without it.' And now he had tiptoed into her private life she felt justified asking him the same question. 'And you? What do you have planned for the weekend?'

Instantly the shutters came down. He looked away and muttered something about it being the usual weekend. 'I wondered,' he followed up tentatively, 'if you'd care to visit the house in Sundorne? See if you come up with anything.'

It was the invitation she had both wanted and dreaded. The images of a twisted, blackened corpse would imprint on her mind again, as they had after her visit to Melverley Grange, but she was unable to resist the chance to inspect what might well be a crime scene. She looked at him. 'I'm not sure,' she said.

Randall must have sensed something of her concern. 'After we've removed the body, if and when we find it.'

'If you think it will help understand what happened,' she said. 'There's no point me getting squeamish in my job. More coffee, Alex?'

Randall stood up. 'No. I should be going. It's going to be a busy day. Well, thanks for the chat,' he said. 'I'll be in touch.'

'You're going there now?'

He nodded.

For Martha the day passed as planned. At five thirty she was outside the football ground, waiting for Sam and Tom. As they burst into the car, full of football chat and laughing about a few of the day's mishaps she stowed their bags away in the boot, thankful that the ground had good shower facilities.

That night she was meeting up with Simon Pendlebury – again. Simon was the widower of one of her very best friends in the world, Evelyn, who had died from ovarian cancer – the silent killer, as the medical profession called it – eighteen months ago. Simon and her husband, Martin, had been friends at university and had remained so until Martin's death from cancer more than ten years ago. Simon had come from a very average background; his father had abandoned the family when he had been a child and his mother had struggled to bring Simon and his sister up, barely managing when he had gained a place in university. The Simon of today was not recognizable as the product of that upbringing. It was as though he had been polished, like a gemstone, over the years and now appeared very suave, very wealthy and very handsome. He had even shed his once-pronounced accent from a rough area in Stoke on Trent. Over six feet tall with very dark hair, penetrating eyes and a perceptive, confident manner. Elegant.

Simon lived in the lap of luxury in a period manor house with an efficient German housekeeper to attend to his every need. He also had two opinionated and selfish daughters with characters as brittle and sharp as shards of glass. Between them they had seen off a couple of their father's unsuitable girl-friends, labelling them 'gold-diggers'. Martha could see none of Evie's gentleness in either of them. Maybe they took after their father.

She and Simon had fallen into the habit of dining together once a week or so. Once or twice Martha had cooked for him and a few more times they had gone out for dinner. On a couple of occasions he had invited her back to his house and his housekeeper had provided dinner. It should have been a romance but it simply wasn't and Martha wasn't sure why not. He was good looking, the proverbial tall, dark, handsome and rich. Intelligent with a wicked sense of humour.

But, as she'd said to Alex, the spark wasn't there, neither for her nor, she suspected, for him. Maybe it was because she had been such a good friend of his wife, perhaps, or because she had witnessed his falling hopelessly in love with Christabel, a girl easily young enough to be his daughter. Or maybe it was Simon's two daughters themselves, spoilt, rich, selfish. Armenia and Jocasta Pendlebury were capable of finishing off any budding romance their father might have and saw any intruding female as a money-grabber, to be disposed of quickly. Martha had never quite worked out how gentle, sweet-natured Evie had produced two such monstrous daughters. Had it been their father spoiling them or the exclusive schools they had been packed off to? Whatever the explanation Martha was sure that Evie would have been very disappointed in them.

In fact, she wasn't particularly looking forward to this evening even though they were booked into Drapers' Hall, one of her favourite eating-places in the town.

They had arranged to meet at Drapers' at seven thirty. Martha had chosen a simple black dress with silver straps, black very high-heeled shoes and had tried to style her own hair (big mistake)!

But as she faced Simon Pendlebury across the table she wondered why she felt so little for him? He was rich, intelligent, handsome, funny and always beautifully dressed. So what was it that made her want to keep him at arm's length when she was perfectly aware that he wanted a relationship?

Could she really blame Jocasta and Armenia?

Or was it something slightly more troubling? Was it the mystery of where his money had come from and that she and Martin had always suspected he was not quite kosher that made her mistrust him and doubt his motives?

Was it the stupid affair he had had with Christabel?

Possibly a bit of all these plus more.

She didn't trust him and had an instinct that he was basically dishonest, the sort of man who would climb over other men's heads to get out of the swamp. Underneath the charm there was something cold, something cruel about this apparently perfect man. If she could not find and love his flaws she could never love him. It is a person's imperfections that make them unique, vulnerable and ultimately lovable. She would never feel safe in his arms as she had in Martin's and those observations explained why.

He was commenting on her appearance. 'You look well.' He reached across the table for her hand. 'But distracted tonight. What is it, Martha?' His very dark eyes seemed to bore into hers so she looked away. She didn't want him to read her revulsion. She started. Revulsion? Had she really used that word?

She drew her hand away anyway.

It was almost nine o'clock before the police, forensic team, firemen (and woman) and the police surgeon congregated at the scene. Another smoking house, another wrecked home. But this time they had a surprise. An omission.

Delyth Fontaine was remonstrating with the unlucky PC Gary Coleman. 'Well, I can't certify death without a body.' She was a blunt-spoken woman who never minced her words. 'It's Saturday night, Coleman. You might have waited at least until you were sure.'

Although he was used to Dr Fontaine's ways Coleman felt bound to defend himself. 'Well, it seemed the most sensible thing to do – have you here, ready. Then we could get on with hunting through and finding the source of the fire.'

'I'm going home,' she said. 'Call me on my mobile if you want me. I've a couple of sheep ready to lamb. It's a bit early in the season and I don't want to lose them to the cold, if you don't mind.'

Delyth's walk was more of a waddle but her exit was still dignified. Coleman stared after her feeling a little foolish. Then he turned to the watching firemen. 'Come on, you,' he said, 'it isn't a free show, you know.'

TEN

Monday, 14 March, 9 a.m.

Martha expected a call to come in at any time about the house fire, either that the police had found a body or that they'd made contact with the missing woman. Had her job not been so absorbing the day might have passed slowly but it didn't. She immersed herself in her tasks and left her office at five. On the way home she bought the *Shropshire Star*, expecting to see something more than she already knew but the newspaper headlines were muted, merely mentioning the fire in Sundorne without making much of it. There was no word of the nurse or whether she was dead or alive, the only reference being that the house which had been gutted by the fire belonged to a retired nurse named Monica Deverill, who was in her sixties. Martha assumed that the police would make no public comment until they had made certain of the woman's fate. She scrutinized the headlines, trying to read the meaning behind the words and noted that no connection was made between the fire in Shrewsbury and the Melverley arson. The modus operandi was not disclosed in either case and she strongly suspected that this detail was being deliberately withheld. She had heard nothing from either DI Randall or Mark Sullivan, the pathologist, so deduced there was no body to make the coroner informed of and no post-mortem in the offing which, again, would have involved her. She was intrigued and, naturally, itching to find out how the investigation was progressing. But it wasn't her role to ring either of them. She had no option but to wait for Alex Randall's call.

Tuesday, 15 March, 12.09 p.m.

Without making an appointment or even ringing to say he was on his way, Alex Randall arrived unexpectedly at her office a little after midday. Jericho rang through, patently resenting the unannounced intrusion. 'Ma'am,' he said a little testily, 'I have DI Randall here. He wonders if he *might* have a word with you.'

The emphasis on the word *might* told Martha everything, that Jericho hoped she would relay the message back (via him) that she was far, far too busy to spend time with the detective. But the truth was that Martha was glad of the interruption. And curious, too, so she asked Jericho to send him straight in. Randall greeted her with a wide grin which provoked her comment, 'You're looking very pleased with yourself, Alex. Does that mean you're getting somewhere?'

He faced her for a minute, looking friendly, but at the same time not overly anxious to respond to her question. His comment, though, was interesting. 'Not really, Martha,' he said, his face breaking into a grin, 'I just knew that you'd want an update and I thought I might share a couple of thoughts.'

'That's nice of you.'

His next comment was even more neutral. He looked at the window and the view outside. 'The nights are beginning to get lighter and brighter.'

She, too, glanced across at the window, wondering why this preamble. 'Yes, they are, aren't they? Almost feels like the beginning of spring. It's a lovely time of year, isn't it, the end of the winter in sight?' As he didn't answer she added, 'Did you come here merely to comment on the weather?'

He smiled back at her, in no great hurry, obviously, and she continued. 'So how are the investigations going?'

'Slow.' He didn't look too bothered by the lack of progress.

'And the house in Sundorne?' she prompted. 'Have you found Mrs Deverill?'

He shook his head. 'There's no sign of her in the house although we can't be absolutely sure until we've combed right through the wreckage.' He stopped, frowning. 'She *could* still be in there.'

She caught the doubt in his voice. 'But you don't think so?'

'I'm holding back my judgement.' He took pity on her then. 'Let's just say that if she walked into the police station in Monkmoor saying she'd been on a last-minute cruise and had forgotten to tell her sons I wouldn't be hugely surprised. She sounds an independent woman who's quite feisty, used to living life her own way.'

She nodded. 'So you think she's still alive.' It was a statement not a question.

Randall nodded, then tacked on, 'But, you know, Martha . . .'

'Do sit down, Alex, you're making me nervous.' She was no dwarf but he topped her by a good few inches and his naturally restless nature made it difficult for him to stand completely still. Something around Alex Randall was always moving, his feet, his hands, his head, his arms, his legs.

He dropped down into the chair. 'Melverley is not a big village,' he began slowly and very obliquely.

She couldn't see even where this was leading but when Alex enlarged on the point it hit her like a bomb.

'Although it was late and very cold on the night of the fire at the Grange,' he continued, 'minus four degrees, it was dry.'

Martha waited, still wondering where on earth this was going.

'Quite a few people were walking their dogs.'

The silence was thick as Randall waited for her to connect.

'No one saw anything,' he continued. 'Not a car or a strange person. You understand, Martha?' Randall's eyes burned into hers.

She did understand now and was silent. So was Randall.

She broke the silence. 'William? But he can't have . . .' Her voice trailed away. 'Nigel?'

But Randall wouldn't commit. 'I'll keep in touch,' he promised. 'If there's any news I'll call in again.' Again his face creased into a grin. 'That is if I can get past your watchdog.' He glanced in the direction of the door. Martha smiled, knowing too that Jericho would be right outside it, trying to glean anything about the case that he could. If she wanted to be cynical she might say that she suspected that Jericho Palfreyman's 'insider knowledge' got him free drinks at his local pub!

Alex left and Martha began to work out a plan of action. Coroners frequently have the luxury of being able to make a difference. She had used inquests before to make a point, anti-smoking, the hidden dangers of alcohol, a warning about neglected illness, soothing relatives of a suicide, a plea against knife crime and revenge. She had tackled greed and selfishness, grief and anger. And she had the feeling that this case would be no different. She started making notes on the Barton family tragedy.

Smoke alarms, she wrote first, before ringing up the fire station and urging them to put out an advertising campaign. She spoke to Will Tyler, the station chief, who listened very carefully to her words. He too knew that tragedy was a good time to focus the public's awareness on safety issues.

But when she had put the phone down her thoughts were not on these wider points but centred on the dual mysteries of the missing nurse and the Melverley Grange tragedy. She rolled her pen between her fingers and wondered. Were they connected? Who would want to destroy first almost an entire family and then an elderly retired nurse with no apparent connection?

Something nibbled away at the back of her mind, like a mouse gnawing through skirting board, noisy, regular, insistent. Something to do with the nurse and the locked doors in Melverley Grange. But for the moment it was eluding her. Martha's face changed so she looked shrewd and thoughtful, her features pointed, her lips thin.

The nurse? Missing? So far.

On holiday? Perhaps.

Or were her charred remains still buried underneath the rubble of her one-time home, waiting to be discovered by the forensic fire team?

Was it chance that first Melverley Grange and then the modest home in Sundorne had been burnt? Were the properties not selected but random? It was, she knew, the big question. The answer would lead them to . . . what?

Alex Randall's thoughts were running almost parallel to hers as he faced his investigating force. 'Right.' He indicated the board. 'This is a free for all.' He smiled. 'Or a brainstorm, if you prefer to call it that.'

There was a ripple of amusement round the room. All the gathered officers were familiar with DI Randall's dislike of jargon.

He continued. 'We can all throw in ideas for who might have done it, either the fire out at Melverley or here in the town. Think

why; think how; think who.' He appealed around the room then
turned back to the board. 'Let's start with the fire at Melverley
Grange and ask the pertinent questions. Why lock the women in
their rooms but not Jude? Was it coincidence that Nigel Barton
was away? What about the old man? What part did he play? And
is it possible that the fire in Sundorne was a copycat arson attack?
Should we be considering the two fires as one incident, the second
fire perhaps a consequence of the first? Or two? OK.' He looked
around the room. 'Here goes.'

With some trepidation Gethin Roberts started the ball rolling
with a wavering raising of his hand, looking around nervously
at his colleagues. 'I don't think it's a coincidence that Mr Barton
was away on business,' he ventured.

'OK, Roberts, what's your thinking? Why not?' And as the
young constable still looked nervous, typically Randall tried to
encourage him. 'Try and take us through it, Roberts,' he prompted
gently.

'Too much coincidence, too much money involved.' He went
red. 'The life insurance, I mean.'

Randall felt bound to point out, 'But Barton's finances were
in good shape. He didn't need the money. Besides, he really was
away on the Wednesday and Thursday nights. We've spoken to
the business associates and confirmed his meetings. At the time
when the fire started he was seen at the hotel bar in York. We've
seen the timed and dated CCTV pictures of the hotel foyer. That
means, Roberts, that if he was, as you suspect, behind the fire,
he would have needed to hire someone to set the fire going for
him – which would put him in a very vulnerable position and
open to blackmail.'

Roberts looked chagrined but Randall wanted the boy to
develop as an officer. To use his brain. Think laterally, put himself
in the place of a fire-raiser. And that would need encouragement.
Not ridicule. Roberts' colleagues, he noted, were not inclined to
jeer but were listening intently and quietly.

Good.

'Don't give up, Roberts,' he urged. 'Just try to think things
through. Are you suggesting that Nigel Barton masterminded the
entire event? I would find it hard to believe that he would murder
his father, wife and daughter and risk his son's life. While we

don't really know what the relationship was between Barton and
the rest of his family, he's clearly very fond of the boy.'

Roberts was learning – quickly. 'Well, I was thinking that he
could have masterminded the entire thing.' He sourced inspiration
from somewhere. 'If he knew about Jude's ladder and that he
was up at all hours' – he was warming to his subject –'perhaps
he'd know that Jude would escape.'

Randall gave the idea due consideration. 'It's one hell of a big
risk,' he said. 'Fire shoots upwards and the boy was on the top
floor. He could have fallen asleep early that night or been trapped
or had his headphones on. If he had been asleep he would have
died alongside his mother, sister and grandfather. Unless he was
in on the act.' He blew out a sharp breath. 'Or.' Randall scrutinized Roberts. 'You saw him trying to rescue his family,' he said.
'How did he appear to you?'

'Distraught,' Roberts said without even thinking. 'He was screaming and shouting. But then he was on fire. He was hysterical.'

'Can you believe he could have known about it?'

Roberts shook his head. 'He wasn't acting, sir. I'm certain of
it.'

Randall nodded and threw the questions wider. 'OK, let's go
back to Mr Nigel Barton.'

The room fell silent as they all considered the guilt or innocence
of the man.

Alex prompted them. 'Is it simply coincidence that he was
absent from home that night with an unbreakable alibi? But is that
in itself something we should be suspicious of? York is miles away
from Melverley. The journey couldn't be done in under three hours.
It's 160 miles. It's not possible that he was there.' He shook his
head. 'No. He's off the hook. So – although it looks as though
the Melverley fire might have been an inside job we can't complete
the circle. We don't think Jude started the fire; neither do we
believe that Nigel would have risked his son's life and there's no
evidence of friction between Nigel and his wife or daughter. And
he appears positively protective towards his father.' He tried to put
his thoughts in order. 'Was he the intended target? Did he just
happen not to be there?' He should have remembered that he was
in a room full of coppers. A ribbon of scepticism threaded around
the room. The police dislike coincidence.

WPC Delia Shaw spoke up. 'Sir,' she said tentatively, 'I went to Mr Barton's office.'

'Go on,' Alex prompted softly, sensing something soft as velvet but ugly as murder was creeping near.

'It's very smart, near the abbey,' she continued. 'It looks prosperous. He has a secretary called Mirabelle. Very attractive, I sensed.' She coloured. 'She seemed a bit . . .' She frowned. 'I wondered . . .'

Alex was tempted to retort, *Spit it out, whatever it is. Don't be coy, Constable*, but it wasn't his way to belittle his officers. He wanted to encourage them. Nurture them. They were his family. He needed to tease this out of the WPC as he had out of PC Roberts.

'Are you suggesting that there was something between Nigel Barton and his secretary?'

The entire room was listening. Now it was Delia Shaw's turn to colour. 'I just wondered. That's all,' she said lamely. 'She seemed a bit – well, considering what's happened she seemed a bit cocky. A bit familiar. A bit casual.'

Randall was still gentle with her. 'Was there any hard evidence of anything?'

'No.' Then her natural defences struck up. 'Well, there wouldn't be, would there?'

A titter did a Mexican wave around the room this time while Randall cursed his choice of adjective.

'Is Mirabelle married?'

'Divorced.'

'On the grounds of?'

'Irretrievable breakdown.'

'Good.' Randall approved. At least the WPC had done her home-work, followed through a lead, checked out a hunch. He determined to speak to her after the briefing and ask her to follow up her idea.

He turned again to the whiteboard and the list of three names. 'Now then, of the three business associates, Karoglan's in the clear. He was with his secretary in his flat in Chester.' Talith couldn't resist grinning at the memory of the lovely and very sexy Teresa Holloway.

Randall continued, oblivious to his sergeant's fantasy. 'The doorman saw them go in around eight and they didn't come out again. He was nowhere near Melverley.' He pencilled a line through the name before moving to the second name. 'Hatton is now living in Slough. Although he's still bitter I can't see him travelling up to Melverley. Besides, he'd know that Nigel was away roughly one night a month. His quarrel was with Nigel Barton – not with his family. I think he would have made sure that Barton was in the house that night.'

Another pencil line then he tapped the tip of the pen. 'And Pinfold lives in Amsterdam, according to his mum. She still lives in Melverley and is very angry and bitter towards Barton. She feels that he ruined her son's life because he never gave him a second chance.' He looked around the room. 'But we know something she doesn't know: her innocent little boy was in the United Kingdom between the dates of the twenty-third and twenty-sixth of February. So what was he doing here? I suggest that we have another chat with Mrs Pinfold.' He hesitated 'And young Jude.'

Gethin Roberts stirred. Randall caught it. 'Go on, Roberts.'

'The boy was burning,' he said. 'He was in a panic. I can't believe he had anything to do with it.'

'Right. OK. It's a valid point.' He paused. 'I have no suspicion that Jude started this fire but I wonder if he knows just a little more than he is telling. Now does anyone else have anything else to add?'

It seemed not. Alex Randall summed up, divided them into teams and wrote a list. 'We need to focus first of all on Stuart Pinfold and his mother. Talith, you and Coleman can head off on that one. Shaw – as you've already an interest in Mirabelle you can pursue that line of enquiry. Roberts, you and I will be searching through all the detail we have to see if we can discover a connection between the Bartons and Monica Deverill. Coleman, take some statements from the neighbours and see when Mrs Deverill was last seen, if there are any clues. OK? Any questions? No?'

He dismissed the briefing.

Wednesday, 16 March, 3 p.m.

It took until the afternoon before the team of firemen working at Sundorne could give him a categorical answer. Alex had returned to the property and found Will Tyler and Colin Agnew in deep discussion.

Tyler spoke up for them. 'We've gone right through with a toothcomb, Inspector. She isn't here,' he said. 'Wherever she is she didn't die here. And her car's missing.'

Randall frowned, met the fireman's eyes and waited for him to enlarge. He'd met Tyler before and found him a wise old fire chief. He knew about fires. Alex trusted his instincts.

'So?'

'So she's either on holiday and blissfully ignorant that she doesn't have a house any more, or she set it alight herself or –'

Randall finished it for him. 'Or,' he said, 'she was abducted by our arsonist.'

Tyler scooped in a deep breath. 'I'd better speak to her sons,' he said.

James and Gordon Deverill were easy to track down by mobile phone. They already knew about the fire and that their mother was missing and Alex Randall felt it was important that they were kept up to date with the investigation.

After receiving a negative answer when he asked them whether their mother had been in touch, Randall asked that they come down to the station 'for a chat'. He suspected they were not fooled as neither of them asked whether their mother's body had been found. He felt a touch of sympathy when Gordon Deverill tried to cover up his upset by repeatedly clearing his throat while his brother stood stiffly by. Randall suspected that James, being the older, was better at hiding his feelings.

They arrived together an hour and a half later, James in a business suit – he must have come straight from work – and his younger brother in jeans and a sweater. They struck him as decent and pleasant young men and they both looked very apprehensive.

Randall showed them into an interview room and ordered tea for James, coffee for himself and the younger brother. He opened the conversation. 'The fire people have now gone right through the house.' He paused. 'They have found no sign of your mother's body.'

'Thank God.' They spoke as one.

But then they started to put two and two together. They stared at him, seemingly unable to take it in. Gordon spoke first. 'So she wasn't at home when the fire broke out?'

'All I can tell you, with any certainty,' Randall repeated very steadily – hand to the tiller in rough seas – 'is that her body is not in the house.'

He could tell from Gordon's widened eyes and James's hand rubbing an already-bald spot on his head that they weren't sure whether to be relieved, puzzled, or even more worried.

'I know you've already been interviewed,' Randall said steadily, 'but I want to go over everything. First of all, when did you last see or speak to her?' Without waiting for them to answer he continued, 'And secondly, has she ever done anything like this before?'

The brothers looked at each other.

James spoke first. 'I spoke to her a week last Monday evening,' he said, 'the seventh. Val and I wondered if she'd like to come over for lunch at the weekend.'

'What did she say?'

'That she was busy that weekend,' James's clear eyes met those of the inspector, 'but that she would be over this coming weekend i.e. the twentieth.'

'Did you ask her what she was busy doing?'

James drew in a long, regretful breath. 'No, I didn't. She didn't like us prying. She had a lot of friends from her nursing days and resented us intruding.' His eyes met those of his brother's and seemed to flash a warning. 'She valued her privacy. Our father used to be fairly possessive. Apart from work Mum didn't really have much of a social life when they were together. When he died it was as though she'd been let off a leash. Weeks in Spain, cruises, visiting friends. She and Dad both had quite good pensions and she's always been good with money.'

Randall nodded. He was building up a picture of the proverbial 'Merry Widow'.

'She worked full time as a nurse?'

'Oh, yes.' This time it was Gordon who spoke. 'More than full time. Nights, weekends. The phone would ring at home and she'd be called in because someone else was off sick. Dedicated. She was dedicated.'

More of the picture. 'What sort of nurse was she?'

'Psychiatric.'

Randall felt a chill. His collar felt tight as though it was choking him. Surreptitiously he undid his top shirt button. Then realized that both men were watching him.

He forced himself to continue. 'Has she ever done anything like this before – gone missing?'

It was Gordon who answered for them both. 'Not for this length of time. Maybe the odd weekend but she'd have her mobile with her. Text or ring and let us know. We've been trying her mobile. It's been switched off. I'm really worried. Even without the fire I'd be worried.' His voice was rising as he carried on, 'As it is I'm beside myself. It's awful.' There was a note of hysteria in his tone now.

'I shall need a list of all her friends and acquaintances,' Randall said.

They looked at one another. 'We don't know *all* of them,' Gordon said awkwardly. 'And I suppose her address book and stuff has been destroyed.'

Inwardly Randall sighed. This would prove to be tricky. 'Is there anything else that might help?' He looked hopefully from one to the other.

They looked glum. 'No.'

ELEVEN

After speaking to the Deverills Randall spent some time drawing up another list of things to do.

For now he was treating the two cases as one and searching for a link. He might be wrong but this was to be his starting point. So top of the list was anything that might help track down the missing woman. And that meant her mobile and landline printouts and an alert on her car. They would appoint one of the junior officers to ring each and every number and see if any of her friends had a clue as to her whereabouts. At the back of his mind he still thought it a possibility that she was fine – just away, somewhere else, maybe with friends and the fire was an unlucky coincidence.

She might not even be in this country. It was all too easy to get away last minute and there were still points on the globe where mobile phones and 'the news' did not penetrate. She might be holed up in just such a spot and unable to inform her sons of her whereabouts. But he couldn't completely discount the theory that she had been abducted by the fire-raiser.

Randall sat, his chin in his palm, and thought. The next priority was to speak to Jude Barton. Again. Randall had a feeling that the boy knew something significant. Which, for whatever reason, he wasn't telling. After all, he was the sole survivor of what the papers were mistakenly now starting to headline as Death House 1. Even if he was not absolutely certain about the connection the local and national papers appeared to have no such doubts.

Randall also felt that he should follow up one small statement, which had seemed insignificant at the time but might be important. It could just lead them out of this blind tunnel and show them a way back into the light. The boy, Jude, had told him he spent time with his grandfather listening to stories. What stories? Randall wondered. Had the old man given the boy any sort of hint that all was not well in his psyche? Had there been forewarning that things might tip him farther away from his sanity? And why was he, Alex, even thinking about Barton the elder when it was patently obvious he could have had nothing to do with the second fire? Why? Why? Why?

And now Randall was wondering why he had not recognized just how important Jude Barton might be as a witness. Because the boy's statement had appeared so very bland and uninformative? He drummed his fingers on the desk. Almost banging out a rhythm, of admonishment to himself and a warning to be more vigilant. He would rectify this situation himself, leaving the rest of the team to focus on the other leads they had outlined in the briefing.

And so, finally, Detective Inspector Alex Randall went home, if not content and optimistic then at least feeling that the scent of optimism might lie just around the corner. He went home believing he had it all planned out.

Thursday, 17 March, 8 a.m.

The morning brought its own surprise. Randall was at the station
for 8 a.m. and was met by Sergeant Paul Talith at the door. And
Talith patently had something to say. He was shifting his not
inconsiderable weight from foot to foot in a dance of impatience
as Randall arrived. Randall had always had a hearty regard for
Talith. Although he didn't look like a particularly thoughtful
person – he was a big guy with thinning hair, meaty thighs and
a double chin, which appeared to increase in size almost daily
– Randall had realized that sergeant Paul Talith was blessed with
a good dollop of common sense. He was a football freak who
was not usually very good at dealing with the general public,
displaying poor humour and impatience. But in spite of all this
there had been times when it had been Talith who had put his
finger right on the throbbing pulse of a case, made an apparently
thoughtless or accidental remark which had led to a train of
thought which, in its turn, had pointed the way towards a conclusion. Randall respected the guy and was always happy to have
him around.

Talith began with a polite, 'Morning, sir,' which Randall
returned. Then the sergeant cleared his throat. 'We've had a bit
of an interesting development, sir.'

Randall felt his interest stir. A 'bit of an interesting development' was just what they needed. 'Go on, Talith.'

'Well, you know the woman who's missing after the fire in
Sundorne, Monica Deverill?'

'Ye-es?' *Wait for it.*

Talith revealed his trump card. 'She's logged on as having
rung the helpline around seven p.m. after your TV appeal.'

'What?' Randall felt his pulse quickening. 'You're sure?'

'We have the tape, sir.'

Without another word Alex Randall followed Talith into the
communications room and slipped on a pair of headphones.
He heard the operator say, 'Can I have your name, please,' and
the woman's answer, clear and precise. 'My name is Monica
Deverill. I heard your lunchtime broadcast. I think I know
something about the fire out at Melverlcy Grange.'

'Really?' The operator sounded only faintly interested.

'Yes, you see . . .' There was almost a cluck of annoyance. 'It's so difficult to put all this sensibly over the phone. It'd be better . . .' A pause, then, 'Can I call in tomorrow morning and speak to someone personally?'

The operator's voice was soothing and polite now, bordering on patronizing. 'Yes, of course, Mrs Deverill. We have a team of officers ready to talk to anyone who thinks they might have information on the case.'

Mrs Deverill didn't even hesitate. 'I'll call in tomorrow then. Around eleven?'

'That's fine, Mrs Deverill. Thank you for your call. Someone will speak to you in the morning.' There was a click and the phone was put down.

Randall put himself in the operator's shoes. After an appeal like this they had hundreds of calls. Most of them had no useful information at all but simply wanted to join in what they saw as a TV thriller. Even if it was on the very edge of the drama, the faint connection gave the general public a frisson of excitement. Monica Deverill would not have been the first phone call of the day; neither would she have been the last. Many callers deliberately affected an air of mystery to focus attention on themselves, pretending they had vital information when often they didn't, merely offering up some trivia about a T-shirt or a car without anything specific or helpful. A phone call didn't necessarily mean that what the caller had was either of relevance or importance. So many were simply time-wasters.

Randall replayed the tape, listening hard for a clue, the slightest inflection, a word, a hint of what it was that Monica Deverill had known – if anything. '*I think I know something about the fire at Melverley Grange.*'

It could have been anything. But during the night her house, too, had been the target of the arsonist.

Randall took a look at Talith who simply shrugged and looked sympathetic.

'Just our luck,' Randall said gloomily. 'If only she'd kept her appointment. At least we'd know whether she did know something significant or not.'

'Well, it's a start,' Talith pointed out. 'It's a real connection between the two fires.'

'Maybe.'

But surely this could be no coincidence? Randall was still pondering the point when the phone rang. Surprisingly it was Will Tyler ringing from the fire station and he came straight to the point. 'I hope you don't mind me ringing you, Inspector,' he said in his slow, Shropshire burr, 'but there's something botherin' me.'

Randall waited. Cases were like this, odd facts surfacing, coming from all sorts of sources. Left drifting they could appear too random to be of any use. But put them together and they started to connect, like a string of pearls. So he listened carefully as Tyler enlarged. 'The staircase was intact enough for William Barton to have descended, so why didn't he?'

'Smoke?' Randall suggested tentatively. He didn't want to appear to be telling the fire officer his job.

'It's possible,' Tyler conceded, 'but he could have run to the back of the house.'

Randall was silent for a moment absorbing Tyler's words. Then he said, 'What exactly are you saying?'

'He could have escaped. The fire was more at the front. It spread upwards from the lounge and the kitchen to the women's bedrooms above. I know smoke would have been billowing up the stairs but I still think he could have got out.'

'But didn't?'

Tyler gave a little cough. 'There's something else. It's about the two women. You see, I've been thinking about the timing. If the women went to bed at eleven and the fire had taken a real hold before twelve the fire-raiser would have to have locked them in as soon as they went to the bedrooms. Waited, as it were, for them to go but not being sure they were asleep.'

'Go on,' Randall prompted, baffled as to where this was all leading.

'Then there's the fact that our second fire was started in exactly the same way – splashes of petrol through a front window, the curtains soaked and a light thrown in but evidence of accelerants in more than one room. And believe me, Inspector Randall, this is not the usual way to fire-raise. It's nearly always petrol through the letterbox which works just as well.' He chuckled. 'For some reason arsonists are about the least imaginative of criminals. It's a strange case.'

'You don't know the half of it,' Alex said gloomily. 'There's something else,' and he related the story of Monica Deverill's telephone call to the police station the night of the TV appeal, a week before her house had been set alight.

'Ah,' Tyler said. 'I couldn't see what but I thought there had to be a connection.'

'Yeah, but what it actually is is still a mystery,' Randall said.

Tyler still seemed to want to offload. 'Do you know how many house fires we had last year?'

'No.'

'Forty. That's getting on for one a week. Do you know how many of those were fatal?' Without even waiting for the detective's response he supplied the answer. 'None,' he said, emphasizing the statement with a, 'not one. We haven't had a fatal house fire for more than three years in Shrewsbury. They're rare, thank God, but a high percentage of fatal house fires are very often arson. Now, all of a sudden, we have two house fires, consequent loss of life and someone missing. Doesn't make sense, does it?'

Randall had to agree with the fire chief and waited, expecting the word *unless,* but Tyler simply advised him to 'think on it'. Randall put the phone down thoughtfully.

Martha's morning, meanwhile, was punctuated by a telephone call from Mark Sullivan, the pathologist who had performed the post-mortems on the three members of the Barton family. And he was having second thoughts.

'I've been looking again at the body of Mr William Barton,' he said. 'There's no doubt that the cause of death was smoke inhalation but there is also some damage to the skull.' She could tell from his tone that he was frowning. 'I could have put it down to fire damage, the heat causing the skull to split, but I've been thinking about it.' Again he paused before adding, 'I think he might have been bashed over the head.'

'Are you sure, Mark?'

'It can be really difficult to interpret,' Sullivan said. 'Heat damages the bones, changes the microscopic structure so it can be hard to know whether an injury was inflicted pre- or post-mortem. To be honest, Martha, I couldn't really swear to either.'

'That's disturbing,' Martha said. 'And it makes the case even more difficult. But . . .' She fell silent. A new and troubling scenario was unfolding in front of her mind's eye. The fire-raiser entering the house, locking the doors on the women, assaulting a confused old man. Then a couple of weeks later the same assault on the home of a retired nurse.

She thanked Mark for his call but sensed he was hesitating. 'Was there something else?' Still he hesitated so she prompted him. 'Mark?'

'I wondered if you'd care to have dinner with me one night?' He'd blurted out the words so quickly she half imagined she'd dreamt them. But she hadn't.

The invitation was so out of the blue and Martha was so taken aback that she couldn't answer at once. And Sullivan took this the wrong way. 'Yeah, I know,' he said. 'Very bad idea to mix business with pleasure. Sorry.'

It made up her mind for her. 'Thank you,' she said smoothly. 'I'd love to.'

'Great. We can sort out a time and place soon?'

'Soon,' she echoed and the phone was put down. Privately she agreed with the pathologist who was a good few years younger than her. This was not a good idea. In fact, it was a rotten idea and she shouldn't have said yes.

Even so, she sat at her desk and smiled. Here she was, a widow in her forties, no great beauty, twin teenagers (was there ever anything more horrible?) and she was being asked for a date by a very eligible divorced/newly single man. She frowned. Maybe before she agreed to a specific time and date she should check out what exactly Mark Sullivan's marital status was. She had no intention of being copped having a sneaky date with a still-married man. Particularly one she worked with.

She glanced at the door. Jericho would know whether Mark Sullivan was still married but she couldn't possibly ask her assistant outright. He would smell a rat faster than a terrier would. And he was incredibly protective – one could say jealous – of her privacy both personal and professional.

She must find a subtle way around it. And if Dr Mark Sullivan was, as he had said, no longer married, well, what was the harm? She smiled to herself, not displeased with the day's work – so far.

Her next task was to speak to DI Randall and ask whether she could visit Melverley Grange again and then take up his offer of a visit to the site in Sundorne. As coroner she had a perfect right to visit the scene of an accident or crime, anything that had resulted in reportable death, even to instruct that a jury do likewise. She didn't really want to go back to the terrible wreck of what must once have been a most beautiful house, the scene of such tragedy, but she was very anxious to learn the truth. She picked up the phone, got put through to DI Randall and made her request.

He was outside her office in forty-five minutes flat, car waiting. While he drove out to Melverley Alex Randall filled her in on the latest events, the connection between the two fires and the puzzling phone call from the fire chief. Martha was both intrigued and reflective. 'I wonder what it was that this Mrs Deverill knew?' she said. Then, 'Do you know anything about this nurse?'

Randall filled her in on the 'Merry Widow's' family, friends, the two sons but she shook her head. 'No – I mean, about her. Where she'd worked, who these friends were. Did she have any close relationships? What was in her past life – her husband, things like that.'

Alex's face was thoughtful as he pulled into the drive. As always Martha was inspiring him, opening doors and windows on to new possibilities and ideas. He pulled up outside Melverley Grange. They sat in the car and regarded the ruin without speaking.

Even from the outside Martha could still see the effects of the fire, from the boarded windows to the police tape which marked out a corridor of access, workmen's vans, and still the forensic vans parked outside. There was an aura of sadness and already neglect around the house that must once have been so beautiful. It was already hard to imagine that a family would ever live there happily again.

Alex Randall followed her gaze. 'Still a bloody mess,' he commented.

Martha couldn't help but agree. 'It is that.' He handed her a hard hat and together they walked inside.

The scent of smoke was still pungent and strong but fading now, the atmosphere inside gloomy. 'It's hard to get rid of the smell of a fire,' Randall commented. 'It seems to seep into the woodwork, the bricks, the mortar.' He gave a harrumph of a laugh. 'You can paint, decorate, put up new curtains and replace the damaged woodwork but you never get rid of the smell of a fire.'

'Or the aura it leaves behind,' Martha added, glancing at the detective sharply. There was a sadness in his voice that made her wonder if he had had personal experience of a house fire. But she said nothing.

The lounge still looked dingy, smoke-marked and hardly better today than it had on the morning after the fire except that now there were new marks, sinister in their significance: white patches where pieces of furniture had been removed for forensic examination, circles marked where accelerant had been found. The broken window had been completely removed and replaced with a sheet of hardboard. The carpet was still cold and sodden. It was obvious that the entire house would have to be stripped right down and redecorated. It was hard to imagine that it would ever be restored to its former beauty or completely lose the smell of smoke.

Martha walked through all the downstairs rooms, not really knowing what she was looking for: some small thing that would lead her towards understanding the sequence of events on that terrible night. Alex followed behind her, keeping quiet, eyeing her curiously, not quite sure what she was looking for either, yet hoping that she would pick up on something he had not.

They climbed the stairs and came to the spot where William Barton's body had been found. At last Martha began to see something. 'Show me again which way he was facing, Alex.'

'Like this.' Alex indicated the feet towards the stairs. 'Head towards the bedroom, arms outstretched.'

And Martha began to wonder if they had misunderstood the evidence they had found. 'So he *was* approaching the women's bedrooms, probably trying to get them out,' she said.

Randall agreed without any idea of what this might mean.

She told him then about Mark Sullivan's call – at least the bit about William Barton's possible head injury – not the bit about dinner. Randall was thoughtful and unwittingly echoed her private thoughts.

'Maybe,' he said, recalling the unspoken detail of Tyler's telephone call, 'we've been looking at this the wrong way round.'

'That was what I was wondering.'

It was as though he hadn't heard her. 'The old man was a victim,' he said quietly.

They were standing in the room where Christie Barton had died. Martha looked down at the bunch of scented white lilies and read the card out loud. 'I'm so sorry, darling,' it read. 'Love, Nige X'

'Sorry for what, I wonder?' Martha commented.

Randall gave a loud sigh and filled her in on Mirabelle. 'The oldest cliché in the book,' he said wearily. 'We'll be getting a statement from her.'

But Martha's attention was distracted. 'The key to her bedroom,' she said. 'Did you find it?'

'Oh, yes. The entire door must have been ablaze. We found the key in the ashes.' Alex looked disturbed as he took in the carnage.

'And you found traces of accelerants in both downstairs rooms and splashes on the stairs?'

Randall gave her a sharp look. 'Yes,' he said.

'Any *inside* either of the bedrooms where the women died?'

Slowly he shook his head.

'Anywhere else?'

'Stairs, hallway, lounge and the sofa in the front room where the blaze was started was soaked in the stuff.'

'Petrol can?'

He looked at her.

'Was there one in the garage – a petrol can, I mean? Or one in the house?'

He scrutinized her. 'What are you getting at, Martha Gunn?'

She gave him an innocent half smile. 'Just trying to get a more complete picture, Alex.'

He grinned. 'I know you, Martha. And I wouldn't trust you as far as I could throw you.'

'I'd better lose weight then so you'll be able to throw me further.'

They both laughed at the weak and silly quip. Then looked around them and sobered up instantly. The sooty blackness gave their surroundings a look of hell. The work of the devil, everlasting flames, purgatory and all the other horrors that religion can throw at you. Behind their natural revulsion crept a sense of doom, of destruction, burning martyrs and the Spanish Inquisition.

Martha voiced both their feelings. 'What an awful sight,' she said. 'How completely awful to die like this, terrified, disorientated.' Disorientated? But Christie Barton had made it to the door. And her daughter to the only place of safety she could imagine. They had not been so disorientated. Merely trapped.

This room was still patently smoke-wrecked, the windows cracked and stained. Even the winter sunshine couldn't penetrate the blackened windows. And everywhere the pall of smoke seemed still to be present. The air was not quite clear and clean but had remained hazy, whispering secrets it had witnessed. Hell itself, in the form of smoke and water, had crept in under that door, like the serpent of Genesis, slithering poisonously towards its victim. Martha took a last look around, conscious still that something was gnawing away at the back of her mind like a persistently hungry rat. She frowned. What on earth was it? *What was here?* She took in the bed between the two chests of drawers, the windows, the curtains, melted and scorched, the layer of wet, oily char that lay over all. A white space where a picture had been removed.

What did it all mean? And now a new question was hammering in her mind. What contribution had Monica Deverill been about to make before she vanished?

Next they entered Adelaide's room, where the poor child had cowered. Pink wallpaper stained with soot. This time Martha couldn't help but imagine Sukey in this situation and found the room unbearably poignant and painful. It almost moved her to tears. She had to leave.

Alex was watching her curiously. 'Found what you were looking for?'

She took a last sweep around the girl's room. 'I don't know,' she said. 'I just don't know. Except . . .' He paused, waiting for her comment. 'It's all here, Alex. It has to be.'

'Do you want to go up there again?' He indicated the door which led to the attic stairs and she nodded. Three people had died in this house. She had a duty to find out the truth.

The rooms still held a vague scent of smoke but it was not pungent and overpowering as it had been on the first two floors. She seemed drawn to the hook from which had hung the rope ladder. 'Interesting,' she said. 'It must have been quite a drama, a boy climbing down a rope ladder through the smoke, escaping from a burning house where his mother and sister were trapped. On that night the rope ladder could only have been used at the back of the house.'

Again, wondering what exactly she was getting at, Randall made no comment but simply waited for her to continue. 'The rope ladder could only have been used at the back of the house.'

Randall's eyes narrowed.

She studied the beam in more detail, noted that the screws had been inserted recently. They were sharp and shiny. 'And it has been put in recently.' She peered round the room. Jude obviously hadn't returned to collect his belongings. It was all still here: computer games, a TV set, random clothes scattered around the place, books, DVDs. In here there was nothing out of the ordinary. It was a typical teenage boy's room. Except the teenage boy was still exiled. 'I take it the Bartons, father and son, are still in the private hotel?'

'And likely to remain there for some months. It may well be a year before Melverley Grange is habitable again.'

Poor house, she thought and wondered whether father and son would ever be able to bear living here again. It would always be a blighted home and for the boy a terrible memory. They descended the stairs and out into the welcome crisp air of a March day. Martha felt relief to escape the atmosphere of the ruined house.

TWELVE

'Shall we move on to Sundorne?' Martha asked shakily and took up her seat in the front of the police car. She was quiet as Randall drove but minutes later as she was chauffeur driven through frosty Shropshire countryside her mood lightened. 'Oh, what it is to be chauffeur driven,' she murmured, enjoying the luxury. The journey was relaxing. Randall was a careful, smooth driver. Twenty minutes later they had reached Battlefields roundabout, entering the town from the north-east, passing Tesco's superstore on the right-hand side. Just past Morrisons Alex Randall turned down a side street and pulled up outside another house wrecked by fire, this time a neat semi. But the destruction was even worse than the damage affected at Melverley Grange. If Monica Deverill had been inside when the fire had torn through her home she could not have survived. It was a much smaller, more modest house than the Grange and a higher percentage of it had been completely destroyed. The roof had fallen in, the joists now blackened ribs bared to the sky. Even the house that joined Monica Deverill's had suffered extensive damage too. It was probable that both would have to be demolished. Two families would lose their homes.

If Monica was still alive.

Detective and coroner stood and regarded the sight, then looked back at one another. This felt somehow strange. Not merely tragic. It was lacking an explanation. Where was she? She had to be somewhere, didn't she? People didn't simply disappear, did they? And where was her car? As they walked up the drive Martha's feeling of disquiet intensified. This felt supernatural, other-wordly. Even this act of simply walking up the drive seemed to represent the spookiness of a sequence in a horror film, the eye sneaking up on the unsuspecting victim, the wrecked house waiting and watching. Martha shivered and Alex Randall noticed. 'The atmosphere,' he commented. 'It's getting to you, isn't it, Martha?'

She nodded. 'I just wish I knew what was going on, and what's happened to her. Even if she'd written a confession to starting the Melverley fire and turned up dead it would feel less threatening.'

Randall nodded in agreement.

'So we're still left with the major questions,' she said. 'We still don't have a clue who set this fire or what Mrs Deverill had been about to tell you about the arson attack on Melverley Grange.'

'Million dollar questions,' he said grimly. 'I just hope we get some settlement on this.'

And Martha could not help but agree.

The fire chief was standing outside the house and they fell into step with him as they approached what had been the front door. Hard hats again and they were inside. The three of them stood in the hall and looked up. It was like the house at Melverley but worse. Overhead parts of the roof still hung on blackened beams. But where the roof had caved in the clear blue sky of a winter's day was visible. The effect was of a broken patchwork, gleams of cold blue air flooding the stricken property with light and softening the smell of the smoke so although the building had been worse affected than Melverley Grange the atmosphere inside was less claustrophobic. Martha looked at the broken steps of the stairs and Will Tyler, fire chief, voiced her thoughts. 'I wonder which bedroom she normally slept in.'

Martha looked up. Then back down again. It wouldn't have made much difference. *All* the bedrooms had been destroyed.

Even to her untrained eye she could see that it simply wasn't safe to explore the house. The front room had been completely destroyed. And much of the furniture from the bedroom above lay skewed, on its side, as the joists beneath them had collapsed. Even as they stood and stared there was an ominous creaking above and an impression of a release of latent heat.

The forensic team, two men from Birmingham, specialists in malicious fire damage, were still taking samples and labelling them carefully. Martha watched them with the fascination and respect she always felt for a professional doing his – or her – job. She spoke to them. 'Can you be quite sure that Mrs Deverill isn't here somewhere? Maybe lying underneath some of the furniture?'

'She isn't here,' Tyler said. 'Even when fire damage is as extensive as this is a human body is quite easy to spot.'

She turned her head. 'So what *have* you found?'

'Same as before,' Tyler responded. 'Petrol-soaked rag through a broken window.'

'We think she must have slept in the front bedroom,' fireman Colin Agnew put in gloomily. 'It's the worst affected.' And as though to underline his certainty he repeated, 'She definitely isn't anywhere.'

As the staircase was unsafe a ladder had been placed against an external wall and Agnew climbed it, making running commentaries to the detective inspector from above, talking him through events. 'The front bedroom has all but been destroyed. Most of the joists . . .' He demonstrated by putting his weight very gingerly on a heavily scorched floorboard, 'have been burned. If not right through, then severely weakened. It was quite a blaze. Took hold quickly. And the gas fire and cooker didn't help. They exploded and took the fire to another dimension.' He grinned down at them. Even on the ground floor Martha and Alex were walking very gingerly, feeling the floorboards move under their weight and listening for that terrible sound of splintering which would herald the floor completely giving way. Above them they could see the bed was still in the centre of the room, dipping down towards them. Agnew drew their attention to the bedding, badly charred. But they knew it was empty. The watchers all knew that she was somewhere else, dead or alive, free or a prisoner but she was not here. They watched Agnew move through the rest of the room, stepping around the perimeter and avoiding the centre which was about to cave in completely. Even as they watched the bed slipped a little farther towards them and they withdrew.

So if she wasn't here, where was she? They all knew that people confused and disorientated by smoke can lose their way even in an environment as familiar as their own bedroom. There had been signs of this in Christie Barton's room in Melverley Grange. First she had headed for the window, not the door, her first mistake being to step out of the wrong side of her bed. People in the dark, in the dead of night, normally find their way from their bed to the bathroom. People disorientated by smoke do not. Tyler led them next to the kitchen which was at the back of the house and less badly damaged by the fire, though still a wreck with laminated cupboard doors melted and burned and the rubber floor tiles burnt right through. Martha could not resist opening the larder cupboard just in case. Maybe Monica had mistaken the door for an exit. Behind was not so badly damaged. Smoke had seeped in but she was not here. The shelves only held packets of food partly scorched and soot-stained. They could not find her. They *would* not find her. Was she playing a macabre game of Hide and Seek? As they progressed through rooms, opening cupboards, Agnew even shining a light into the downstairs shower cubicle, it felt like it. That the woman's presence was here but eluding them. It was Agnew who spoke up first, his voice both timorous and feisty, holding anger and frustration. 'So where the hell is she?' His eyes turned to Randall. 'There's been no sightings of the car?'

Randall shook his head, his face grim.

Martha felt a sudden flash of hope, a conviction that Monica Deverill was wherever her car was but safe. She smiled at Alex. Perhaps? But the warm feeling quickly chilled as she read his expression.

He stepped towards the back door. 'We'll just take a peek inside the garage,' he said, 'in case there's something there.'

Apart from checking for the car and a very superficial search the SOCOs had largely left the garage alone, concentrating their efforts on the house. They stared around a neat and empty space, a few boxes stacked neatly at the back, a chest freezer. It was obvious that Monica had sometimes garaged her car – there were oil stains and the garage was relatively clear, leaving plenty of room for it, and just as obvious that the vehicle was not here.

Randall did a cursory search, moved a couple of token boxes. Martha knew exactly what he would be looking for – a petrol can. One of those with a screw top and a long spout.

He didn't find one.

Their attention was diverted by a second police car pulling up and Sergeant Paul Talith and WPC Lara Tinsley climbing out. Or at least that's how Talith's awkward manoeuvres could better be described as he 'eased' himself out of the car.

Even as Randall was greeting them the unpleasant thought Martha had voiced earlier was worming its way through her mind. The two fires had been started in the same way. Exactly. It was an unusual operandi and the results in each case had been catastrophic. Was it possible then that the *nurse* had, for some reason, burnt down Melverley Grange and then, in an attempt to disguise this, set her own home alight? Surely not. It had simply drawn attention to her. 'The nurse and the Barton family,' she asked, frowning. 'Was there any connection between them?'

Randall met her eyes with a gaze of his own which was hard to read. 'Not that we've found out yet,' he said, mirroring her frown. Then he drew in a deep breath. 'But it's early days yet, Martha. I'm confident all this will make sense finally.'

'I suppose the fact that the car is missing points us in the direction that Mrs Deverill drove herself away from here,' she ventured.

Randall turned to her. 'We can't make any assumptions yet, Martha. The arsonist could have taken it.' He paused. 'Even with her inside, dead or alive. All we know is that her body is not in there.' He indicated the wrecked semi then added, 'Anything's possible,' he said, 'at the moment.'

'If it was our arsonist he or she would have to have got the car key somehow,' Martha pondered.

Alex continued with her reasoning. 'And before he ignited the fire. The back door was bolted and the front door would have been in flames.'

'Unless the car was stolen earlier,' Lara Tinsley suggested.

Talith gave a lopsided grin. 'Bit of a coincidence, isn't it, Lara, two crimes in one night? Besides, if Monica had been aware her car had been stolen she would have reported it.'

She persisted. 'What if they were committed by the same person? He stole the car and then came back?'

'To torch the house,' Martha extrapolated. 'Perhaps she saw him steal the car and ran out. And he came back later to torch the house.'

Talith pursed his lips as he considered this option. 'It's possible,' he conceded.

'There's another thing, Alex.'

He looked up.

'There was quite a time lapse between your broadcast and her telephone call. You say she'd heard your lunchtime broadcast but didn't call until the evening. Why do you think that was?'

He drew in a deep breath. 'Sometimes it's because they didn't realize the significance of what they knew.'

'Is that what you think is the case here?'

Randall shrugged but everyone watching knew that the action was not because he didn't care but because he didn't know. And when he did speak they could hear the frustration in his voice. 'Well, wherever she is, Mrs Deverill is not here.' He thought for a moment then fished his mobile phone out of his pocket and connected with James Deverill, the older of Monica's two sons. He told him where he was and outlined the current situation quickly: that the forensic team had failed to find his mother's body so she was listed as missing, that her car was too and that they had put a stop and apprehend order on both vehicle and person.

'Naturally,' he said quickly before Deverill jumped to an unfavourable conclusion, 'it's imperative that we find your mother and make certain she's safe. I wonder if you've had any further thoughts? Is it possible your mother is perhaps staying with a friend? Do you have any contact details that have been so far omitted?'

'She would have told me,' James Deverill insisted. 'She'd know I'd worry. I've been trying her mobile phone all morning but she isn't picking up.' He paused. 'It isn't even ringing. It's going straight through to answerphone. I take it you haven't found anything at the house that would give you a clue as to her whereabouts?'

'There isn't much left of the house, James,' Randall responded gently. 'I'm afraid it was a very bad fire.'

'I was thinking of going round later.'

'That's fine by us but it isn't terribly safe. I'm afraid the combination of the fire plus the firemen's hoses have pretty much destroyed it. You'll have to wear a hard hat and you'll be supervised but there may be things you can salvage,' Randall said doubtfully. He added: 'James, there is something else.'

'Oh?'

'Your mother rang us the night before the fire in connection with the blaze at Mclverley Grange. She said she knew something about it. Have you any idea what it might be?'

'Not a clue.'

He did sound genuinely confounded.

'Did she know the Barton family?'

'Not to my knowledge.'

'Did she say anything to you about the fire at the Grange?'

'Not to me.'

'To your brother?'

'You'll have to ask him but I doubt it.'

'Can you think of any connection between Melverley, the Barton family and your mother?'

'No. I can't think of any connection except that she simply loves going to the old black and white church in the village. I think she found it peaceful and rather beautiful. She was upset when she learned that the banks were slipping and helped with a couple of charity events to raise money to shore it up.' He paused. 'She may have met the Barton family through that but I think it's unlikely. If she did, as I said, she never mentioned them.'

'Really?' It was, at best, a very tenuous connection. But it was still a potential connection. 'Your mother wouldn't have been in touch with your brother and not you?'

'No.' Deverill was patently irritated by the question. 'She would never do that. If she'd spoken to one of us she would have spoken to us both, I'm sure. Mum was a thoughtful person. And she had a conscience. She would have hated to cause us worry. This simply isn't like her.'

Randall tried to retrieve the situation. 'Look, James,' he said, 'I wouldn't worry if I were you. She could have gone somewhere in the car, somewhere perfectly innocent, and while she was away someone torched her house.'

The attempt at consolation didn't work. James fired up. 'Bit of a coincidence,' he said sarcastically. 'If that's all, where is she now? And why hasn't she been in touch?'

Randall tried to pour oil on the troubled waters. 'We'll continue our search of your mother's property, do house-to-house enquiries, see if we can ascertain when the car was last seen in the drive. A team of officers is ringing down the list of her friends' numbers. She has to be somewhere, Mr Deverill. We will find her.'

James Deverill was unconvinced. 'I hope so, Inspector,' he said grimly.

Again Randall tried to reassure the worried man. 'In a way the news is good, James. We haven't found her in the house. She isn't there. If she had been she would not have survived. We're looking for your mother – not a body.'

'But –' Even James Deverill couldn't quite finish the sentence. Randall knew exactly what he would have wanted to say. If she is alive – and free – why has she not been in touch?

Randall was finally beaten. There were too many questions he could not answer – yet. He thanked James Deverill and rang off, then glanced at Martha who was waiting at his side. 'Sorry,' he said. 'I'd better run you back to your office.'

As soon as DI Randall had arrived back to the station he rang the younger brother, Gordon, who sounded much less disturbed about his mother's disappearance than did his sibling. Particularly when Randall told him the car was still missing.

Gordon Deverill was obviously reassured. 'Then she must have gone off somewhere on a jolly,' he said, sounding initially relieved, then cross. 'She could have saved us all this worry. And switching her phone off – well, it's just selfish. Thoughtless. Not like Mum at all.'

It was as though he had completely forgotten that his mother's house had burnt to the ground two nights ago. Not for the first time Alex Randall was astonished at the perspective of selfishness. He was at a loss what to say. 'We've put a "stop and apprehend" on the car,' he said finally, 'but there have been no sightings yet. If – when – it turns up we'll let you know. In the meantime if she does get in touch please do contact us immediately.' He felt he must say something more. 'We are concerned as to her whereabouts.'

'So am I.' His voice, now, was broken.

This was a bit more realistic.

Randall ended the call with a polite goodbye and looked up to see Talith and WPC Tinsley watching him. 'We'll play it like this for now,' he said quietly. 'Low key, and escalate the investigation if we find anything suspicious. Huh?'

They both nodded.

Martha had had a busy day and the visit to the two burnt-out houses hadn't really helped her. In her quieter moments she would keep wondering whether Mrs Deverill had been found but she resisted the temptation to ring Alex Randall. He would have enough to do without her pestering him. It wouldn't have been professional. So she ploughed her way through the piles of work in front of her.

Gary Coleman and Gethin Roberts were, meanwhile, in Melverley village, speaking to the Pinfolds, mother and son. Stuart had, his mother explained, returned from Amsterdam for a 'flying

visit'. It was opportune for the police except that the presence
of her son gave Mrs Pinfold added confidence. In fact, she looked
triumphant and was proving less than helpful. Her manner could
better be described as covertly hostile. Felicity Pinfold was an
unusual-looking woman in her mid-forties with very fair hair
– almost white. Today she was wearing a shapeless brown
cardigan over a flowery shepherdess dress which billowed around
her knees. The ensemble was oddly completed by bare legs and
grubby trainers. She probably wouldn't have won a Best Dressed
Woman award, Gary Coleman reflected, putting his head on one
side and studying her. She returned his scrutiny with a bold,
defiant expression. Coleman turned his attention to the son.
Stuart Pinfold was a slim, pale man with rounded shoulders and
a shifty gaze. Neither policeman was surprised he had lost his
job. They wouldn't have wanted to employ him. There was
something slippery about him. And his mother didn't help,
strongly defensive towards her son who could patently do no
wrong in her eyes. She was very bitter towards Nigel Barton,
whom she blamed for all that had gone wrong in Stuart's life.

Each time they mentioned something she had her answer ready
to challenge them. The conviction for possession? 'He planted
it there.' Current employment status? 'Who would employ him
without references?' Depression? 'His life's gone down the chute.
I know who's to blame.' Fiddling expenses? 'A trumped-up
charge. Stuart would never . . .'

On and on went the catalogue of complaints against Nigel
Barton.

Coleman had to bring it to an end. 'And Mrs Barton, did you
know her at all?'

It brought a renewed tirade.

'Did I know her? Everyone in the village knew her. Lady
Muck, driving around in that flashy car, always expensively
dressed, looking like someone out of *Hello!* magazine.'

It was interesting to get some reality and perspective on the
dead woman. She was no longer a 'sainted martyr burnt at
the stake' but someone whom other people might dislike.

Coleman pressed on. 'And the old man, Mr Barton senior?'

Felicity Pinfold looked disappointed. Even her vitriol could
not spread this far. 'He never went out of the house,' she said

sourly. 'I never met him. Only heard about him. From what I've heard they hid him away.' She grimaced. 'He was probably barking mad.'

'Right. What about Adelaide?'

Quite out of the blue, Felicity Pinfold's face softened. 'She was a lovely kid,' she said sadly. 'I can't get it out of my mind what happened to her. Poor little thing.'

'How did you know her?'

'She was in the local Wildlife Society. Always trying to sell raffle tickets or raise money for some Animals' Rescue centre. She was a sweet little thing.'

All this time Stuart Pinfold appeared to have been taking his cue from Mummy. Now he started nodding vehemently. Of all his mother's statements this was the one he agreed with most.

'And Jude?'

Mother and son looked at each other. Felicity frowned. 'He was a dark one,' she said. 'I could never quite work him out. He was quiet and deep. You never knew what he was thinking.'

Her son nodded his agreement.

Roberts eyed him curiously and inserted a few of his own questions. 'Where were you last Thursday night?'

They both stared at him. Felicity spoke first, eyes narrow, suspicion hardening her face. 'Why?'

Then the penny dropped and her face cleared. 'Oh, I see,' she said. 'Not content with trying to pin the Melverley Grange fire on us you want us to confess to arson on the nurse's house. Well, I don't know her. I never met her and we didn't set fire to her house either. Constable,' she mocked, 'if you're wanting to find someone to pin both fires on then you'll have to look elsewhere. Understand?'

Roberts ignored her outburst and turned to the son. 'Stuart?' he prompted.

Stuart grew even paler. In fact, he looked distinctly unwell. He cleared his throat and jerked.

His mother spoke for him. 'He didn't do any of those things,' she said flatly.

Again Roberts addressed the son – not the mother. 'So when *did* you arrive from Amsterdam?'

'I just got here a couple of days ago.'

Roberts waited and Pinfold finally supplied the answer.
'Tuesday afternoon,' he said grumpily. 'I wasn't in the country
for either fire.'

Both Coleman and Talith knew Pinfold had been in the country
at least for the Melverley fire and, looking at Stuart's shifty gaze,
they suspected he knew what they knew. But for now they kept
their cards close to their chests. They stored the interview away,
ready to share with Detective Inspector Randall and the rest of
the team at the briefing later on.

Delia Shaw, meanwhile, was at Nigel Barton's very smart office
and 'chatting' to his secretary, Mirabelle, wondering what exactly
was the relationship between the boss and the very attractive but
hard-faced young woman who seemed as brittle as cinder toffee.

After some preamble Delia asked the question outright. 'What
exactly was the relationship between you and Mr Barton? Your
boss,' she added.

Mirabelle didn't answer straight away but seemed to be deciding
what to say. She lifted her heavy eyelashes to stare straight into
WPC Shaw's, as though she was setting up a line of communication. Then she shrugged her slim shoulders and tossed her head.
'I think,' she began, and tried again. 'Mr Barton . . .' And again.
'He was a married man,' she said, as silkily as a lawyer. 'He isn't
the sort to play at flirtation when he has a wife.'

It didn't seem to occur to her pretty little head that this was
a motive for murder. And WPC Shaw didn't feel the need to
remind her. Mirabelle gave another smug little smile and pressed
her lips together. But WPC Shaw didn't let her off the hook that
easily. 'Have you ever gone out together – not in connection with
work?'

It provoked another smug smile. 'We've had lunch together a
few times.'

'Alone?'

A coquettish nod. 'Purely business.'

'When was the last time you had one of your "purely business" meetings?'

'We met at The Armoury a couple of weeks ago.'

'And how do you feel about him?'

The girl almost drooled. 'Mr Barton is a very attractive man,' she said primly. And volunteered no more but turned her gaze back to the computer screen.

Attractive and wealthy, Delia reflected. *Even more so now he'll be entitled to a cool million pounds compensation for the loss of his family.*

She stood up. The interview was over.

Friday, 18 March, 10.05 a.m.

Alex rang Martha's office at a little after 10 a.m., again to Jericho's evident disapproval. Martha took the call at once. Palfreyman may as well get used to these – she fished around in her mind for the word, finally snagging it on her line – interludes.

'I've got some surprising news for you,' Randall said. 'And if it's all right with you it'd be nice to pop over and tell you face-to-face. OK?'

'Naturally. I'm intrigued.' She couldn't hide that she was pleased to hear from him again and wondered what had turned up.

He appeared at midday. 'You say you're intrigued,' he said. 'So am I.'

He folded his lanky frame into the chair, stretched his long legs out in front of him and gave her a very straight look. 'We have some answers,' he confessed, 'but more questions.'

'Go on.'

'There definitely isn't a body in the house,' he said. 'We've had a thorough look and she's not there. Before you ask,' his face held a tinge of amusement, 'she's not buried in the garden. There's no freshly dug earth there. She is not walled up in the garage which is completely empty, nor is she in the small wooden shed behind the apple tree. And her car has not turned up anywhere. We've looked through airport car parks, put out a stop if seen. And nothing.' He crossed and recrossed his legs. Then grinned. 'It's more difficult to hide a car than you'd realize.'

'Tell me about it,' she said. 'I got ticketed last week in the town centre. Ten tiny minutes over my time.'

'You should have . . .' His eyes were warm but his voice tailed away. It wasn't her way to use her influence to get off a parking ticket. He continued. 'Her mobile is switched off or dead and goes straight through to answer phone without us getting a hit on it. We've had a team of officers ring every single telephone number and contact that Gordon and James gave us. They are naturally frantic.'

'Hospitals? Maybe she was confused, hurt, ill, made her way . . .' Her voice died away as she interpreted Alex's slow shake of the head correctly.

'The fire was started deliberately,' he continued. 'Accelerants – petrol-soaked rags. According to the forensic fire team the property caught fire so well partly because she'd apparently used some proprietary carpet cleaner, which was highly inflammable, to clean her hall carpet. We can't know whether our arsonist knew this or whether he just hit lucky. But it worked in his or her favour all right.'

'So where do you think she is?'

Alex's shrug told her all. 'I think she's dead,' he said bluntly. 'It's been a week now. She hasn't been in touch with her sons. There has been no activity on her phone since the night of Monday the seventh when she spoke to James. According to him, she sounded perfectly normal and promised to call in this weekend. Since then nothing.'

'So you think she's been abducted and murdered.' Something struck her. 'Of course, *she* would have known about the carpet cleaner.'

Randall looked up. 'What on earth are you saying? That Monica Deverill set fire to her *own* house?'

This time it was Martha's turn to shrug. Then looking straight at Alex Randall, she followed up with, 'How were her finances?'

'I've got a team of officers on the job at the moment, checking her passport, bank statement, mobile phone stuff.' He gave a deep sigh. 'All the usual. I still think that her fate holds the key to the Melverley fire.' He paused. 'Do you want to visit the scene again?'

'I don't see how I can, Alex,' Martha said. 'This isn't a case for a coroner – yet. It's a missing person and therefore a case for you.'

'I just thought –'

'If a death is involved I'll be happy to work with you,' Martha said, 'more than. But in the meantime I should concentrate on the inquests for the three members of the Barton family who died.'

'So I'm on my own,' Alex finished, getting out of the chair. 'Well, thanks anyway.'

'Keep in touch,' Martha advised.

The minute he had gone she felt cross with herself for being such a pedant. Why was she being so linear? Sticking strictly to guidelines had never been a feature of the way she had conducted enquiries before. Besides, she enjoyed Alex Randall's visits to her office, the way he stretched out those long legs and relaxed. Maybe that was the real reason she felt she should draw up lines, build fences, so she could hide behind them when necessary. But Randall did seem more relaxed these days, happier. She had always suspected that behind the formality of a Detective Inspector Alex Randall was a man with a troubled personal life. Although lately it had seemed as though that was melting away.

Curious, she thought, then sat forward and put her chin into her cupped hand, staring straight ahead, seeing not her organized room or the view over the town, not the telephone, the files, the books or the computer screen, but Alex Randall's warm eyes and crooked, sometimes apologetic grin. This was every woman's nightmare, she decided: early forties, widowed, twin teenagers – and she had a schoolgirl crush.

She felt her face flush with humility. This was ghastly. She had to work with the man. He was married, for goodness' sake. Besides, he'd never given her one crumb of a hint that he felt anything for her but as a valued colleague.

'So stop dreaming, Martha Gunn,' she admonished herself, 'and wake up – to the real world.'

THIRTEEN

She almost forgot about the arson cases over the weekend, which was spent in a frenzy of activity. Sam was playing in a match and Sukey wanted to come along, together with a gaggle of friends. Martha watched the girls pile into the back of the car and knew this was the way it would be in future for his sons and their friends. This glamorous world, the word, *'footballer'*, whispered in the back of the car, accompanied with giggles, told her it all. Yet as she stood, shivering on the touchline, watching the players muddy themselves over a game that was scrappy to say the least, she wondered. What was it about footballers that made them so glamorous? Purely their income? It made headlines, sure. But was that it? So many players didn't get paid anything like the Premier League boys, her own son included. They did it for the love of the game – or perhaps because they couldn't think of anything else to do and had pent up energy that needed spending. She smiled as she watched her son slither towards the goal, lift the ball up – and watched it bounce off the bar to the agonized groans of the Stoke City sympathizers and delighted whoops of the opposition. Already she could feel commiserations and platitudes spilling out of her mouth. Sometimes it seemed a tough way to make a living.

Two hours later she was cooking for the still-giggling girls and Sam and his two mates, who seemed oblivious to the female interest, concentrating instead on a detailed post-mortem of the game. Kick by kick, pass by pass. Martha slid two lasagnes on to the top shelf of the oven and started to make the salad and garlic bread. But, as she watched the beginnings of flirtation on the girls' part and oblivion to the females' interest on the boys' part, she felt that sudden wash of isolation when a parent realizes their offspring are no longer their sons and daughters but about to emerge, butterfly-like, into adulthood and that the parental role would dim and fade until it barely existed except in times of extreme trouble. It wasn't the same feeling as she had experienced when Martin had died. That had been loneliness, yes, and grief too. No, this was different. Sukey and Sam who had been her focus for so many years, were now inching away from her, drifting down the river of life, while she was left standing on the banks, waving them off with a white handkerchief. Even more strong than the feeling that they were moving downstream was the consciousness that she stood on the bank perfectly alone. No one was at her side. This, then, was true loneliness.

She wandered into her study. No messages on her phone. She pressed the button and the voice confirmed this with a touch of spite. *You have no messages*. No messages. *Absolutely no messages* it might have added. She felt a sudden urge to confide in her mother and spent the next twenty minutes in deep conversation.

Laura Rees, Martha's mother, was Irish and now in her late sixties, a quirky, funny, unpredictable woman who was 'all heart'. She listened to her daughter's outpourings without comment then said drily, 'Well, now you've come round to your senses let's just hope you haven't left it too late.'

The result was that Martha felt even more down that evening, sitting in, hearing Sam and Sukey's lively and excited conversations with their friends, bursts of music as doors opened and closed. The giggles of the girls and the gruff voices of the boys. She felt excluded. Old and alone with her mother's words ringing in her ears. She gave a deep sigh and then was ashamed of herself. It was not like her to be self-pitying and it was not how she wanted to be. '*You've just been too busy with the twins and your work*,' her mother's voice continued scolding her. Martha made a face and was tempted even to stick her tongue out.

So now what? Having indulged herself quite shamelessly she squared her shoulders and sat up, a burst of energy propelling her into action as now she plotted and planned.

She couldn't Internet date. She just couldn't go through with all that. She'd heard of a website called Ivory Towers, was even tempted to go online and check it out. But five minutes later she was still sitting with her chin in her hands, staring into space. Love wasn't like that, she reasoned. It was special and personal. One could meet hundreds of men the right age, background, even ones who shared the same identical pursuits, intellect and interest.

But it took that magic spark to fall in love. And without love there was no point, was there?

She answered her own question. No, mouthing the word. Emphatically the answer was no. Then, with a gasp of irritation at herself, she went and fetched a novel. It might be escapism but for now she had no better ideas.

Sunday, 20 March, 9 a.m.

Sunday started a little better. There was breakfast to be made for the exhausted 'sleepovers' before ferrying them home. Somehow the tradition of keeping Sunday as a family day had persisted amongst the twins and their friends. Then there was the dog to walk, through a muggy, damp, cold day, which seemed to tell you that the sun would probably not shine for a few months yet. There was lunch to cook, a traditional roast, of course. There were school clothes to be ironed before a classic serial on the television.

But even through all the normal busy jobs, the empty feeling would not leave her.

Monday, 21 March, 8.45 a.m.

She was glad to return to work on the Monday morning, aware that March was slipping away. The bulbs were peering out of the soil and any moment now the trees would start to turn green. She locked her car and stood, looking up at the office building, a large Victorian property to the south of the town. She'd worked here for fourteen years now, handled death after death, 'happy releases', tragedy, murders, accidents, suicides and natural death. She'd spent time considering them all and explaining them, as best she could, to relatives who were sometimes angry, sometimes grief-struck and occasionally relieved – though they invariably tried to hide that one. There were mysteries and misadventures. A few had remained puzzles. Would this be one of those? Would there ever be a satisfactory explanation to these two cases of arson which had resulted in three deaths and, so far, one disappearance? Would there be more arson attacks? Had something terrible and destructive been unleashed? Shiva, the Hindu god of destruction.

She approached the door, still reflecting. No one could call death in a burning home misadventure and certainly not a 'happy release'. And the missing nurse? Would she ever turn up? Would she remain forever a mystery or would there be a banal explanation?

Why the fire then, Martha reasoned, so carefully laid, so quickly destructive? Why the fire which had drawn attention to *her,* suggested a connection between two families when there might have appeared none? *Someone* wanted to draw attention to the link between the two families, even if it was little more than a silken line, fine as a spider's web. And now Martha sat perfectly still, convinced that she was tiptoeing around a pool, deep and dark but not bottomless. In her mind she was leaning in towards it, peering down into waters that had no reflection. Yet.

She shook herself and walked inside.

The hallway of the coroner's office had deliberately been left unspoilt, terrazzo tiles, a high, moulded ceiling, panelling halfway up the walls. It had the power to dwarf and overawe which, in a way, it was meant to. The coroner represents the crown, the law and justice at its most solemn and there was never a time when Martha was not aware of this status. Except . . . she sometimes bent the rules just a little to allow herself to pursue her own investigations – off the record, of course.

Downstairs were offices for clerical and secretarial staff.

Her office and Jericho's were on the first floor, up a wide and sweeping staircase carpeted with a narrow red stair carpet held by polished brass rods.

Without any idea of what had been passing through her mind Jericho Palfreyman, Coroners' Officer, greeted her as normal. She enquired whether there was any news in the double arson case.

'I haven't heard anything,' he said, his eyes bright as a robin's. 'It seems to have gone quiet for a while, doesn't it, Mrs Gunn?'

'It does.' She paused and then decided. 'Jericho,' she said, 'I thought I might have a word with young Jude. Do you have a number to contact him?'

'That I do,' Jericho said, patently pleased to see her pursuing her own enquiry. 'I can get him at the hotel they're staying at. They're at the Lord Hill, you know.'

'Thank you.' She smiled. There was nothing Palfreyman liked better than 'imparting information', as he pompously put it.

She walked into her office, glad of the coffee, but still aware of a lingering depression which threatened to creep back in unless she kept herself very, very busy.

'Oh.' Exasperated with herself she smacked her hand to her forehead. She had to click out of this. She sat at her desk, rolling a pen backwards and forwards. It was OK to suddenly decide that you were ready to start a new relationship. But how *did* one go about meeting eligible unmarried men when you were in your forties? It made her smile. She and Miranda, her best and only single friend, could hardly go hitting the discos or tea dances. Her smile broadened. This was getting ever more ridiculous. Speed dating certainly wasn't her style. She sat and stared until the phone rang and Jericho announced that he had Jude Barton on the telephone.

She introduced herself and explained that she would like him to come in with an adult of his choosing to talk to her. He hesitated for a moment before asking if it was OK to bring his Dad. 'Of course,' she replied calmly. This was what she had anticipated.

He was off the phone for a minute or so, presumably while he discussed it with his father, and finally arranged to come in at three p.m. At last Martha settled back down to work.

Not for long.

At ten thirty she had a pang of conscience and asked Jericho to get DI Randall on the phone. 'Morning, Martha?' He knew she would have rang about something.

'I ought to tell you that I've arranged to speak to Jude Barton this afternoon.'

'Really?'

'Yes. I thought it might be helpful.' She waited for a comment even braced herself for an acerbic, *to whom?*, but perhaps wisely Alex Randall made no comment at all.

'Alex,' she said, 'was anyone watching when Jude descended the rope ladder? It must have been quite a spectacle.'

'I don't know,' he said, obviously surprised by the question. 'I can find out.'

'Yes.'

'Was there anything else?'

'I take it you haven't found the missing woman?'

'No.'

'Her car?'

'No.'

'But how can you hide a car, Alex?' Her mind tracked along car parks and her recent experience of sticky labels which appeared on the windscreen if you overstayed your welcome.

'Well, it can be done. There are places and there are ways.'

'Such as?'

'Hidden in a garage or a building, an isolated spot,' he said thoughtfully.

'Could have been set on fire, like the houses?'

Alex gave a snort. 'You must be joking,' he said.

'But surely it destroys forensic evidence?'

'It might do that,' Alex said, 'but it also draws attention to itself. People report burning cars. Fire engines scream in and the police are soon involved.'

'Oh, I suppose so,' she fell in dubiously. But couldn't resist tacking on, 'And you still have no activity on her mobile phone?'

'Nothing. We've gone through virtually all her known family and friends and drawn a blank. There's been good coverage on the national news and . . .'

Martha interrupted. 'I know about the phone call on the Monday but when was she last actually *seen*?'

'Not since the previous Saturday afternoon – that would be the fifth of March, according to the information so far. She went shopping with a friend.'

'The Sunday?'

'She appears to have spent the day alone. We can't find anyone who saw her.'

'During the entire week?'

'That's right.'

'Not even her sons?'

'No.'

'Or her friends?'

'No.'

'So she was on her own all week?'

The phrases rang hollow inside Martha's head. When the twins had left home – for university or wherever – that would be her lot. *She was on her own all week.*

'Are you still there, Martha?'

She rallied. 'Yes. Yes, of course. Sorry. I thought you said she was a "Merry Widow"?'

'Yes, she had a lot of friends around the town. There's been no shortage of them coming in to give us what they consider to be information. But she also, according to several of them, "liked her own space".' He continued. 'She'd had a couple of holidays over the winter and had gone away on her own. She was a very independent woman.'

'Obviously.'

'One particular friend, a rather sharp lady called Betty, seemed a little put out by the fact that Monica was so happy with her own company – took it rather as an insult.'

'Really?'

'Really.'

Martha thought for a moment then asked, 'She had lots of friends?'

'Yes, many of them from her nursing days.'

'Any boyfriends turned up?' She almost hoped.

'No. She seems either to have mixed with female friends of roughly the same age, sometimes with her two sons and their families and often went on cruises on her own.'

Again Martha felt that hollow, panicky feeling. Went on cruises on her own? Was that going to be it? She had a vision of herself, fading hair, blanket over legs, reading a paperback on the blustery deck of a cruise ship.

On the other end of the line Alex, too, was silent.

'Have you any other lines of enquiry?'

'A few.' He chuckled.

She waited.

'I'll let you know if they turn anything up.'

'Thank you.'

'Well,' he finally said, 'good luck with young Jude this afternoon.'

'Thanks.' She put the phone down.

Thank goodness the telephone did not allow him to read her thoughts or see the desperation in her face.

*   *   *

At a little after three Jericho Palfreyman was opening the door to father and son. Martha took stock of them as she moved forwards to greet them.

Nigel Barton still looked shell-shocked. His face was fish-pale and he walked slowly, almost an automaton. He lifted his eyes to meet hers then lowered them but not before she had read a hopelessly tortured grief behind them. He said nothing and his handshake was like his walk, automatic, with no thought or direction behind it. Martha wondered if he had been prescribed some sedation. After muttering a greeting she turned her attention to Jude. He, too, was as white as death, his shoulders bowed like an old man's. His hands were still bandaged; she didn't even try to shake them but simply smiled a greeting at him. Jude didn't even return the smile but stared at her, straight-lipped. There was an expression of pain on his face. She was aware that both father and son were suffering raw grief and wondered how they were managing – not only emotionally but physically. Particularly Jude. Washing, dressing, eating – anything would be difficult with bandages round his hands. His father must be helping.

Nigel Barton was dressed in mourning, sober-suited and black tie. It was almost Victorian to see someone dressed in funereal black. The boy was in jeans, a black T-shirt and a padded jacket. He looked as though he was cold and his skin still had the same sickly green tinge. At her bidding they sat down in unison. Father and son then sat back, eyeing her and waiting for her to take the lead.

She began, as she often did, by offering them both a drink which they refused, continuing to watch her expectantly. 'Jude,' she said, 'you must be wondering why I've asked you here?'

The boy shrugged.

'I want you to tell me about your grandfather. I've heard you two were close?'

The boy nodded with confidence.

'How would you describe your relationship?'

Jude's brown eyes, so light they were like two fly-flecked pieces of amber, were suddenly wary. He moved his bandaged hands up in front of him as though to remind her to focus on them, so she did as he wanted, focused on them and asked how they were.

'They're getting better every day,' he said.

'Are they still painful?'

He grunted. In well-known teenage boy's language this meant, 'OK.' It meant, 'I'm coping.' It also meant, 'Don't go there. Don't intrude.' And finally a savage and decisive, 'Back off.'

It was time she took the initiative. 'Jude,' she began, 'I know that the police have already gone through the events of that terrible night. And I don't want to add to your grief.'

He was watching her with heightened awareness.

'I simply want to learn a little more about your grandfather. Tell me, what was he like?'

The boy shot a swift look at his father. Searching for approval? Martha wondered and watched curiously. Nigel's eyes met hers with sudden understanding. He must know that even though there had been a second fire there were still some who wondered if a confused old man had lit the fire which had killed his daughter-in-law and granddaughter.

Jude Barton put his head on one side and appraised her but didn't answer the question.

She needed to prompt him. 'I know you were very fond of the old man.'

He nodded. But still wary. And she was aware of Barton senior's eyes on her.

She was going to have to be very subtle about this. She checked her tone, made it conversational, softened her features and smiled. 'What did you particularly like about him?'

Jude grinned and relaxed. 'His stories,' he said enthusiastically.

'What did he tell you stories about?'

'I don't know,' he said. 'Things he'd done in his life. He was in the war, you know, a Desert Rat, fighting out there in Africa with Montgomery and stuff. Against Rommel. He drove a tank right across the desert.'

'Really?' She was seeing the real Jude Barton at last. And behind him, his grandfather.

'He was a hero.'

Martha was surprised. The boy was naïve. He lacked cynicism and insight. How many grandfathers span these stories, embellished them, polished them up like medals on a soldier's chest, purely to impress their grandchildren and enforce the image that once they had been young, fit and heroic? Not always ancient, confused and frail. Martha thought quickly. By her calculations William Barton would have been just fourteen years old when the Second World War had broken out. Only twenty when peace had been declared. She'd be very surprised if he had met either Rommel or Montgomery. And though the image of driving a tank right across the desert was a powerful one it sounded more · like a story than the truth. She sneaked a glance at Nigel. He was looking equally surprised and sceptical. But all that had mattered to the old man was not the truth but that his grandson had believed his stories. Now Martha had unearthed this angle of the relationship between grandfather and grandson she needed to find a way back to her own agenda. 'Would *you* like to be a soldier?' she fumbled.

Jude shook his head. 'I wouldn't be brave enough. Not like him. I'd like to think I would be but . . .'

He looked suddenly upset, as though he had remembered something. His father must have picked up on this too and warned her off with a growl in his throat. Martha gave him a quick, sideways glance.

She ignored this animal caution at her peril. So she changed tack. 'You know there's been another house fire in Shrewsbury?'

Jude nodded and shot a swift glance at his father to check.

She could skip around the truth. 'The house belonged to a widow named Monica Deverill.'

Jude looked even more wary. Had he had whiskers they would have twitched, like a cat's.

'She was a retired mental nurse.'

Barton senior shifted in his chair.

Martha looked innocently at both of them. 'Do you know her?'

This time it was Barton senior who answered. 'We don't know any mental nurses.' He made them sound like vermin. And low-class vermin at that.

Martha smiled and addressed her next question to Barton senior. She inched a little closer. 'The way the fire was set was identical to the fire at your house, Mr Barton, at which your wife, father and daughter died.'

He looked up, startled but – in Martha's opinion – not quite startled enough.

She played another card. 'Do you think it's coincidence?'

The response was a heavy silence.

She tried another card. 'The night before the fire at her house Mrs Deverill rang the police incident desk and said she knew something about the fire at your home.' She didn't ask them the direct question which could have followed, instead simply looking at them both expectantly.

Barton shrugged. 'I can't think what that might have been.'

'No?'

Father and son both looked blank.

'Can you think of anything else that might have a bearing on the fire at your home?' She watched without great hope but the question, to her surprise, bore fruit.

The impasse was broken, quite suddenly, by Barton senior, who gave away the first nugget of information.

'It's ironic,' he said, 'that my father should die in a house fire.'

'Ironic?' It was an odd choice of word. 'Why so?'

'Because he was a fireman.'

Martha stared at him and Nigel Barton looked pleased with himself at having gained the higher ground. 'I thought coroners were in possession of *all* the facts pertaining to a case.'

It was she now who was thoughtful and silent, needing to chew and chew before she could digest. But she also knew she should divert from this piece of information and pursue another line of enquiry. Tactfully. She turned to Jude. 'Your father tells me that your grandfather had Alzheimer's,' she said, resisting the temptation to insult the boy by explaining what Alzheimer's was.

Jude thought for a while. Then looked at her. 'He was *strange*,' he said. 'But that made him exciting.'

'In what way strange?'

'Unpredictable. You never knew what Grandad would do. And that made him exciting.' She realized that he was trying to get her to see the old man in the favourable light he had viewed him in. But the word interested her.

Unpredictable.

'I notice that you put the hooks for the rope ladder in recently. Why did you do that, Jude? Was it anything to do with the fire your grandfather set six months ago?'

'Yes and no. It was my grandfather,' the boy explained. 'In his job he'd been used to thinking about fire safety. It was he who said to me that if the staircase caught fire I'd be f—'

'Jude.' Ironic that the father disciplined the boy for his own father's bad language.

Jude's eyes flashed an apology towards his father who nodded his acceptance as heavily as a mandarin. But the boy's loyalty to his grandfather still stuck fast. He pressed his lips together, speaking in jerky words. 'Grandad saved my life in the end with his ladder, didn't he, Dad?'

Nigel Barton nodded. But it was a qualified agreement. He spoke up stiffly. 'The days in the fire service were Dad's glory days. You know how Alzheimer's sufferers go back in time. It was like that with him. He used to tell Jude stories about fires he'd attended.' He gave a sad and perceptive smile. 'Somehow Dad was always the hero, even though he only ever achieved the rank of a junior officer. He was always the one who rescued everyone, knew how the fire had been started, who'd taken batteries out of the smoke alarms, got drunk and dropped a cigarette down the back of a sofa or neglected safety responsibilities. Sometimes he voiced the most idiotic ideas.'

'And he had threatened your wife.'

Barton defended himself. 'I tried not to be away from home.' He felt bound to add, 'That was why I combined the meetings in York. Otherwise I'd have been away for longer.'

Time to take the bull by the horns. 'Jude,' Martha said, 'was it your grandfather who set fire to your house?'

The boy looked wary. And significantly he didn't answer. And his father, who should have looked furious, didn't respond at all except to look at her.

When Jude did respond it was an oblique reference. 'Grandad had changed in the last few months,' he said. 'He used to be fun and . . . well, just fun. But lately he'd got a bit more unpredictable. You'd think you knew what he was going to do then he'd do something completely different.' He looked a bit cross.

Nigel Barton shook himself and Martha knew she needed to wind this interview up. She turned back to the father. 'Is there anything either of you wants to know?'

They looked at one another and shook their heads.

'Right,' she said. 'The inquest will be opened a week tomorrow, the twenty-ninth, at nine a.m. and will be adjourned pending police investigations. You understand?'

Barton was frowning. 'And what about the other fire? The other woman?'

'She is currently missing.'

Barton's frown deepened. 'What do you mean, she's missing?'

She let the question ride.

'You mean that she wasn't burnt to death.' He spoke the words cruelly.

She could have corrected him, pointed out that neither his wife, daughter nor father had 'burnt to death'. She had already informed him of the results of the post-mortem. They had died of smoke inhalation. Mark Sullivan had told her that the actual fire damage to their bodies had been minimal. Christie Barton's legs had been burnt by the nylon melted in the heat. It was a different image from that of a charred corpse.

She watched them leave, after a very formal goodbye, still sensing their anger but also with a feeling of frustration.

She didn't believe they were being entirely honest with her.

FOURTEEN

I t was after they had left and she had heard their car drive away that she began to analyse what had been said. The old man had been a fireman, concerned with safety enough to advise his grandson to put in a fire escape of sorts, a rope ladder. He had been right about the narrow staircase boxed in behind the door. Fire streaking up that would have meant certain death for the boy. She wrenched her mind away from that and focused on another word.

Stories.

The old man had told his grandson stories. How much was true and how much fantasy? Had he really driven a tank across the desert as a teenager? Had he really saved all these people's lives as a fireman?

Alzheimer's sufferers in general do not make up stories or fantasize. They are beyond boasting to impress their listener. They simply want to revisit the past. But it is a real and truthful past, not a place invented to impress. They don't seek status by boasting but recall the truth with a clear mind and without embellishment. Usually.

Martha was cross with herself. She felt she had just missed an opportunity. She should have asked him outright and in more detail about these stories. She felt she would instinctively have known what significance they would have had. And more importantly, what bearing they might have on recent events.

And now she was wondering. Besides tales of the Second World War what other stories had William Barton related to his impressionable grandson? She leaned back in her chair, needing to think, to clarify this new information, sort it and use it. The whole thing about William Barton setting fire to the house previously made a lot more sense now. He had simply been reliving the past. Putting himself into the part of hero. And who would know better than an ex-fireman how to set a fire? But at the same time it gave someone else an opportunity to shift the blame for any fire back on to William Barton. And Barton senior was dead. He could not defend himself. Martha sat, frowning into the distance. Something was still nagging at her. And now there was the added complication of the missing nurse. She felt a great temptation to ring DI Randall and tell him this latest little nugget of information. But when she rang the station she was told he was out. And she didn't want to tell anyone else. She looked out of the window. It was late afternoon but the weather was fine and dry and in a sudden burst of energy she needed to walk. Telling Jericho that she was going out for an hour she took her car to the bottom of Wyle Cop, parked in the NCP and walked up the hill. It was a steep hill, lined with shops, most of them still with the crooked black and white facades they had worn for centuries.

And then. Halfway up the hill she was standing outside the antiques shop with a *For Sale or To Let* sign over it. She stopped dead. Finton Cley saw her through the window and came out. She looked up at the board then back at him for an explanation.

'Time to move on, Martha Gunn,' he said equably. 'I've spent enough time here living in the past. I need to get on with my life.'

She read the pain behind his eyes and nodded. 'It is a good thing to do that,' she said. 'I wish you luck, Finton.' Then she smiled mischievously. 'I don't suppose you're having a closing-down sale, are you?'

His eyes, too, were merry as he shook his head. 'I said moving on,' he said. 'Not giving up.'

'So where to, Finton?'

'New York,' he said surprisingly. 'It's been on my mind forever. I have a friend over there who already has an established business. I was in school with him. He's been trying to get me to join with him for years. I want to go.' He glanced behind him. 'I can ship this stuff out and will have a good start.'

'And your sister?'

'Comes with me.' His chin was firm. 'I couldn't possibly leave her behind.'

She put her hand on his arm. 'Then good luck,' she said with sincerity.

She continued right to the top of Wyle Cop, stopping at Appleyards, the Deli, where she bought some Comté cheese and olives and peeped in the window at the shop opposite which had a window display of antique jewellery then wandered back down 'the Cop', eyeing up the window of Oberon and wondering whether Sukey would like one of the charm bracelets that were currently popular. The twins' birthdays were looming. Sam had already asked for an exercise bench.

She returned to the NCP. It was getting dark now. Lights were being switched on. It was time to return to the office, tidy up the day's paperwork and go home. But the encounter with Finton Cley had unsettled her. His father's death had been one of her early cases and the knock on effect of her suicide verdict had been brought home to her – rather forcibly – by Finton, who had played some bizarre and occasionally macabre, even threatening, tricks on her. Initially she had been intrigued and then disturbed. But when she had understood who was behind these events and why, it had made her even more aware of the nature of her work and the impact of her verdicts on the victims' families. It had been his *Message for Martha,* a hint manifested by the depositing of the Adam Faith record on her doorstep. And now? She had thought she had always been fully aware of the effect of violent death on its survivors. Now she was even more so. So Finton Cley's tricks had achieved their desired effect.

Just as she arrived at her car her mobile phone rang. It was Simon Pendlebury who, once he'd greeted her, cut straight to the chase without preamble, as was his way. 'Can I persuade you to have dinner with me again, Martha? Fairly soon?' There was urgency in his voice.

She agreed to have dinner with him on the Friday, climbed into the car and sat, hands on the wheel, reflecting. Simon Pendlebury, widower, wealthy, attractive. So why wasn't she jumping up and down for joy at the dinner invitation? And what was the urgency? Was he feeling the same desperation that she was?

Ah. Who knew? She leaned forward, turned the ignition and put the car into gear. Time to go home.

Back at the station DI Alex Randall was holed up with a few of his officers, Gethin Roberts, Paul Talith, Gary Coleman and WPC Lara Tinsley. It was meant to be a brainstorming exercise but so far there hadn't been much evidence that any one of them had a brain. And there were no storms in sight. There had still been no sightings of either the missing nurse or her car and the case felt dangerously close to limbo, the doldrums, or any other place where absolutely nothing happened. Sometimes Randall felt he lived in these very places.

Like Martha herself DI Randall was tempted to pick up the phone and brainstorm with the coroner but that was not the way it was done. His mouth twisted with frustration. Something needed to happen. They needed a break. The problem in the police force was that you could not force the pace in an investigation. One had to hope that any vital piece of evidence or a statement from a member of the general public didn't get lost in the gigabytes of information that soon surrounded any major investigation. One could only go so far and all the time new cases would continue to arrive, each one of them distracting you. Crimes did not tidily wait for the previous one to be solved to present themselves. *Positive* crime solution figures were what the politicians wanted but these statistics did not always reflect the severity of the crime or the complexity of the investigation.

Randall gave a loud sigh. And now it was time to go home. Sometimes he felt like Sisyphus. He spent all day rolling a boulder up a hill only to find in the morning it had rolled all the way back down again. He knew what Sisyphus had done to warrant the punishment. He was a thoroughly nasty piece of work, a cheat and a murderer. But what on earth had he done?

Martha, meanwhile, while driving home, had been struck by a thought and was now dancing with her own demons. Something else was triggering her interest. A new angle. For some reason her mind had homed in on the keys to the two women's rooms. Because of the women's fate they had made the assumption that Adelaide and Christie had been locked in their rooms. That while Adelaide had cowered beneath her bedclothes, presumably because she was frightened of the fire, Christie had been frantically trying to get out when the blaze had taken hold. But to try and escape their rooms would have propelled them into the heat and the smoke which would have been funnelled up the staircase. Would they have realized that in their state of confusion and panic? And now, for some reason, her mind was asking another question completely. What if the reverse was true, that far from being trapped in their bedrooms they had been sheltering from some perceived danger outside, terrified of something or someone who was in the house and their place of safety had been their bedrooms? Had they locked themselves in rather than out? Was there evidence whether the doors had been locked from the *inside* or the *outside*? The truth was that the evidence was unclear. The doors had been both damaged by the fire and forced open by the forensic crew. The keys had dropped to the floor and landed in a pile of rubble. If they had locked themselves *in* what had they been so frightened of? Had it been the fire? What had happened earlier, prior to the blaze? It had been early. Not like the dead of night when they would all have been deeply asleep. What had they been individually protecting themselves from? If they had been . . .

Unable to stop herself she picked up her mobile phone and connected with Colin Agnew, Fire Chief.

He saw what she was getting at instantly. 'I hadn't thought of that,' he said slowly. 'I simply made the assumption that they were locked in and couldn't get out – not the other way round. Why lock it? A locked door wouldn't keep a fire out. They would have to have been fearful of something else.' He paused. 'Something more like a threatening human presence.'

Martha needed to check. 'You're sure the doors were locked?'

'Yes. The bolt of the lock was still shot back on the inside of the doorframe. There's no doubt about it even though the damage to the doors, both doors, was quite extensive and the keys were found on the floor. It's possible,' he said after some thought, 'that having to axe through the door meant that the keys would have fallen. But,' he added then, 'I can understand why they would cower behind their doors when there was a fire outside, on the landing, but not lock them?'

'It must have felt safer that way.'

'But the damage was worse in their bedrooms than outside.'

'They wouldn't have known that. They would have been confused – disorientated.'

By his silence she could tell he was thinking.

'One more question, Colin. Did any of your personnel actually see Jude Barton climb down the ladder?'

'Inspector Randall asked me that. I've questioned everyone who was at the Melverley fire. They were all concentrating on the front of the house where the fire was worst. No one saw the boy descend. Only the ladder, hanging there. And then of course, PC Roberts . . .'

'Mmm. Thank you.'

'Any time, Coroner.' Even as she ended the call another picture seemed to drop in front of her vision. Neither of the women had tried to get to their windows. Both Christie and Adelaide's rooms were on the first floor, a gravel pathway beneath them. The evidence was that Christie had approached the window before the door. Why hadn't she exited through the window? Had the flames beaten her back? Had she tried to reach her daughter? The fire had been well underway before the fire engines had arrived. The image that now impressed itself into her mind

was of Adelaide cowering under her bedclothes, terrified not
only by the fire but perhaps by another threat, something outside
her door and Christie, breath held, also listening at the door.
Maybe not confused and disorientated then – simply terrified.

Alex Randall, in the meantime, was not concentrating on the
Melverley fire but on the missing nurse. With the other officers
they reviewed all they knew so far. He turned back to the
whiteboard.

Credit cards not used, mobile phone switched off; the car had
become invisible, her two sons frantic. No friends or family had
seen or heard from her for two weeks. Her passport hadn't been
used. Ergo she was still in the country either dead or alive, free
or a captive. Her house had been burnt down in the same way
as Melverley Grange. Randall felt frustrated. It was sitting there.
What?

Nigel Barton denied ever having met the nurse and yet . . .

There must be a connection. There must be.

Sergeant Paul Talith was watching him, waiting for a response,
some direction. At last Randall looked up and Sergeant Paul
Talith spotted a spark in those hazel eyes. Enough to prompt
him. 'Sir?'

Randall looked at him. 'We have to find the connection between
William Barton and Monica Deverill,' he said slowly. 'And the
best way to do this is to speak again to her two sons.' He knew
that many of Monica Deverill's friends had been interviewed by
local police forces up and down the country. All had drawn a
blank. But who knew her best? Her sons.

Talith stood up. In spite of his increasing bulk he hated
inactivity. The time was six o'clock. But it felt later. Much later.
It was a cold, dingy evening, the weather having lost the spark
that had deceived them into believing that spring was on its way.
But they all felt the urgency. They needed to press on. Talith
volunteered to stay with the inspector who'd said easily and
truthfully, 'I'm in no great hurry to get home. I'm more anxious
to get some answers in this wretched case.'

So it was Randall and Talith who stayed. James and Gordon
Deverill were located within minutes.

How had the police managed without mobile phones? Randall

mused, as he sat and waited for them to arrive. It took *hours* off locating someone, saved *days* of police time, *hundreds* of wasted visits to empty properties, waiting, waiting. But there was a downside to this useful little toy. Pay and Throwaway phones were a lifeline to those who wanted to remain anonymous. He toyed with his pen, wondering whether this last thought was significant.

Straightaway Randall could see both Monica Deverill's sons were really worried about her so he didn't bother asking whether she was still missing but simply assumed it. James made a brave attempt at optimism but it was a transparently, almost pathetically thin one. 'I suppose no news is good news?' he said faux-cheerfully.

In Randall's more pragmatic outlook no news was exactly that – no news. No ruddy news at all. And as a result there was nothing good about it, he was tempted to growl. But the purpose of this interview was not to depress the brothers further but extract information – even information they might not have realized was relevant. And he knew exactly the tack he would take.

'Can you think of any connection between your mother and Mr William Barton?'

They looked at one another, puzzled. 'No.'

'He was a fire officer in the Shrewsbury force until his retirement about twenty years ago,' Randall prompted.

They still looked at him blankly.

Randall felt like giving up. They weren't being deliberately unhelpful. If there was a connection between Barton senior and the retired nurse they may well not even know it. He was going to have to think this one over.

He tried again. 'Do the names Yusuf Karoglan, Ben Hatton or Stuart Pinfold mean anything to you?'

They looked uncertain. Not illuminated. Simply uncertain. Gordon Deverill frowned. 'I'm not sure,' he said, before making an attempt at a joke. 'They sound a motley crew. Who are they?'

'Ex-employees of Mr Nigel Barton,' Randall supplied. 'We wondered if any of the names was familiar to you?'

Both sons shook their heads.

'Did your mother have anything to do with the Shropshire Wildlife Trust?' He was clutching at straws now.

They looked at each other as though each was thinking the same thought. *This detective's finally flipped it.* And shook their heads. 'Oh.' It was James who pursued this thread irritably. 'And this has what exactly to do with my mother's house being subjected to an arson attack and her having gone missing?'

'The MO of the two fires was the same.'

James kept coming. 'So, based on this, you're assuming our mother had some connection to the Barton family?'

Slowly Randall nodded.

Gordon's shoulders went up to around his ears as he shrugged. 'What?' he challenged bluntly.

'We don't know.' Randall wanted to give another deep, deep sigh but he glanced at Talith who was looking bored, gave an almost imperceptible shrug and resisted. 'That,' he said, 'is what we are trying to find out.'

The brothers looked at each other blankly.

FIFTEEN

Alex had a quick chat with forensics and another with Dr Mark Sullivan whom he just caught before he left for the evening, but no one seemed to have turned anything up. So he had only one real live lead to pursue – Jude Barton. He had never quite shaken off the feeling that Barton junior was keeping something back. It was something to do with the relationship between Jude and his grandfather. And he was wondering why Martha had asked whether anyone had witnessed the boy's descent of the rope ladder. DI Randall had a healthy respect for the coroner's instincts so when she asked a question he knew the answer might well be significant.

Jude Barton, however, was a minor, still injured and he'd already interviewed him. There was no new evidence to justify interviewing him again and he was well aware that the press and Jude's father might well interpret a further interview as harassment. He needed to tread carefully and he wasn't hopeful. He switched his office light off.

Tuesday, 22 March, 9 a.m.

First thing in the morning Alex Randall discussed the matter with his senior officers and the consensus was for him to interview the boy again using a bit more of a shock tactic. And so he summoned father and son in, without relish or optimism.

The bandages were off the boy's hands, leaving only smaller dressings now, but the look of pain and confusion in his eyes still lingered. He looked pale but resolute, his lips pressed together in a thin line, his brows drawn in and his eyes staring ahead blankly. Jude Barton was even more traumatized by the events than he had realized. There was a look of hopelessness about him, a droop of the shoulders that seemed to signify abject failure. Misery.

It was Nigel Barton who opened the conversation, speaking in a quiet and controlled voice. 'We've decided to return to Melverley just as soon as the Grange has been renovated,' he volunteered and, although his voice was quiet it was firm, repelling any challenge or criticism of the decision. Randall made no comment. This was their choice after all, nothing to do with him. So he simply raised his eyebrows and sympathized. 'I'm sure it'll be hard for you both – at first,' he said, 'it being the scene of . . .' There was no need to finish the sentence.

He drew in a deep breath, ready to delve a little deeper, knowing he was about to embark on a risky plan. 'Jude,' he began, addressing the boy directly, 'we're working on the premise that it was your grandfather who started the fire, rather than an outsider.' He waited for the boy's response, wondering if this had been such a good idea. A shock tactic had seemed right when he was thinking about it. But it was patently risky, particularly as the boy was so traumatized by events. He had lost three members of his family, after all.

Jude froze, his slightly almond-shaped eyes narrowed making him appear Oriental, inscrutable, unreadable. He seemed to shrink into himself and looked at Randall without blinking. Alex risked a swift glance at Barton senior and noted no response apart from a slightly pugnacious squaring of his shoulders.

'I don't think Grandpa would have set a fire,' Jude muttered finally, staring at the floor, his shoulders bowed. 'He was a fireman.'

Alex tried not to react to this titbit of information. But he knew it slotted in neatly – somewhere. 'But he did set a fire six months ago, didn't he?'

'That was different.'

Nigel Barton interrupted. 'And how exactly do you explain the *second* fire?' he asked, his voice heavy with sarcasm. 'Are you suggesting that my father returned from the grave to victimize some nurse?'

'I'll get to that,' Randall said, trusting that at some point he really would. He returned his attention to the boy. 'Jude,' he said, 'we were wondering about those stories your grandfather used to tell you.'

The boy looked directly at him then, a frank question in his gaze.

'We know he had some dementia,' Alex continued gingerly, giving Nigel Barton a very swift glance to check he was not crossing the invisible line. 'The way we're thinking is that he wasn't really responsible at all for what he did, not any more. He must have attended so many fires as a younger man. And perhaps it was these memories that preyed on his mind and persuaded him to act as he did.'

Barton senior finally chipped in. 'You're putting all the blame on my father,' he asked brokenly, his face twisted, 'saying that he was responsible for what happened to Addy and Christie?'

'We might never be able to prove anything,' Randall said, uncertain whether he was being challenged or agreed with. He knew right after Barton's next challenge.

'Did you find petrol splashes on his clothes?'

Alex was forced to admit that no, they had not.

'Burns on his hands?'

'There was a lighter in his pocket,' Randall said tightly. 'And he was in the hallway.'

Barton looked angry now. 'I'm sorry, Inspector, I think you're using my father as a fall guy because you really haven't got a clue how the fire happened or who started it or why. You need someone to blame and he can't speak up for himself. He's dead,' he burst out. 'He can't defend himself. Thinking about it more carefully, particularly since the fire in the nurse's house, I can't believe he did it for a moment. My father wasn't really like that. In his job he knew exactly what fire did to property and to people. He was careful.'

Randall played the card he'd kept up his sleeve. 'And the fire he set six months ago?'

It silenced Barton for only a minute. And then he found Randall's weak spot. 'What about the missing nurse?' he taunted. 'You told me that the two fires were started in a similar fashion. You cannot allege that my father torched her house too. He – was – already – dead.' Barton emphasized the words as though to a naughty two-year-old and Alex was forced to agree. But he had one further card up his sleeve.

'It could have been a copycat arson attack,' he said.

It took Barton aback. But he soon rallied. 'So where *is* she, this missing nurse?'

The taunting continued. Randall drew in a deep breath, which gave Nigel Barton further opportunity to mock him.

'You mean you haven't found her yet? According to the papers she wasn't in the house, was she?'

Randall simply waited.

'And you haven't managed to track her down, have you? Talk about incompetent,' Barton sneered. 'I ask you.' He turned to his son then. 'Come on, Jude,' he said. 'Let's go.'

The boy shot Randall a swift, unhappy, almost desperate look as they left. But for the life of him Randall could not fathom its meaning. He sat for a while, pondering. Something about the relationship between father and son seemed askew, but he wasn't sure what it signified. They were close, for sure. So close that he couldn't quite place a wife and daughter between them, picture the family dynamics. Or a father/grandfather, for that matter. The father/son relationship struck him as exclusive, very private and not altogether healthy. Or was this closeness something that had developed *since* the terrible fire? Only they were left. Sole survivors. He puzzled over this for a while but nothing quite slotted into place. A minute later he slapped his hand on his desk in frustration and gave up. But irritatingly, instead of moving on to other things, his brain tracked towards . . . Almost without conscious thought he found the phone in his hand and the number already ringing.

Jericho Palfreyman's gruff voice responded with frank hostility. 'I'm very sorry, Inspector,' he said politely but obstructively, 'the coroner is very busy right now. I'm sure she won't want to be disturbed. She's talking to the family of a road traffic incident.'

Randall smothered a smile. It was so typical of Palfreyman to use the current politically correct title. However, even Palfreyman was not going to stand in his way. He continued silkily, 'Then would you ask her to give me a ring when she's free, please, Jericho?'

Jericho was still playing hard to get. He was very aware of his status as coroner's assistant and used to using it to its fullest capacity. 'She may not be free at all today, Inspector, she's having a *very* busy day of it. Is it *so* urgent?'

Randall caved in under such intransigence. 'No, not really,' he admitted. 'It'll keep.'

And he replaced the phone. He had already called a briefing but it was a mere formality. No one had anything new to report, until WPC Delia Shaw stepped forward, her brown eyes bright, alert and sparkling with information. 'I've been working through the list of Mrs Deverill's friends,' she said. 'One of them, a Mrs Moncrieff, volunteered the information that she used to work with Mrs Deverill in the late sixties.'

'Go on,' Alex prompted, sensing something.

'They worked together in Shelton Hospital, which was the same then as these days – a psychiatric unit. In February 1968 there was a huge fire there, on Beech Ward. It was a locked ward,' she added. 'The patients were all severely disturbed, suffering from a range of complaints, obsessive compulsive disorder, schizophrenia, severe depression, what's called bipolar disorder these days but then was called manic depressive disease.'

Randall frowned. He couldn't work out the connection here. Yet. 'Go on,' he prompted.

'Mrs Moncrieff said that she hadn't been on duty the night of the fire but Mrs Deverill – she was Monica Gowan then – had been working. I've looked it up on the Internet, sir,' PC Shaw said. 'There were forty-three female patients resident on Barton Ward the night of the fire. Twenty-four of them died and eleven were seriously injured. It was the highest hospital death toll in fourteen years. The deaths were due to carbon monoxide poisoning and asphyxia. The patients on the general ward were the ones who died; their beds were placed top to tail because of overcrowding. The more severely disturbed patients survived because they were doubly locked, not only behind the ward doors but behind further heavy doors which were also locked. The doors provided a fire break and kept the smoke out.'

Randall waited, trusting that this awful story would somehow lead back to the two recent fires.

'The staff who were on duty that night were initially praised for saving the lives of some of the patients and for the way they handled the fire. But as the enquiry progressed and the journalists worked on the story *behind* the story the public mood changed and they came in for a lot of criticism.'

'Yes,' Randall prompted impatiently, still wondering what bearing this long-ago drama had on recent events. 'And what was the *cause* of the fire?'

Again, WPC Shaw bent over her notebook, determined to relate only the exact facts. 'That's the interesting bit,' she said, looking up. 'Although the wards had open fires it was not believed that this was the cause of the fire that night. There was talk that a lighted cigarette smouldered in a sofa for some time before igniting,' she looked up again, 'and releasing toxic fumes into the air. It was before the legislation for fireproof furniture.'

'Go on.'

'Patients were led to safety via the fire escape but it was difficult as many were heavily sedated due to their mental illness. Others were bedridden. And some who had OCD refused to leave without certain rituals being observed, shoes on, sweaters on the right way, slippers under the bed, all their buttons done up correctly.'

Alex Randall was interested now. 'It sounds a nightmare situation.'

'It was. Several members of staff were subsequently awarded bravery medals. One returned to Beech Ward six times to rescue patients at the height of the fire at obvious personal risk to himself. It appeared that the staff were all heroes and to be commended. But as the enquiries progressed contemporaneous newspaper articles started to paint a slightly different picture.'

The assembled officers listened intently.

'The subsequent accident investigation found that no night staff had had fire training for more than twenty years. A report five years earlier from the Shropshire Fire Service had stressed the need for proper fire training for the night nurses but none had been carried out.

'It also blamed a delay between the nurse in charge first noticing smoke and ringing the fire brigade. They blamed the high number of deaths partly on this delay, as well as the obvious difficulties of persuading women with mental illness to leave their beds.'

She had everyone's rapt attention.

'There was also some mention that the staffing levels were on the low side.' She met Randall's eyes and continued almost with an apology. 'Locked wards were the norm in those days although the 1959 Mental Health Act had stressed that as few patients as was possible should be locked up. Following the fire safety procedures in the Midlands were reviewed.'

'I should hope so,' Randall said, appalled at the image of disturbed patients in locked wards unable to escape the toxic smoke. It was as bad as the fire at Melverley Grange with its tragic result. 'Is there anything else?'

'Not factual, sir.'

Randall waited.

'But there is something *unofficial*.' She paused. 'A year after the fire and a month after the enquiries had been wound up a rumour started. A story was leaked. No one knew where it had come from. It was cited as "an unimpeachable source". It started in the local paper and suggested that the fire had been started deliberately and that traces of accelerants had been found. There was nothing official. The fire service denied it and so did the health service.'

'So where did the rumours come from and how did they spread? Was there any truth behind them?'

'No one knows the original source and the paper subsequently printed a retraction but, you know,' her brown eyes sparkled but behind them was a note of seriousness, 'no smoke without fire.'

Randall was tempted to scoff, but the old cliché held true. 'That's really good work. Well done, Shaw.'

'There is one last thing,' she said quickly, and the entire force knew that WPC Shaw was keeping the best little nugget for last so she could fling it to the floor with the maximum dramatic effect. 'One of the firemen cited in the recommendations was . . .'

They could guess it. But they could hardly deprive the WPC of her moment of triumph.

'William Barton.' She flung the name down like a trophy.

But after their initial exhilaration they all realized this didn't really tell them anything more. No one in the entire room could thread these facts into their current investigations. OK, they had found a tenuous connection between William Barton and Monica Deverill and fire: she had been a nurse on duty the night of the Shelton fire, he had been a fireman attendant on the tragedy. But where did it take them? They looked at each other blankly.

Randall dismissed them with a few words of appeal to think this through and thanks to WPC Shaw for her investigative work. Then he stood in the room, chewing his lip and knew that now he really must speak to Martha again. This time he got past the bulldog at the door and was put straight through.

She listened to Shaw's revelations without comment, only saying when he had finished, 'The Shelton fire was before my time but I heard about it. It became something of a cause celebre, a teaching tool, something we all learned about.'

'I knew it would be before your time. It's more than forty years ago.' Randall wanted to make the quip that she would have been a mere child then but it seemed inappropriate and a little dangerous. Their relationship had hovered near the boundary that stands between a work colleague and a friend but whenever they neared the line they both stepped smartly back and it had become something of a habit now.

'The thing is, Alex,' and he could hear gravity, humour and a challenge in her voice, 'what can it possibly have to do with the fires at Melverley Grange and at Monica Deverill's, and will it help you find her?'

He was frowning as he responded. 'Well, surely it has to. It's the only connection we've found so far between the Barton family and Monica Deverill. And the connection is a fatal fire.'

'So your next move is?'

'To find her.' He spoke through gritted teeth, avoiding adding the cliché, *Dead or alive*, but thinking it just the same.

'Then I wish you luck, Alex.'

He thanked her and they rang off. DI Randall sat for a while not even seeing the phone but a pair of wide green eyes, a ready smile and thick red hair, and he wondered why life always felt so much better when he'd talked to Martha Gunn. Why did he feel soothed, as though she was a balm? Was it her voice? Her presence? Her optimistic/realistic approach? Her motherliness?

He couldn't answer, probably because it was a cocktail of all these things.

The next thing he did was to pick up the phone and speak to both the Deverill brothers, in turn. He asked them both the same question. 'Did your mother ever mention the Shelton Hospital fire?'

And they gave the same answer. An emphatic NO.

But, he noted, neither of them asked *why* he was asking this particular question about an event that had happened so long ago. Apart from the obvious connection, which was a very tenuous one at best: their mother plus a fatal fire. He hadn't mentioned William Barton's connection with the Shelton tragedy but surely they might have wondered why his enquiry had taken such an unexpected turn. There would be no reason to make it the subject of a specific telephone call two weeks after their mother had disappeared. But neither of them had asked. Strange.

Alex felt a sudden gust of irritation sweep through him. Where the hell was the woman?

The initial elation at Delia Shaw's revelation was fast beginning to evaporate. It had seemed such a promising lead but had led nowhere. It was a blind connection. Somehow he needed to piece all these fragments together and make a coherent case. Sense out of a ragbag of facts. He made a face. Who'd be a detective?

He wanted to talk to Martha some more. Not simply ring her

with the latest development but talk over it face-to-face, chat around it, drink coffee as they bounced ideas around. Alex Randall sat still for a moment, troubled. What exactly was he wanting? Friendship? That was outside the remit of a coroner. Too much to ask. It wasn't part of her role. As realization started to seep through him he knew exactly what he was asking for. Her as a woman, not as a coroner. And then he remembered.

It wasn't possible. None of it was possible.

He had a wife.

SIXTEEN

Alex Randall sat late in his office that night, thinking about what fate had dished out to him. Some people might have called it a rough deal but he was not one to indulge in self-pity. He only had one real regret. Realizing he was staying late a few officers knocked on his door, asked if they could do anything if he needed them, even if they could fetch him a coffee or some tea. He fended off all offers of help or sustenance until his mobile phone finally buzzed in his pocket and he looked at the caller ID.

His wife. And that was the end of it. The familiar dark cloud wrapped around him. Dutifully he responded and went home.

Martha spent the evening listening to Sukey reading out her lines in the school play, *The Monkey's Paw*. To Sukey's delight she had landed the lead female part of Mrs White which gave ample scope for all her actress skills: horror, excitement, hope, terror and grief and Martha had to admit it, she really was good. She was proud of her, though a little like Sam's footballing skills she could not work out where these talents had come from. It was another one of life's little mysteries, she thought, as she watched Sukey's eyes widen with horror at the 'thing that knocked on the door'. She gave her daughter's blonde hair a little stroke, feeling its youthful silkiness under her fingers. Upstairs she could hear Sam bashing around on his weights. It made her reflect on how wonderful it felt to have the place noisy and boisterous and how very awful it would be when the pair of them left home and all fell quiet.

She cooked spaghetti bolognese for tea, watched the twins eat – Sukey daintily and Sam forking it in hungrily as she sipped a glass of Rioja, feeling mellow and glad to leave the day's tragedies behind.

Her feeling of contentment lasted right up until bedtime, when she threw back the duvet of the double bed it seemed vast, empty and cheerless.

Randall, on the other hand, was feeling increasingly frustrated with his home life. In fact, sometimes he felt he almost wanted to explode with the sheer awfulness of it. He sat in his sitting room and wondered how life had landed him in this place.

Wednesday, 23 March, 8 a.m.

Randall was in his office early the next day and again called for a briefing.

He perched on the edge of his desk and scanned the watching faces. Still alert. But if not glum they were lacking the optimism and excitement which hit them initially during a case. They all knew that an early breakthrough was helpful on all counts – financial, forensically and socially. It rescued the police's too often tarnished reputation and reflected well on the balance sheets. But this had never even looked as though it was going to be simple – even with WPC Shaw's discoveries. Fires were a tricky business. A lot of forensic evidence was destroyed. They'd spent a fortnight working out at Melverley and there was nothing more to find there. Besides, the fire at Sundorne had made it sensible to move the incident room back into the station. Alex's instinct told him there must be a connection between the two fires. It wouldn't be found in the small village but elsewhere so they may as well 'work from home' and they had moved back to Monkmoor Police Station.

'Let's summarize,' he said, addressing the assembled officers, 'starting from the very beginning.'

'Monica Deverill hasn't been seen since Saturday, March the

fifth, nine days after the Melverley fire. She speaks to her son, James, on the seventh promising to visit him and his family over last weekend but on that Friday night, the eleventh, her house too was set ablaze. Her car's been missing since then.' He glanced across at Gary Coleman. 'Did you find out when her car was last seen?'

'Nobody could be sure. She always garaged it.'

'Mmm. No sightings of either her or the vehicle anywhere in spite of a Stop and Search going out countrywide. Neither she nor the car has gone through any borders and she hasn't flown out of any of the airports. So she's still in the country, dead or alive. She told no one she was going away, which is out of character; her mobile has been switched off since then and there's been no activity on either that or her bank account. The phone could have been in the house and destroyed in the inferno or it could be with her but switched off.' He was thoughtful. 'Her house is gutted using exactly the same method as at Melverley Grange. That fire resulted in three deaths. No one died in Monica Deverill's house.' Randall scanned the room and caught the eyes of DS Talith, whose intelligent gaze beamed back something of his own thoughts.

He continued: 'The only connection we can find between the two families is, coincidentally, another fatal blaze, which took place more than forty years ago at Shelton Hospital, and resulted in twenty-four deaths and eleven serious injuries. As far as we know the fire at Shelton was not started deliberately. Though inevitably rumours started to circulate no evidence was ever found that this was so.'

Randall stopped speaking for an instant and began to ponder the words he had said. *But what if*, he thought, *the fire at Shelton was started deliberately? What if?*

Followed by, *Who would know?* when the official version was that it had been started by a cigarette left to smoulder in a sofa which was not fireproof, emitting noxious fumes which quickly killed the patients in the upstairs ward. Forty years ago was quite a while. That, then, might be an area to work in.

He continued: 'We find that two of the victims of the arson attacks were involved in the hospital fire, one as a *fire officer* and the other as a *nurse*. We have no evidence of contact between these two people either then or since. So what role, exactly, did

Monica Deverill, née Gowan, play in that other fatal fire? Is she connected, somehow, to the fire at Melverley Grange? If so how and why? Why did William Barton set that other fire in his own house six months ago? How did he set it? Are there any similarities to the two recent house fires? Were the Barton family certain that it *was* William who started that fire? Is there a possibility it could have been someone else? Maybe our arsonist. Perhaps, even, the missing nurse, however unlikely that seems? And, I suppose, the sixty-four-thousand-dollar question is, where the hell is she?' He was tempted to thump the desk to emphasize his words. But looking around at the alert faces of his team he knew there was no need for this. They were one hundred per cent attentive.

He scanned the room slowly, looking at each face in turn, hoping for some spark of inspiration to ignite one of the faces. He saw nothing. So he threw a last question into the room. 'Does it strike any of you as odd that after that fire last year, instead of reviewing whether William Barton might be better in a residential home with more supervision, Nigel Barton stands by and watches his father help his son to set up an escape route i.e. the rope ladder which is not without its dangers and leaves his wife and daughter to fend for themselves?'

Suddenly he saw it. *The locked doors.* Obvious. The women locked themselves in to protect themselves from William Barton's wanderings or assaults.

He shared the idea together with the fact that they had looked at the locked doors from the wrong perspective. Not locked in. They had been locking something out.

Most of the officers adopted a thoughtful look. A few of them nodded.

Randall came to a swift decision. 'Roberts, go and speak to Nigel and Jude Barton. Ask if William ever mentioned the fire at Shelton. Talith, you and I will go and have tea with Mrs Deverill's erstwhile colleague, Mrs . . . umm?'

'Moncrieff,' WPC Shaw supplied. 'Stella Moncrieff.'

'Quite.'

Gethin Roberts was always proud when he was the one to be chosen to pursue a delicate investigation.

He screeched to a halt outside the Lord Hill Hotel in a squad car, storing every detail in his mind ready to relate to Flora, his adored and adoring long-term girlfriend who had a very distorted view of his job, partly through watching too many TV crime dramas and partly fuelled by Gethin Roberts's embellishments of the parts he played in investigations. Every detail of his day's activities, plus a generous dollop of imaginative drama, made their evening chats quite exciting.

Having forewarned the Bartons that he would be arriving they were ready for him in a corner of the hotel lobby, father and son leaning forward, deep in conversation. He introduced himself and plonked himself down on the sofa opposite them, questions primed and ready to go. 'Mr Barton,' he began, angry with his voice for giving a small squeak at the end of his words, 'your father set fire to the house six months ago?'

Barton frowned. 'That's correct,' he said curtly.

'How did he do it?'

'In a very inept way,' Barton said tightly, 'considering he had been in the fire service.' Roberts smiled expectantly and waited. 'He had a pile of paper in his room,' Barton finally admitted. 'He simply set fire to it.'

'Was there much damage?'

'More than you would have thought.'

Roberts waited for him to enlarge and reluctantly Barton did. 'The bedding caught fire. There was damage to the ceiling and the rafters above.'

Roberts resisted the temptation to whistle and satisfied himself with a dry comment. 'Quite a blaze, then.'

Barton dipped his head. 'As you say.'

'Were accelerants used?'

Barton shook his head.

'How did he light it?'

'With a cigarette lighter,' Barton said through gritted teeth.

'You didn't think it would have been a good idea to have had more supervision for your father?'

Another shake of the head.

'You didn't worry about the risk to your wife and daughter? Only to your son?'

Barton drew his brows together, chewed his lip and attempted some sort of explanation. 'I thought being on the top floor that Jude was the more vulnerable. Obviously,' he added, 'I regret that decision now. But I had promised my father that he would not be put in a home. I didn't judge him a risk,' he added.

'And you thought a ladder might be helpful?'

For the first time Barton looked almost sheepish. 'It was my father's idea,' he said. 'A fire escape.' And then the instinct to defend his father's decision won. 'And it worked, didn't it?'

Not for your wife and daughter, Roberts thought and knew that to say this blunt statement would be to put him right in front of police complaints. He recalled his brief. 'Did your father ever mention the fire at Shelton Hospital in the late sixties?'

'Yes, he did. What's that got to do with . . .' Barton was no fool. He soon supplied his own answer. 'The missing nurse,' he said. 'Did she work there too?'

'Yes.'

'And you think there's a connection? After all these years?'

Roberts was about to say that it was one line of enquiry they were pursuing but he didn't get the chance. Barton supplied it for him. 'That's preposterous,' he said. 'It doesn't make any sense.'

And Roberts was inclined to believe him.

Stella Moncrieff proved to be a smart, energetic woman wearing a business suit who lived in a small, neat detached house on one of the estates that were springing up all around the ancient town of Shrewsbury.

She opened the door to them with a bright smile, her eyes gleaming with the whisper of scandal and drama.

After the inevitable introduction Randall launched straight into the reason why he had come. 'Tell me anything you remember Mrs Deverill saying about the Shelton fire.'

Stella Moncrieff gave a sharp, explosive chuckle. 'Monica Gowan, you mean,' she said, giggling like a girl. 'Oh, she was a one. You know? We all were. Not like these days. Things weren't so serious. There weren't the lawyers and complaints systems watching our every move.' She gave another delighted chuckle. 'You only had to say you were a nurse and everyone . . .' Her shoulders bunched up in recalled excitement. 'Everyone

just trusted you. We were the little angels of the health service.'
She opened her eyes very wide. 'You have no idea, Inspector. It
was so very different. The entire atmosphere was so much less
suspicious. Less litigious.'

Randall wanted to tell her to get on with it but he had the idea
Mrs Moncrieff would not be hurried. However, he did try. 'Mrs
Moncrieff,' he began severely, 'we are really concerned about
your one-time colleague who is still missing.'

She waved a hand in front of her. 'I know, I know,' she said.
'You want to know about the fire.' And then suddenly, quite
abruptly, she stopped her chatter, changed gear and became sober.
'Monica blamed herself,' she said, looking around as though
someone might be eavesdropping. 'The subsequent enquiries
went on and on. They were looking for someone to blame.
Anyone. Fingers were pointed at all sorts of people, half of whom
had nothing to do with it at all.' She leaned in. 'Monica was
probably just one of those unlucky ones.'

'Probably?' Randall probed gently.

'Well, I'm sure it wasn't her fault,' Stella snapped. 'It just
wasn't.'

'Why don't you start at the beginning, Mrs Moncrieff,' Randall
prodded gently. 'Exactly what part *did* she play in the events of
that night?'

Stella drew in a deep, regretful, sighing breath. 'She was on
duty that night, the only trained nurse. It was her job to make
sure all was well. One of those duties was to check out the day
room. The day room,' she explained, 'was underneath Beech
Ward.' She seemed to be losing confidence by the second.

'And?' Randall prompted gently.

She looked panicky. 'I don't know,' she said. 'Not really.'

Randall waited.

And got his answer. 'Not another human soul knows this,' she
said, 'and if Monica hadn't – wasn't,' she substituted, 'missing'
. . . Her eyes looked guarded. 'I don't know where she is, you
know.'

Randall still waited patiently. He knew he had *something*
wriggling on the end of his fishing line. And then it burst out,
like a boil.

Stella Moncrieff spoke slowly and reluctantly, the words

dragging out of her. 'Earlier that evening Monica had been in the day room with some of the patients. She'd been using nail varnish remover although it was banned but the patient was making a fuss.' She gave a rueful smile. 'Some of the patients were very hard to nurse, Inspector. Everything always had to be done in a certain way. And this patient had been making a fuss about something. So Monica . . . Well. She told me afterwards that she'd spilt half the bottle of nail varnish remover on a cushion on the sofa. When she discovered the fire she panicked and tried to put it out.'

And Randall began to understand. Acetone. Flammable. Acetone plus a smouldering cigarette equals major fire. Add in the non-fire-retardant sofa and you had a recipe for toxic smoke. And like Adelaide and Christie Barton there had been locked doors. It didn't make sense. Not yet – but it was beginning to have a certain rhythm to it. No wonder Monica Gowan had delayed summoning help. She must have realized she'd be implicated and had tried to contain the fire herself.

But even with this new knowledge, where did it leave the investigation now?

'Where is she?' he asked.

DI Randall had thought the blunt question might provoke hard rebuttals, denial. Outrage. But Mrs Moncrieff took the question perfectly seriously. She didn't proffer an answer, simply opened and closed her mouth like a fish out of water then bowed her head. 'I told you. I don't know.' Randall didn't sniff much conviction in the words.

'I know what you *told* me.'

There was no further response so Randall replaced the question with another.

'You say no one knew this – about the acetone?'

A firm shake of the head.

'I've read the reports. There was no mention of an inflammable substance furthering the fire.'

'No.'

'So who do you think burnt her house down and why?'

Again she gave no answer but her features altered slightly to a shifty look and a loss of the preening confidence. And still no response.

Randall tried again. 'Mrs Moncrieff, do you think there is a connection between the three fires? The arson attack at Melverley, your friend's house and the fire at Shelton in the sixties?'

This time the answer was a slight, jerky nod. 'There has to be,' she muttered.

'How?' In reality Randall's question was not how but who?

'I don't know any more,' she pleaded. 'Honestly, I just don't know. I really don't. We didn't see so much of each other until we found out a couple of years ago at a reunion that we were both widowed. That's when she confided in me about the acetone. It had always been on her conscience.' She opened her eyes wide. 'I honestly think she was glad to tell someone else and I tried my best to reassure her, to put her conscience to rest after all this time.'

'Could anyone else have heard her confession to you that night?'

'I don't think so.'

'Think carefully, Mrs Moncrieff. Could anyone else know about it?'

Stella Moncrieff obviously had to think about this one, wonder whether to say anything. Her eyes flickered towards him then looked away.

'She is missing,' Randall reminded her. He was really having to drag this out of her.

Stella Moncrieff frowned. 'One of the firemen said something a bit odd to her, asking her questions about who'd been in the day room that evening and if she'd noticed anyone with something that might have made the fire worse. It worried her.'

And another of the odd-shaped pieces in the puzzle slotted into place. '*Might* have made the fire worse?'

'He said something to her about the cigarette suddenly igniting and a whoosh of flame. The way he said it made her wonder if he had picked up on the spillage of nail varnish remover.'

He almost didn't need to ask the next question. 'Did she give you a name?'

But that was too much to ask. She shook her head so mentally Randall inserted the name himself.

William Barton.

SEVENTEEN

Wednesday, 23 March, 10 a.m.

As always when they neared answers in a case, Alex was feeling restless so, although he'd resolved to stop involving her in his cases, he decided that he wanted to speak to Martha again. No. He was more honest with himself. He *needed* to speak to her. He needed her matter-of-fact response to the dark place he was fumbling through. He also needed her sense of perspective and humour. This time he didn't even bother to try and go through Jericho but simply turned up at her office unannounced. Jericho opened the door to his knock, disapproval leaking out of every single pore. 'Inspector Randall,' he said severely, 'I don't recall you making an appointment.'

It was an accusation to which Randall responded tersely. 'I didn't.'

Jericho Palfreyman folded his arms, blocked the doorway and opened his mouth ready to object but Alex Randall got in there first. 'Don't tell me,' he said, his lips curving into a smile, 'the coroner's very busy.'

Palfreyman's lips twitched. He flicked a hank of grey hair away from his face and picked up the internal phone.

Alex heard Martha's voice respond and then Jericho put the phone down and without another word strode to the door and flung it open.

'Detective Inspector Randall,' he announced pompously.

Martha was not sitting at her desk but was standing at the window, staring out. She turned as Alex Randall entered and suddenly he felt embarrassed, as though he was intruding. Then he caught the glint of humour in her wide green, Irish eyes. 'Alex,' she said, moving forwards gladly. 'Jericho makes it up. I wasn't really working hard, you know.'

Behind him Palfreyman closed the door with an irritable snap.

She gave a sigh. 'To be honest I was tussling with a personal problem.' She gave another sigh and felt compelled to confide in him. Bugger the consequences. 'It's so much harder dating when you're middle-aged,' she said ruefully. 'And I don't even feel I know the rules any more. It was all so instinctive and natural when we were younger,' she said frankly. 'Now it feels stilted, forced. To be honest, I'm not enjoying it.'

He moved closer. Whatever he had been expecting it had not been this. He scraped his throat noisily and with acute embarrassment. 'I take it you're talking about a specific man?'

She nodded. 'Someone who has all the attributes.' She laughed and sank back into her chair; her chin rested on her cupped hand and she met his eyes with a regretful smile. 'A complete recipe book of all that a woman might want in a man. Handsome, rich, single. And yet . . .' She folded her arms and shook her head.

Randall dropped down into the seat opposite her. 'He isn't the right one then, is he?'

A shadow darkened her features and made her face look pinched and unhappy. 'I wonder if such a person as "*the right one*" even exists. He did. But –' She glanced at the corner of her desk and the photograph of Martin with the twins that had stood there for so many years. Then she scooped in a deep breath and recovered the customary brightness in her voice. 'Anyway, you didn't come here to listen to my whingeing and ruminations, did you, Alex? What is it?'

He related the conversation he'd just had with Monica Deverill's friend, adding, 'You can see it opens up all sorts of possibilities.'

'I do see that,' she said. 'It not only links Monica Deverill with the Barton family but – why – it opens an absolute can of worms.'

He frowned and nodded. 'If we find *her* we'll know about the fire at Melverley,' he said.

She looked at him curiously. 'You think she's alive?'

'I honestly don't know,' he said. Then smiled. 'I *know* we're near to breaking it but –' Although he emphasized the word 'know' there was no inner confidence in his voice.

Martha leaned back in her chair, half closing her eyes. 'As I see it, Alex, you have two ports of call here.'

He raised his eyebrows.

'One,' she continued smoothly, 'Monica Deverill's sons.'

'I did wonder about checking their mobile phone records.'

'That seems a good idea to me. If she's alive she will have been in touch. I'm a mother and I know it.' She met his eyes. 'Believe me. If she's alive she'll be in touch with her sons.'

'And the other one?'

She laughed. 'You know it yourself, don't you?'

He grinned back at her, held that grin for a fraction of a second too long and she flushed.

Damn her red hair and florid colouring. And the blush had embarrassed him.

'I'd better go,' he said, struggling to his feet.

'Wait.'

But as he turned she knew that had been a mistake too. His eyes warmed and then he drew back a step, frowning uncomfortably.

'I just wanted to say thank you for listening, Alex,' she said, putting her hand on his arm. 'It's good to have a friend.'

'My pleasure.' And he was out of the door before she could say another word but she knew he would have understood her second point. The old man's stories.

Mobile phone companies were necessarily obliging when it came to surrendering their records to the police and WPC Delia Shaw and Sergeant Paul Talith spent a while checking back for details of the accounts of Gordon and James Deverill. The two brothers were busy little bees on their mobile phone lines. There was a great deal of activity. It was going to take some time to cross-reference all their contacts.

'Look for a number,' Talith advised his colleagues, 'that only appears recently.'

In the meantime, Martha had been correct. Randall had understood her second point perfectly but he still had his work cut out persuading Nigel Barton that he needed to talk to his son – again.

Barton was in a foul temper. 'I'm sure you've squeezed

everything out of Jude, Inspector,' he barked down the phone. 'This is just making things worse for the boy. I really can't see that yet another interview is justified. Do I have the right to refuse?'

Unfortunately, yes, Alex thought miserably, unless he arrested the boy. Sometimes he decided that the law was not on the side of The Law. 'We still haven't found out who started the fire that killed your father, your wife and your daughter,' Randall reminded him deliberately.

It didn't do a lot to help his cause. Barton snorted derisively. 'Well, that's your shortcoming.'

Randall didn't respond to the jibe so Barton took up the cudgel again. 'And you think my son has the answer?'

'I think there are things that he knows which will help us, Mr Barton,' Randall responded, affecting a mildness he did not feel.

On the other end of the phone there was silence. It felt as though Nigel was going to refuse permission for the police to interview his son again. Randall felt he must push a little harder.

'If I had lost my family in that terrible way, Mr Barton, I think I would do anything in the world to find out who had committed the crime.'

'My son is alive and has been through a dreadful experience,' Barton said tightly. 'As his father I have a duty to protect him.' His face changed. 'He's all I have left. I must put him first – above all else.'

Alex empathized. He could quite understand the man's dilemma. 'I understand that you may be torn in your decision, Mr Barton,' he said, 'but please, we really think he may be able to help us. I wouldn't ask otherwise. We are as anxious to find out the truth behind your house fire as you almost certainly are.'

On the other end of the line there was silence. And then Barton spoke in a much softer voice. 'My son has already been traumatized by the events, Inspector. I have engaged the services of a counsellor who tells me Jude is suffering from what they are calling Survivor Guilt, a feeling that he could, should have done more to help his family. It's difficult knowing three family members did not survive the carnage and that you are the sole survivor of the family.'

'Apart from you, sir.'

And for some reason Alex Randall felt that the remark needled Nigel Barton.

There was a tense pause and then he said, 'Very well then, Inspector, but if he shows signs of any distress. *Any distress*,' he emphasized, 'the interview is to be terminated immediately. You understand?'

'Perfectly.'

'When would you like us to come?'

'As soon as possible, please, sir.'

'Then we may as well come at once and get it over with.'

Fifteen minutes later they arrived at the station. Randall greeted the boy with a warm handshake and a swift glance at Nigel, whose lips were pressed firmly together. He locked eyes with him for a second and gave a terse nod as though to underline the conditions of this interview.

Randall chose one of the interview rooms which had been brightly painted in yellow. Yellow for sunshine and optimism. It was often used to speak to children, hoping that 'nursery yellow' would minimize the impact of being interviewed by the police.

Jude glanced around him and settled back into one of the two chairs covered in red leatherette. Alex used the coffee table for the tape recorder and settled back in his chair which was Mastermind Black. He smiled again at Jude Barton. 'You don't mind if I record the interview?'

The boy gave his father a swift glance then shook his head vigorously.

'I'm interested in your grandfather, Jude,' Randall began.

The boy's expression was as alert as an eagle's. His shoulders bunched up. He was wary.

Randall continued in a conversational tone. 'I found it really interesting that he was a fireman.'

The comment agitated the boy. He licked his lips which were so dry the action had a rasping sound to it.

'He must have told you a few stories about his work.'

Jude gave a jerky nod. 'I already told you he did.'

Alex Randall leaned forwards. 'Did he ever talk to you about the fire he attended in the sixties at Shelton Hospital?'

Jude dropped his gaze. 'He might have,' he said, shrugging. 'I can't remember every story he told me.'

Randall persisted. 'I think you would remember this one. Shelton Hospital is a psychiatric hospital. Some of their patients were disturbed so they had to be in a locked ward.' He continued in a softer voice. 'There was a fire. A lot of patients died in that fire.'

Jude shrugged. 'He might have told me that one. I seem to remember something about some mental patients dying. I couldn't remember the name of the hospital – or any other details about it.' His eyes slid along the floor towards Randall's feet – and upwards, stopping somewhere near the detective's chest.

Randall continued. 'As your grandfather got a bit older his recent memory would have faded and his past memories become clearer. Also his judgement of what was politic to tell you would have been impaired.'

The boy paled and shot a look at his father. It was a silent appeal for help in a difficult situation. But Nigel Barton was looking at his son with some abhorrence, almost as though he was a stranger and this was the first time he had really seen him.

Again Randall lunged his question forward. 'He told you something else, Jude, didn't he? Something he really shouldn't have told you. Something he'd never told anyone else.'

Jude said nothing but his eyes swivelled upwards right into Randall's face with a look of suspicion, as though he suspected the DI of sorcery. He nibbled his lip and shook his head. 'No,' he said flatly.

There was nothing to be gained here so Randall turned his attention back to Nigel. 'Tell me more about the fire your father started.'

'There's nothing to . . .' And then a further penny dropped; both father and son's shoulders jerked as though both were held by an invisible puppet master. The same idea had occurred to both of them simultaneously.

And Randall began to see through the gauzy film that had hidden the truth so tantalizingly and effectively from him. He tapped his forehead with his fingertips in the old gesture of comprehension. '*He* didn't start it, did he?' His eyes met those of both father and son. 'That's why you couldn't banish him to an old people's home, isn't it? He'd done nothing to punish, had he?'

Barton was regarding him with a frozen look, as though he dreaded Randall's next sentence. Randall continued sadly. 'It wasn't your father, was it?'

He looked back to Jude. He leaned forward, switched the tape recorder off and regarded father and son. 'Thank you for your help,' he said. 'I appreciate it.'

'So what now?' It was Nigel who spoke.

Randall assumed the blandest of expressions. 'You're free to go.'

They scuttled out like crabs on the beach. Ungainly: feet, legs everywhere. Alex sat back in the chair, steepled his fingers and had a long ponder. He was going to need evidence or a confession, preferably both, to put in front of the CPS like a fresh and juicy bone. He smiled again. The image of a bone pleased him, something bloody to gnaw on.

WPC Delia Shaw arrived opportunely. 'We have something for you, sir,' she said.

EIGHTEEN

As the door had closed behind Detective Inspector Alex Randall Martha had drawn in a deep breath. She was unsettled. She needed to talk. She needed lunch with a friend and there was only one friend who fitted the bill. Miranda Mountford. She sent her a text, reflecting that these wonderful ways of communication had transformed friendship. Instantly accessible. A minute later her phone was responding. She read the message, smiled and felt better already.

Miranda had had a disastrous marriage to a guy named

Steven who had practically turned psycho, threatening her, stalking her, playing tricks on her, appearing and disappearing until her friend had wondered about her sanity. At one time Martha had fretted for her friend's safety. Steven had been so very unpredictable. But all that was behind her now. A restriction order had been placed on him and it appeared to have worked. So far.

While Paul Talith followed up his own lead Delia Shaw was checking through the numbers on the Deverill sons' mobile phones. It was tedious work. There were eighteen which coincided with both of them, a cluster of calls, both to each other and to these numbers around the time that their mother had last been seen. There was four days' silence and then the number cropped up again. Comparing the two lists it looked as though Gordon and James had rung round the same people at the time when the police had been looking into their mother's house fire. Probably a frantic hunt round relatives and friends when they had realized that their mother was missing and not dead inside her house. She cross-checked them with the numbers the brothers had given the police of possible locations for their mother. Some were landlines, others mobiles. The numbers danced in front of her eyes, seeming to mock her. Who would have thought there could be so many different combinations of ten Arabic numerals? She yawned and stretched, deciding that concentrative computer work was more tiring than an hour or so at the gym. She peered again at the list of numbers. It was perfectly logical that the brothers would have been ringing the same numbers. And comparing the printouts there were a lot of duplicated calls. Looking more closely at the timing they must have been dialling the numbers practically simultaneously. Shaw gave a smirk. Typical male behaviour. Women would have sat down and divided the list, not gone scurrying around like rats in a cage, stepping on one another's toes. They had phoned each other frequently too, probably to check whether the other had found the missing mother.

Shaw had begun by concentrating on the beginning of March, the time when Monica had last been seen, rather than the time around the fire at Sundorne. Previous to that they had rung their mother, either on her landline, or on the mobile registered to her, about twice a week and the pattern of calls the brothers had made had been different. Gordon and James wouldn't have been ringing round relatives and friends then – there had been nothing to alert them to the situation until March the eleventh, the night of her fire. They had been in contact with each other before then but infrequently. Shaw sat and stared at her computer screen. Well? They were brothers. Nothing abnormal about that. Then she went back into late February. There was one number which particularly interested her. It had appeared first on Friday the twenty-fifth of February, the evening after the fire at Melverley Grange, and it cropped up fairly regularly after that, both incoming and outgoing and the calls had lasted for up to thirty minutes to both brothers. Shaw's pulse quickened. She had an instinct about this 077 number. She checked both statements back into early February and then January. This number initially appeared just once in the early evening on the night of February twenty-fifth on James's phone and cross-checking the statements he had immediately called his brother. For four days the number did not appear again on either James or Gordon's phone but from the Monday, the day they were assuming Monica Deverill had disappeared, there was activity on that number. It began to appear quite regularly on both Monica's sons' phones. Delia Shaw cupped her chin in her hands and thought.

Monica Deverill had claimed that she knew something significant about the fire at Melverley. She had been convinced enough to ring the police and had been due into the station the very next day. The fire at her house was patently no coincidence but cause and effect. The fire-raiser must have realized she knew something important that she was about to relay to the police. Monica had left her home. She had been running from the arsonist who had torched her fire, maybe knowing, maybe not knowing, whether she was inside. WPC Shaw thought further. Her car had probably been missing at the time the fire was started so the arsonist might have realized the bird had already flown.

Shaw tried to work it out by asking herself questions. What if the fire at Melverley had created panic in the ex-nurse? She

had bought the phone and then – poof – Delia Shaw's hands
went up involuntarily. Like a magician's assistant she had
disappeared. She glanced across at Talith, who was also peering
into his computer screen with the absorption of an online
gambler. She returned her attention to her own screen. She was
going to need a bit more than this to impress her sergeant, giving
a little smirk to herself. Talith's shirt was getting tight around
his middle. He'd popped a button and a bulge of hairy stomach
protruded. She peered closer at her own screen, searching for
some clue, some indication that all this was worth the little
frisson of excitement she was experiencing. Then she sat back.
The *timing* of the calls from the mystery number was interesting
too, always either a little before nine a.m. on weekdays, when
the brothers would have been out of the house, away from wives
and families who might have been curious as to the call. Or
around six p.m., again at a time when they would probably have
been on their way home from work, out of the house, away from
eavesdropping ears. And they had often phoned each other shortly
afterwards.

She had three alternatives. One: she could ring the number
and see if anyone answered. That was obviously the simplest.
Two: she could speak to the mobile companies to see who this
phone was registered to, although she suspected this would prove
to be a pay-as-you-go phone on a false address. Three: she could
ask the brothers who was on the end of this line.

She sat back; allowed herself a little dream. What if *she* was
the one who broke through this case? For some silly reason she
visualized herself standing on a podium, being cheered on by
her colleagues, a laurel wreath on her head. A laurel wreath?
She made a face. How classical. Classical and silly. It was a
great thought but about as likely as winning the Euro Lottery.
Still – she may as well try. She picked up the phone and dialled
the phone company. Then pulled her hand back. Number one
was the most instant and dramatic action. She reached out and
dialled and wasn't surprised to be put straight through to an
automated answer phone which repeated the number in a
monotonic, robotic voice and invited her to leave a message.

WPC Shaw did just that, asking whoever was at the other end
of the phone to contact her at the Monkmoor Police Station in

Shrewsbury. She left her name and number twice and replaced the receiver thoughtfully, her mind analysing the time frame before she confided her suspicion to Paul Talith, who was still absorbed in his computer screen, frowning and muttering to himself as he cross-referenced data.

Delia Shaw concentrated on her job in hand. Randall was always emphasizing the point that you couldn't look too closely at dates and times. She smiled to herself. Truth was she had a bit of thing about DI Randall. He was one of the best detectives she had ever worked with, with his methodical way of analysing data. He might be considered by some a cold fish, a loner, someone who did not join in the frolics of the Force but he was a damned good officer, loyal to his team, good at bringing out their talents and correcting their shortcomings. He also had a talent for homing in on the weaknesses in their prosecutions way before they faced the humiliation of the CPS doing what they did best, their vulture act: picking flesh from bones and ultimately their cases apart. There were senior officers who enjoyed belittling their juniors, focusing on their shortcomings and mocking their inexperience. Randall was not one of these.

She glanced back at Talith. Should she confide in him her instinct? She thought for a minute then decided it would be much better to present him with a *fait accompli*. She dialled the number again. And received the same response. She looked harder into the phone detail and sat back, mentally sending a *Thank you, God,* prayer heavenwards. That clinched it. From the fifth of March neither James nor Gordon had rung their mother's mobile or her landline. In other words, Shaw tidied it up in her mind before confiding in her sergeant, six days before the fire James and Gordon had known their mother wouldn't be around to pick up the phone. And the call to James would have been made from her new mobile.

The Armoury was quiet that lunchtime. Miranda was already sitting down at a small table in the corner when Martha arrived. She smiled. She didn't know why or how it was but Miranda was one of those women who had never really changed her style since the sixties. And yet she always managed to look fashionable. Her hair was the same dark, shining bob that she had always worn. And she was dressed in classic black trousers with a white silk shirt. The only change Martha could spot was that today Miranda was wearing forties-style siren-red lipstick. Miranda gave her a sparkly grin. 'Well,' she said as Martha reached the table and kissed her cheek. 'You sounded desperate. Whatever is it?'

Martha sat down. 'I don't feel so bad now,' she said. 'Having a pal to chat to makes quite a difference.'

Miranda grinned even wider. 'Was the problem that easy to solve?'

'Yes, I was just being silly. Tell me about you first. How's Steven?'

'Well – that's why I'm feeling so good,' Miranda said. 'He's finally buggered off to South Africa. For the first time in years I feel safe.'

How different from her own story, Martha thought. Steve had been a violent, difficult, bullying, unpredictable man and Miranda had been initially intimidated and finally terrified by him. How different from Martin's gentle ways. Martin, whom she mourned for no longer.

'And what about you?'

Martha's tale began to unravel, her desire to meet someone else, her difficulties over confused emotions, her failure to feel anything but friendship for the one man who should have felt eligible and finally her absorption in a work colleague she *knew* to be married. Her friend listened without interruption. Then she reached out and touched Martha's hand. 'Poor you,' she said. 'Poor you.'

Martha felt a combination of better and worse. 'Hey,' she objected, 'I don't want your pity.'

'You're not getting it,' Miranda said stoutly. 'You're getting empathy not sympathy. Don't confuse the two. You're not stupid. You know as well as I do these things just happen, encounters turn into relationships, relationships into love.'

Martha laughed, now feeling much, much better. 'At our age?'

The pair of them giggled like teenagers and then Martha leaned in towards her friend. 'The question is,' she said, 'what about Internet dating?'

'Ah, well,' Miranda said. 'That's where I can advise you.'

NINETEEN

In the end, in spite of Delia Shaw having made her own discoveries it was Talith who burst into *her* thoughts. 'She's alive,' he said suddenly, and with conviction, tapping the computer screen with his index finger.

She turned in her seat. 'How do you know?'

'She withdrew five thousand pounds from her building society account on Saturday the twenty-sixth of February,' he said, not looking at her but staring intently into the computer screen. He continued, 'After the Melverley fire she knew something would happen to her. Probably guessed that her house would be torched too.' Talith's face was thoughtful.

'The five K could have been blackmail money.'

But Talith looked at her and grinned. 'Oh, no. Cause and effect, Shaw. There's only one definite connection that we know of between the two households and that is the fire at Shelton.' He stood up. 'I'm going to have a word with DI Randall.'

'Before you do,' WPC Shaw put in quickly, 'there's something *I'd* like to show *you*.' She ran her finger down the lists of mobile numbers, trying to make her thoughts as clear as possible to her colleague. When she'd finished speaking he nodded. 'It fits in with my ideas,' he said. 'Let's go.'

Randall listened carefully to his two officers, his thick eyebrows tangling in the middle of his forehead as he frowned in concentration, thought for a while, then spoke. 'Good work,' he said to them both. 'Good ideas but even better conjecture.' His eyes rested on them each in turn. 'And that's what it is, the pair of you.' His words were robbed of any sting by his grin. 'Make no mistake, this is just an idea without, so far, any corroborative evidence.' Then his face changed again, his eyes warming. 'But it's the best idea anyone's come up with so far. And if it helps I think you're on the right track. So now we've come to that conclusion let's build on it. Sit down, the pair of you. Let's review what we know for sure. The unmistakable facts. She hasn't gone through passport control and her car hasn't been found.' His hazel eyes lightened. 'Yet. So unless the combined forces of the country are being singularly obtuse and unobservant she's hidden the car somewhere. Right?'

They both nodded. Randall looked at Talith. 'And the only connection we've found so far between the Barton family and our nurse is the fire on Beech Ward in Shelton Hospital in the late sixties. Monica Deverill was a nurse on duty on the ward that night and William Barton was one of the attendant fire officers. It's not much of a connection and doesn't exactly suggest foul play. Also, Barton senior was already dead by the time of the second fire. It's at best a tenuous connection but it's all we have.' He looked at them. 'Right so far?'

'Yes, sir,' they answered in unison.

'There is another possibility,' Randall said slowly. 'And until we're more sure we shouldn't jump to conclusions, should we?'

This time the two officers shook their heads and waited for him to continue.

Randall focused his gaze on WPC Shaw. 'I agree. The five thousand pounds she withdrew from the building society *could* have been blackmail money,' Randall said. 'Her house *could* have been destroyed to muddy the waters of her disappearance either by the blackmailer or by her. If the connection *is* with the Shelton fire it's possible that William Barton and Monica Deverill were targeted by a relative of someone who died in it.' He paused. 'Though why they should exact their revenge on two people who tried to help so long after the event is beyond me. Unless . . .' He looked at the two officers. 'There hasn't been some recent release of information about the tragedy, perhaps over the Internet, has there?'

'Not that I know of,' Delia Shaw answered. 'The stuff I got over the Internet about the fire was years old.'

'Quite so. Maybe that isn't such a great idea. But if the money she withdrew was to tide her over while she hid, who was she hiding from?'

He gave them both a grin. 'You know,' he said in a friendly, confiding tone, 'this is one of those cases which seems to get more complex and throw up more complications the further your investigations go. She could have been kidnapped and her car disposed of or hidden.' Another grin, rueful this time. 'There are endless possibilities but one, I can assure you, will fit all the facts like a handmade kid glove.'

'Who would the kidnapper be, sir?' It was Talith who asked the question.

Randall laughed. 'Obviously the same person who torched her house. Don't worry, Talith. I'm playing Devil's Advocate here, opening up scenarios. I'm only pointing out that there is more than one potential answer. We must look at them all, keep our minds clear and our investigations broad. And there is always the possibility that Monica Deverill herself is our arsonist, though why she should draw attention to herself in this way – well – it could only be the result of a very sick mind.'

They were all silent at this. The term *sick mind* brought the terrible vision of the disturbed patients on a locked ward banging on the doors, begging to be let out, finally succumbing to the dreadful coughing and the inhalation of toxic smoke which would finally kill them. Was it really possible that Monica Deverill set the fire and watched, sadistically, as her patients died? It was a hideous thought and one which silenced them.

It was WPC Delia Shaw who finally broke the silence. 'Well, we know who has the perfect alibi, don't we? William Barton.'

Randall and Talith looked at each other. Neither could resist a smile accompanied by an inevitable groan. Shaw felt flat.

'I wish he was alive,' Talith grunted. 'He'd help us out, I'm sure.

They all nodded gloomily. Randall knew he needed to keep them focused. 'There are a few more questions you should be asking yourselves.'

They eyed him expectantly.

'Is there anything to indicate that Mrs Deverill might have been kidnapped?'

They shook their heads dubiously.

'I agree. I would say it's unlikely. It is much more likely that she has gone underground. Why? Try this for size: because the very thing that she has feared for more than forty years has happened? When Melverley Grange was set on fire, for some reason, she believed that she would be subjected to a similar assault. And that is exactly what did happen.'

He waited to let these words sink in before continuing. 'Now then, it would be tempting to look around for someone who could have been at Shelton Hospital on the night of the fire and decided to repeat the act. Perhaps an ex-patient, someone who would have been fairly young at that time. Or the family of a victim of the Shelton fire. I would have asked you to check the list of the dead. But forty years later? I'd take some convincing.'

He paused. 'Next question. Was it necessary that *Nigel Barton* was away from home on the night of the fire?' He looked at them as though waiting for them to provide the answer, before giving it himself. 'I would say yes, that it is no coincidence. In his statement he said that he was away from home roughly once a month. That's not very often. There would have been much more chance that he would have been at home than away.'

Talith and Shaw waited for him to continue.

'Did you find any connection between the three business associates who had a grudge against Nigel Barton and Monica Deverill?'

Talith answered this one. 'No, sir.'

'But what about Pinfold's flying visit to the UK?'

Talith grinned. 'Not surprising he didn't go to see his old mum – unless she was after some of the supergrass he was importing from the Netherlands. Don't worry, sir, all that's being investigated.'

Randall grinned. 'Good,' he said. 'And Nigel Barton's alibi is unshakeable?'

Shaw responded. 'Yes, sir. We have corroborated evidence from two independent witnesses that on the night of the fire he was in the hotel grill until ten and then in the bar until after eleven, as the CCTV pictures suggest. And he wasn't alone. A young woman was with him – at a guess, the lovely Mirabelle. It's a three-hour trip from York to Melverley. Not a fast road. The fire was phoned in at 11.38 p.m.'

'Right.' Randall smiled at her. 'Then it leaves us with only one person.'

The response from both officers was surprise. 'Sir?'

Randall stood up. 'Work it out for yourselves,' he said and left the room.

He went outside the station to ring Martha from his mobile phone. He didn't want his colleagues listening in. As soon as she picked up and without a word of explanation he said, 'I thought I might pop up and have a cup of tea with you.'

The pleasure she felt was quite disproportionate to the invitation. 'Wonderful, Alex,' she said warmly. 'That'd be lovely. I'll ask Jericho to put the kettle on and . . .'

He interrupted her. 'I'll bring jam doughnuts.' And put the phone down before she could quip that he knew the way to a woman's heart. When she heard the click of his phone she was glad she hadn't said it.

Even before he arrived she'd known from his jaunty tone that the case must be near to some resolution. Then it would be her turn again to reopen the inquest and finally pronounce a verdict on the three family members who had died at Melverley Grange. And the nurse? she asked herself. Well, no body no inquest. She corrected herself. There were cases where an inquest had taken place when there had been no body but these were rare and unusual cases. This wouldn't be one of them. Alex would be able to solve this. Monica Deverill's fate would not elude them for ever. She couldn't deny it. She was intrigued and looking forward as much to seeing him as to the jam doughnuts he'd promised.

And the broad grin he gave her as she opened the door to him confirmed all her suspicions. He stood in the doorway, tall, slim almost to the point of thin, his features irregular enough to make him attractive. Large nose, wide mouth, sharp chin. But there was a warmth in his hazel eyes, a kindness in his spirit and an honesty in his words that made her heart give a little skip in his presence.

She cursed herself. What was the point? DI Alex Randall was a professional, a colleague and a married man. She listened very carefully to every single word before responding. 'So what do you propose to do next?'

'We have three points of enquiry – the three fires,' he said.

She hesitated before, in a measured voice, she began asking him questions to clarify the suspicions that were sprouting in her mind. 'Can you explain to me exactly where the splashes of petrol were found at the Grange?'

He didn't answer straight away but regarded her gravely, then, 'Landing, up the stairs. The carpet in both front rooms was pretty soaked.'

Martha nodded. 'And did anyone see Jude Barton descend his ladder?'

This time Randall didn't even make a reply. He knew she was prodding him. He stood up, smiled and took a step towards her. For the briefest of seconds Martha panicked, thinking he was about to kiss her. But he didn't. He simply smiled, said his goodbye and left.

TWENTY

Detective Inspector Alex Randall called the briefing for six o'clock, his plan being to rein in all the facts, interviews, review the evidence and make contact on the following day. He also wanted to book all his interviews and make sure everyone was available. He had a feeling of danger, of impatience and sudden urgency that he couldn't quite figure out. It wasn't really like him. He was normally a patient man, happy to construct the evidence before diving in with an arrest. But this was different. He had a feeling of anger at the fate of people unable to defend themselves, frightened as this home went up in smoke. And at the back of his mind was the terrible picture, not only of the two women who had died at Melverley Grange and the old man who had tried vainly but bravely to help them. But there was also the sepia image of the patients at Shelton Hospital, trying, in their confused way, to escape. Maybe beating on doors, screaming. It was horrible.

As the officers filed in, he glanced across at the board with the pictures of the bodies of the three victims of the Melverley fire pinned next to two photographs they had of Monica Deverill. Appropriately enough, one was of her in her starched uniform in her Shelton nursing days which James had handed over reluctantly. 'I really like this photo of Mum,' he'd said. 'She looks so . . . professional.'

And the other photograph showed Monica as she was today, fun-loving, the grandchildren cut out of the picture, her in slacks and a loose fitting T-shirt – a little weightier than in the earlier photo but she still looked fiercely energetic. She was staring towards the camera, a half smile on her face. Her eyes still large, dark and intelligent. Randall peered closer and tried to understand her psyche. She looked a perceptive woman, practical, a pragmatist and far-sighted. There was around her an aura of no nonsense, a roll-up-your-sleeves sort of energy. And it lasted right through from the early photograph to the later one.

He felt he knew her. She would be the nurse on the ward who would make the brave decisions, shoulder the blame, take responsibility, clean up messes and chin-up to authority if it was in her patients' interest. Yes, he knew her. He also had the feeling that he would respect her.

If he ever met her.

The officers were watching him, each one with his or her own take on the moment. Gethin Roberts watched him with a sort of hero worship, wondering whether he would ever be the senior investigating officer on such an important case and stand up in front of junior officers, just like him, who would hang on every word. Give press releases. Roberts was a dreamer. In his mind he was already there, solving difficult cases, inspiring junior colleagues. He dreamed right on, to a moment when he would propose to his adored Flora and slip the ring on her willing finger.

Finally Randall broke into his thoughts. 'I want an initial interview with young Jude,' he said. 'Roberts, stick with me.'

Gethin Roberts turned slightly pink as though Randall had peeked into his fantasy but he still couldn't resist a quick scan of the room to gloat. *He* was the one who'd been picked.

Randall had already moved on swiftly, feeling the pace of the investigation quicken, like jungle drums, intensifying as they increased in tempo to match his own sense of urgency as they neared their quarry and prepared to pounce. 'Then we'll move on to the Deverill brothers.' Randall stopped and he too looked around the room, realizing that most of the officers didn't have a clue just what road he was following. He gave them some explanation almost out of sympathy. *He* was the sighted leading the blind. He addressed them. 'This has been a difficult case mainly because its cause is rooted in history. However, that will make it a learning curve for all of you, how to investigate seemingly unrelated cases and search for some connection.' He relaxed and smiled at them. 'You won't always find one but that shouldn't stop you from looking.' He dismissed them with his customary, 'Thank you.' And as soon as the officers had dispersed he spoke to PC Roberts who was hanging around the edge of the room as though he did not know what to do next.

Then he made the first of his phone calls.

It was as though Nigel Barton knew that something was afoot. He did not object when Randall asked him to bring his son down to the station – again. Neither did Nigel comment when DI Randall asked him whether he would like to bring a solicitor. Barton rejected the idea of a solicitor and simply acquiesced as though he was defeated.

Thursday, 24 March, 9 a.m.

But when father and son arrived Randall understood. If Nigel Barton had diminished in size and bluster the opposite was true of his son. Jude looked different now. Not the skinny, frightened teenager. He walked tall. He almost had a swagger. He had grown in confidence, appeared cocky. But when the boy's eyes met Randall's the detective realized that the truth was something quite different. The boy was bluffing. In reality he was putting on a show.

Randall decided to put the case square on to him. 'Let me tell you a story,' he began. Predictably, like most teenagers, Jude Barton affected boredom. Randall had anticipated an objection any moment from Nigel but after an initial 'Tut', of irritation the boy's father continued to look defeated and very, very tired. This was taking its toll on him. He, too, had had enough. He didn't even point out how many times his son had been summoned to this station any more. His gaze drifted around the room as though looking for some assistance. But he found none. He licked dry lips and made strange clicking noises in his throat as though he was choking. Nervousness, Randall guessed. As he meandered through a story of an old man who had returned to the past when he had been a hero, Randall sensed that Nigel Barton had travelled along much the same road to reach probably the same destination. So now they were in the same place? Except they weren't. Randall was in no way to blame for the events whereas Nigel? The detective leaned far back in his chair – almost far back enough to topple. And Gethin Roberts watched, listened and learned.

Talith and Delia Shaw, in the meantime, were in another interview room, along the corridor, speaking to Gordon Deverill, while in a third interview room WPC Lara Tinsley and PC Gary Coleman were interviewing James Deverill. All with good results.

Delia Shaw had opened the questioning. 'Gordon, you've said,' she glanced down at the printout of the phone bill, knowing he would be able to see what it was, 'that you haven't heard from your mother since sometime in early March?' She looked up, eyebrows raised, questioning, giving the suspect a chance to redeem himself.

Gordon Deverill knew exactly what she was up to and consequently he looked wary, his eyes flickering around the room as restless as a butterfly, searching for not nectar, but inspiration. Inspiration, WPC Shaw thought? All he needed to do was confess the truth.

She gave him an encouraging smile. 'Would you like to revise that statement, sir?' she asked gently and very politely, fixing him with her big brown eyes. Gordon startled; his shoulders twitched, his eyes opened wide, his forearms tensed.

'Shit,' he muttered, dropping his face into his hands. Then he looked up. 'Look,' he said. 'I don't know exactly but Mum knew something about the fire at Melverley. For some reason when she heard about it she completely flipped. There's something terrifying her.' He paused. 'She didn't just go underground on a whim, you know. She just had to get away.'

In the other room Tinsley and Coleman were provoking a similar response. But unlike his brother James Deverill looked angry. It was only as they proceeded with the questions that Lara Tinsley and PC Gary Coleman realized that the anger was not directed at them but at his mother.

'I don't know why she had to go into hiding,' he said for the nth time. 'I only know something seemed to . . . She was *paralysed* with fright. And then, without any explanation, she drags us into her deceit and made us promise not to tell you where she was.'

'It's imperative that we speak to her,' Lara Tinsley prompted gently.

Suddenly James Deverill slapped his mobile on to the table with a clatter. 'Go on,' he said flatly. 'Ring her. She's listed under Mum.'

Coleman did just that. Picked up the phone, found the number, pressed the call button and had a surreal conversation with the 'missing woman'.

'Is that Mrs Monica Deverill?'

The reply was wary. 'Who is that?'

'This is Police Constable Gary Coleman of Shrewsbury police. We've been looking for you, Mrs Deverill.'

For a moment there was no response except a relieved release of breath. Then Monica gave a weary sigh. 'I know,' she said.

'Where are you?'

'With a friend.'

Somehow Coleman knew that she would not give him either the name of her friend or her whereabouts but he asked the question all the same. And got the anticipated response. 'I'm not prepared to tell you that.'

'We need to speak to you. I take it your sons have told you about your house?'

'Why do you think I fled? I knew what was coming, Constable.' Her voice was harsh with emotion. There was another tired sigh and then, 'I take it you want me to present at the police station?'

'Please.'

'Then I surrender.' Said, surprisingly, with a hint of humour. 'I'll be with you –' a pause – 'soon.'

Coleman glanced at James Deverill who looked relieved. 'Thank God,' he muttered, 'for the end of that bloody farce.'

At no time when Randall related his story did he read anything but an affected boredom in Jude's face while his father stayed very quiet and still, not interrupting or even responding. It was almost as though the story was of no great surprise to him. He'd already guessed it. When Randall finally stopped speaking Jude's eyes lifted to the detective's face and there was a subtle change. Respect.

Then Gary Coleman knocked and entered the room, spoke in a low voice to his chief and Randall knew that at last that they were nearing their quarry.

TWENTY-ONE

E veryone in the entire station was waiting, as though for a royal visit, not knowing how long it would be before Monica Deverill turned up. It could be a long wait. She could be in the Isle of Wight or the Highlands and Islands of Scotland, the Westernmost point of Anglesey or the toe of Cornwall. She had deliberately given them no idea where she had been for the last couple of weeks. They did not know how long they may have to wait. They could have kept calling her mobile number but sensed she would not answer.

Likewise, they could have alerted police forces up and down the country. It was probable that she would be in her own car. But they decided simply to sit it out.

And wait.

At last, a little before nine in the evening, the desk sergeant brought in a woman. Randall stared at her. She was solidly built, square with a thick waist, but not fat. She merely looked strong. The phrase, *as an ox,* flittered into his mind and he smiled. Yes. That described her very well. Strong as an ox. Both physically but also, he suspected, morally and mentally. She had a plain, scrubbed face, but met his eyes with an unflinching gaze from direct grey-green eyes as he greeted her. 'Mrs Deverill, I presume?'

'Yes,' she confirmed, her voice, like her persona, firm and decisive without being harsh.

He shook her hand. 'I'm Detective Inspector Alex Randall, senior officer investigating the house fires at both Melverley Grange and your home.'

'Yes,' she said softly. 'I understand that.'

They offered her a cup of tea and then Randall took Talith and Roberts with him into the interview room and they started their interrogation.

It was hard to know where to start. Like Barton, she refused the attentions of a solicitor, saying she was happy to speak to them alone.

'I take it you know about your house?'

She nodded and leaned forward. 'I knew it would happen, you know.'

'I thought you might,' Randall replied gently. 'Don't you think that you'd better start at the beginning? It all begins with the fire at Shelton, doesn't it?'

'Yes,' she answered, apparently unsurprised that he was cognisant of this connection.

Randall sat back, switched on the tape recorder, fed in the names of all present, folded his arms and listened. 'In your own time,' he prompted.

'You already know about the fire in Shelton,' she began. 'I was on duty on Beech Ward that night. William Barton was one of the fire officers who attended. He was a very clever man. And brave. Many of the patients there that night owe their lives to his heroism.' She smiled at a memory. 'There was one particular patient, Dora Robinson, who had OCD.' She smiled at Randall, maybe sensing some empathy. 'Obsessive Compulsive Disorder. You know what I mean, Inspector?'

Randall's answer was a heartfelt, 'I do.'

'Anyway, he dragged her out. But she was screaming she didn't have her slippers on and her feet would get dirty. Do you know what, Inspector?' Even more than forty years after the event her eyes showed her respect for the man who was now dead. 'He went straight back in with his breathing apparatus and brought out her slippers. Everybody cheered.' She laughed and Randall had the image of a nurse cheering a hero. Then her face grew sad. 'Isn't it awful to think that that fantastic man became the person who slagged me off in the middle of Shrewsbury, shouting abuse on a Saturday afternoon, saying I had murdered twenty-four people.' Her face had now changed. 'Twenty-four of my patients.' She looked pinched and unhappy. 'You see it wasn't just the fire, Inspector, it was all the people who were caught up in it. Quite a few patients had OCD and had to be persuaded to leave their beds without their slippers or their dressing gowns on. He couldn't go back for *all* their stuff. Others wouldn't leave because it wasn't morning yet. Plenty were too confused or sleepy to cooperate at all because of their medication. It was chaos.'

Monica Deverill gave him a sharp glance before continuing.

'Officially the fire was put down to a cigarette smouldering in a sofa in the day room which burst into flames. The day room was directly beneath the locked ward, Beech Ward.'

Randall nodded.

'Naturally the firemen were around the hospital quite a lot in the aftermath and I chatted a bit to William Barton. He made a few little hints to me that all was not *quite* as it had been presented, that the fire was not *exactly* an accident and that there had been a delay in raising the alarm.' Her face was frozen. 'He hinted at there being traces of an accelerant and made the comment that he was surprised at the speed and ferocity of the fire's spread. It unnerved me.'

Randall glanced at Talith and frowned.

Monica explained. 'I'd been in the day room earlier and had spilt a bottle of acetone – nail varnish remover – over the sofa. So when Fire Officer Barton started saying that an accelerant had been used, I knew that it was my acetone.' She made a face. 'I knew I'd get into terrible trouble so when I discovered the fire I tried to put it out myself instead of raising the alarm straight away. Everyone knew about the delay. It was mentioned in the press but only I knew about the acetone. Or at least not just me but William Barton too. He was going to take this information to the authorities.' She turned her head. 'Inspector Randall,' she said, 'I was terrified. It was strictly against the rules to have anything inflammable in the day room as there was an open fire. I would have lost my job if it had all come out. Even worse, I would have been held responsible for the loss of all those lives. That terrible night. Murder. I didn't know what to do. In the end I confided in him that I had *accidentally* spilt some stuff and that was why I'd tried to put the fire out myself. He said it needn't go any further.' Her eyes appealed to Randall for understanding. 'I couldn't have borne it, Inspector – all the headlines and stuff in the media blaming *me* for all those deaths when the images of bodies being brought out of a hospital ward were so graphic. I really could not have borne it,' she said again. 'I forgot about the whole thing once the enquiry and the inquests were over. And as the years passed I thought I was safe. But then six months or so ago I was out in the town, shopping in the Darwin Centre and I bumped into William. He was with a youth I took to be his grandson. I think he had some dementia because he started telling the boy that I was responsible for the famous Shelton fire where he had saved so many lives and had been decorated for bravery by the fire service. He was speaking in a really loud voice and people started stopping and listening. He called me a murderess. And then he told the boy my name and asked if I was still living in Sundorne which was where I'd been based at the time of the fire.' She shuddered. 'The boy looked at me with the sort of curious fascination you might give a Black Widow Spider on her wedding day. It gave me shivers down my spine. I was shaking by the time I got home. I felt more frightened than at any time since the fire. When I heard about what happened at Melverley Grange I just knew that boy, as he was the only one to survive, was responsible. But then he rang me,' she said, 'the afternoon of the appeal and told me he wanted money or he'd go to the newspapers and give them the full story about the Shelton fire. I knew that if I gave him money it would never stop. He would want more and more until I had nothing left. And then he'd go to the press. I wanted to disappear. But you can't do that when you have a family. I was also frightened he would torch my house. The date, Inspector. February the twenty-fourth – the anniversary of the Shelton fire.'

'Is that why you rang?'

She nodded. 'I wanted to tell you about him. But I couldn't say anything without implicating myself, could I? So it wouldn't have done any good. There was no point. I dread to think what else William said to the boy but even in the middle of the Darwin Shopping Centre on a Saturday afternoon he said some pretty awful things, describing the people locked in the ward that they were unable to reach in time, the charred bodies, the screaming, the sheer terror of that night. I put my hands over my ears but I could still hear him accusing me. The way that boy looked at me I knew he meant trouble. When Melverley Grange was burnt down I was really, really frightened. And then when he rang I panicked, took some money out of the building society and ran to a friend's house far away. She put my car in her garage and I felt safe. When I heard about my own house I knew I'd done the right thing.' Her eyes met Randall's. 'If I hadn't gone I would be dead.'

'Why didn't you confide in us?' Randall demanded. 'Keep your appointment?'

'I suppose because I bottled out. You're the police, aren't you?
If you had known about the spilt acetone and the reason I didn't
sound the alarm you might still hold me responsible.'

'But you couldn't have hidden for ever.'

'No. I realized that at some point I had to come out of hiding.
I suppose I sort of hoped that you'd arrest Jude. Then I'd be safe.
But nothing seemed to be happening. And James and Gordon
were getting increasingly annoyed with me and . . .'

Randall interrupted. 'How much do they know?'

'Very little. Not about the acetone. Only that I was on duty
the night of the fire and that Fire Officer Barton somehow blamed
me. In fact,' she said with a rueful smile, 'it's a relief that you've
found me. I don't know when I'd have emerged.'

Randall glanced at Talith. They had the story from Monica.
Now it was time to face Jude Barton and his father with the
truth. They arranged for her to be reunited with her disapproving
sons and sandwiches and a pot of tea be provided. The panacea
for all ills.

And so, again, now they faced the boy. Randall studied his face,
wondering at the psyche of the teenager who returned his gaze
with an air of defiance, throwing out a challenge to the
detective.

'Mrs Deverill, the missing nurse, has just arrived here, Jude,'
Randall began, watching for the boy's reaction. 'We know a little
bit more about the fire at Shelton Hospital where your grandfather
proved such a hero.'

'She started it,' Jude muttered. 'It was her fault.'

Randall affected ignorance. 'What do you mean exactly?'

Jude's eyes glittered with the fanaticism of someone watching
martyrs burn. 'She soaked the sofa with something inflammable,'
he said steadily. 'Deliberately.'

'Who told you that?'

'My grandfather. He told me the story.'

'Did he say it was done deliberately?'

Jude dropped his eyes, evading the question. 'He said she'd
hidden the off-duty rota,' he muttered, 'trying to pretend she wasn't
the nurse whose job it was to check the day room. The fire was
her fault and instead of calling the fire brigade she had a pretty

inept go at tackling the blaze herself.' He gave a smirk. 'As if,' he said.

Nigel Barton was watching his son with his mouth open and an expression both of growing horror and a sort of cowed acceptance.

'How do you know all this detail?' Randall asked Jude, already anticipating the inevitable answer.

Roberts was busily storing every tiny detail of the interview in his memory ready to relate to Flora. *Soaked the sofa with something inflammable.* He noted the father's stunned amazement, the boy's brazenness, Randall's cool questioning.

'Grandad told me that starting a fire isn't easy. And once it's got going it's even harder to put out.' Jude hesitated, as though wondering how much he should enlarge on this and gave a swift, checking glance at his father. 'We did the little fire in his room just for him to show me,' he said. 'That's when he told me that there had been an accelerant used in the Shelton fire. That it was deliberate murder, arson. He said he was the only one who knew it and what was more he knew who'd put it there. Who was responsible. And why. I asked him who and he said it was pretty obvious – the nurse in charge that night who'd put the lights out in the day room, turned the key to *lock in* the patients. Twenty-four people died in that fire, Inspector. Eleven were seriously injured. *Maimed.*' He said the word with a sickening relish. 'Grandad said that when they'd had the enquiry he could see that she was feeling pretty bad about something. It wasn't only delaying calling the fire service. It was all her bloody fault. He said he knew a guilty look when he saw one and there was something she wasn't telling and that's what it was. She finally confessed to him and asked him not to say anything. And he didn't – not for years. But then we bumped into her in the Darwin Centre and he told me. He told me everything.'

Randall's mind stopped dead. Monica Deverill had said the spilling of the acetone had been an accident. But if Jude's statement was a true version of his grandfather's story she had missed out something vital. Had it been deliberate? Was there something else?

He tracked back over her statement, searching for a black hole of lies but came up with nothing. On balance he was more inclined to believe Monica Deverill than the boy.

'Everyone knew she'd been the duty nurse but she hid the off-duty rota.' It was turning into a rant.

Randall frowned, unsure where this was leading. He leaned forward. 'You say your grandfather knew *why* Mrs Deverill would have deliberately set a fire at the hospital?'

'Well.' Jude was still trying to win his father over, but it wasn't working. He tried harder. 'Maybe she had an issue with the hospital authorities. Maybe . . .'

And Randall knew Jude Barton was running out of ideas. He was finding it hard to concentrate on the boy's words now and the hour was late. He decided to resume the interrogation in the morning. 'I think we'll leave it there for now, Jude,' he said. 'One of my officers will get you a drink and if you're hungry something to eat.'

Nigel spoke stiffly. 'So we're not free to go?'

'Not just yet, sir.' Randall spoke almost apologetically. 'We'll make you as comfortable as we can.'

Friday, 25 March, 8 a.m.

Monica, too, had spent the night at the station. She had no home to go to and had appeared happy to stay. Neither of her sons had offered to put her up. When they went in the next morning she was looking bright, surprisingly well rested and was cradling a large, plain white mug of tea. She looked up calmly and shrugged. 'I don't suppose my boys will ever forgive me,' she said. 'They're not terribly wonderful at understanding my point of view.' She sighed regretfully. 'But still . . .'

'The fire was years ago,' Randall said, sitting down opposite her. 'I don't really understand why Barton reacted as he did. Why now? And in that way?'

The question threw her. Randall could tell that she was wondering how to answer that question. In the end she came to a decision and gave a little smile. 'Remember I'm a nurse,' she said. 'And he appeared to have some dementia. He knew me all right but it was as though the intervening years had been erased, as though the entire event had happened yesterday. That's why he responded to me like that.'

'OK, it's an explanation.' Randall felt he would never fully understand dementia, what memories stood out bold, and what slipped away downstream. 'Let's go back to the enquiry after the fire. When did Mr Barton speak to you about his suspicions?'

She coloured. 'It was in the initial few days. We were all shocked and the patients disturbed. It was very difficult.'

Randall waited.

'I confided in him. When he started talking about an accelerant and looking for someone who'd started the fire deliberately I knew I had to stop him. I did convince him that it had all been a terrible accident but he mentioned the fire extinguisher they'd found. Inspector,' she said frankly, 'we all know what to do in the case of fire or suspected fire. Raise the alarm. We are not supposed to make any attempt to tackle it. But none of this was important until that day when we met in the Darwin Centre with his grandson.' She frowned. 'Then he said things that he hadn't even mentioned before, some of it not true.'

Randall interrupted. 'Like hiding the off-duty?'

'Yes,' she said. 'I couldn't believe it. I didn't know where he'd got that from. I didn't. There would have been no point. Everyone knew I was on duty that night.'

'But not everyone would know that you were the nurse responsible for checking the day room.'

Monica coloured.

Not quite so truthful, Randall thought. 'What were you doing with acetone anyway?'

For the first time Monica's eyes dropped away. She had no explanation. Randall let it ride – for now. He didn't mention the explanation Stella Moncrieff had given him. It could wait for now.

'When Jude rang me he demanded three thousand pounds. He told me to read the papers. He said the same would happen to me unless I coughed up.' Her face was anguished now. 'I read about the three deaths. So I had a choice, Inspector: pay up – for ever stay in my house and wait to smell the smoke – or go. I chose to go.'

'Why didn't you come straight to the police?'

Again her eyes slid away, then she answered softly. 'I was going to,' she said, 'but then I thought, would you believe me?'

Randall started to nod but checked himself. 'Well, we'd have looked into your story.'

'Would you? It would all have come out.' She gave a cynical harsh laugh. 'You know how the newspapers sensationalize things. They'd have made mincemeat of me.' She eyed Randall dubiously. 'I didn't want to be involved.'

'You could have saved us a lot of trouble.'

She gave him a sweet smile. 'I *was* responsible, Inspector. I didn't start the fire but I should have checked that no cigarettes were left burning. And it took hold because of me.' She thought for a minute, then added, 'If the Shelton fire hadn't happened, I don't think Melverley Grange would have burnt down. And if the Grange hadn't burnt down those two women and William wouldn't have died.'

There wasn't a lot Randall could say. He left the room with a feeling of depression. Time was running out. The PACE clock was ticking and he still hadn't broken Jude.

He entered the interview room without optimism and sat down opposite the boy, Talith at his side. But instead of speaking straight away, he was silent. Was it really possible that this slim, pale-faced boy had sent his mother, sister and grandfather to a hideous death? Even now he had his doubts. He linked his fingers and started. 'Tell me more about your grandfather,' he began.

As before Jude was eager to talk about his hero. His pale face lit as he spoke. 'He said that it wasn't as easy to set a fire as people thought. I asked him what about the Shelton fire and he told me that the nurse had set the fire herself.'

'What about the fire at your home in which your mother, sister and grandfather died?'

'It was my idea,' Jude said proudly. 'I just had to get my grandad to understand what excitement, what a coup it would be but it didn't go according to plan. It wasn't meant to happen like that.' He was frowning and his voice was tight with irritation.

Irritation? Randall thought. Irritation when he had condemned three members of his family to hideous deaths?

'How was it *supposed* to happen?'

Nigel Barton could hardly bear to look at his son. His hands on his lap had a slight tremor.

'The ladder,' Jude said, dropping his eyes. 'I was going to rescue them.' He frowned. 'But it didn't work out.'

'The stone through the window?'

Jude looked proud of himself. 'Made it look like an outside job.'

Randall didn't even bother to point out that no one could open a window when the glass was shattered. He had a feeling of unreality as he continued with his questions, a feeling that Jude's world was some nightmarish place. Not here. 'So what did go wrong?'

'The silly bitches had locked themselves in their rooms, as usual, so we couldn't rescue them.' Jude slapped his palm to his forehead in a gesture not of grief but of incredulity. 'Can you believe it?'

'Why did they do that?'

'After the fire six months ago they started locking their doors before they went to bed whenever Dad was away, so Grandpa couldn't hurt them. It just made it more of a challenge. But when we came up the stairs we couldn't get at them, even though we were yelling. Grandpa was going to save Addie and I was going to take Mum. We'd have been heroes. *I* would have been decorated like Grandpa.'

'But the fire took hold a lot quicker than you'd thought,' Randall prompted.

Jude gave a curt nod.

'And your grandfather . . .?'

'It was great. We ran up the stairs, shouting and screaming like in *Braveheart*.'

Randall pictured the old man, hardly understanding what on earth was happening, simply following his grandson's directions, arms outflung, pointing in the direction of his daughter-in-law and granddaughter's bedrooms, trying to reach them, some pathetic reliving of the 'good old days'. But Jude had known the doors were locked.

'And you couldn't persuade either of them to leave their rooms?'

The boy pouted. 'It was Grandpa's fault,' he said sulkily. 'He kept shouting and it frightened them. I had to bash him to try and keep him quiet.'

Randall couldn't bear to look at the crumpled defeat in Nigel

Barton's face. He looked crushed. Destroyed. 'Let's move on now,' he prompted. 'The nurse. You tried to get some money out of her.'

Jude looked sly. 'It seemed a good idea,' he said. 'In the end it was all her fault. Why shouldn't she pay?'

Why indeed? was Randall's distorted response. In a crazy world, why shouldn't the nurse who had accidentally started a fire pay three grand to someone who knew her little secret, was prepared to blackmail her and murder three members of his family?

'Why did your grandfather die?'

'He was an old man,' the boy said contemptuously. 'He was overcome with the smoke. He couldn't move fast enough. And he was muddled. I'd have thought he could have found his way in the smoke as a firefighter.'

That was forty years ago and you bashed him over the head, Randall thought, but said nothing. 'But *you* could have saved him.' He felt he had to enter the distorted world of Jude Barton and reason with him in his own language. 'You could have saved him with a fireman's lift.'

The boy bit his lip. 'He might have—' he blurted out, glanced at his father and the two officers and changed his story to, 'I did try.'

No one in the room believed him. They knew what he had been about to say, that the old man, in his simple state, might well have blurted out the entire plot.

Randall had stopped listening. His mind was going through the details, trying to make sense of it all. The women had locked themselves *inside* their rooms so Jude and William could not rescue them as planned. But Jude had tried, which was when he'd sustained the burns to his hands.

He allowed his mind to wander and fill in the colour background. Jude Barton had been fed these fantastic stories of heroism by his grandfather who had told him tales of fires and bravery awards, of dramatic rescues, and had embellished the Shelton fire with a story that only he knew – that one of the nurses had spilt nail varnish remover on the very sofa where a cigarette smouldered and then, instead of ringing the fire alarm she had tried to contain the fire herself which had done no good at all, merely set up a delay which had allowed the fire to spread. Fate then that Jude had been with his grandfather on that chance encounter. That had led to 'The Big Idea'. They had waited for Nigel to be away from home otherwise the plan could not have worked. And so that fatal encounter, in the Darwin Centre, had led to the loss of a family. Randall was struck with another thought. William Barton had kept quiet about the Shelton story until dementia had released his inhibitions and judgement. His status with his grandson had then been elevated from doddery ancient to youthful hero. But he had not known his grandson. Not really. Randall looked at the boy and wondered. Was he mad? Bad? Or both?

TWENTY-TWO

Monica Deverill was released to the mercies of her two sons. Randall watched the three of them drive away in their separate cars, heading for James's house for a family council of war. He would love to have been a fly on the wall when they ticked her off. Which son would prove the most forgiving? he wondered.

Two hours later he was sitting in Martha's office, relating the entire saga to her. 'What a story,' she said when he'd finished. 'And what a tragedy. I suppose Jude will have to be examined by a psychiatrist to determine his state of mind. Perhaps the old man had too much influence over him. He was young and vulnerable and believed the stories. He would appear to have a complete lack of reality, understanding and empathy. A very distorted mind. And as William was demented he must have fantasized over past events, embellishing and exaggerating them so, to the rather strange boy, he appeared a superhero.' She smiled. 'Though why his father didn't spot it, I really don't know. Particularly after that first fire.'

'Wrapped up in his business,' Randall hesitated, 'and his secretary.'

Martha nodded.

'I still don't really know what Monica Deverill was doing with the acetone.'

'Well,' Martha said, 'doing a bit of detective work and feeding in what we know of her nothing to do with nail varnish, I suspect.'

Randall waited, sure she would supply the answer.

Which she did. 'Plaster marks,' Martha supplied enigmatically. 'Almost certainly she was removing plaster marks from a patient's arm. It's just the sort of thing you'd do in the day room. Psychiatric patients are sometimes nervous of any sort of physical contact. At a guess that's what she was doing and how it got spilt, patient jogged her arm.'

'But why not say?'

'She's the sort of woman who would carry guilt like Christ's cross. She wouldn't even try to mitigate herself.'

'I see – partially anyway.'

'Ask her,' she suggested. 'Oh, those poor women, Alex – and William. And, of course, the people who suffered in Shelton that night.'

Randall looked up. 'Suffered? Oh, you mean the fire.'

She nodded. 'Not just that. I was thinking of the patient faced with what must have been a dramatic blaze wailing because she didn't have her slippers on. People with OCD suffer, not with physical pain, but with mental pain. It's suffering all the same.'

'I know only too well.'

Martha held her breath and waited for Alex Randall to continue.

'I perhaps should tell you this,' he said, not looking at her. 'My wife suffers from OCD.'

She knew this confidence was a huge step forward in their relationship. DI Randall was a notoriously private man.

'She finds it hard to do things except in a specific way,' he added.

As before Martha didn't comment. She knew now he had begun to confide in her it was better she simply listened.

Alex looked at her. 'They've tried cognitive behavioural therapy,' he said, 'and various medications which practically knock her out. Nothing works.' He paused, swallowed. 'And she's getting worse. Fortunately we live in Church Stretton. She's under a consultant in Hereford and a specialist in Birmingham but –'

He left it at that.

Martha put a hand on his arm. 'I'm so sorry, Alex,' she said.

'She's quite tortured,' he said quietly. 'She's attempted suicide more than once. One of these days . . .'

Did she imagine a question in those deep eyes?

Friday, 25 March, 8.30 p.m.

She studied Simon Pendlebury surreptitiously.

Simon met her eyes, sat down, carefully adjusting the knees of his suit trousers. 'What are you smirking about, Martha Gunn?'

She could answer him truthfully. 'I was thinking about Jocasta and Armenia.'

He raised his eyebrows and peered at her. 'Ah,' he said. 'And what exactly were you thinking about them?'

She could be frank with him. 'That they will never take kindly to a stepmother, Simon.'

Simon's lips tightened. He looked angry and sulky. The well-known thunderclouds were forming. 'You think they will condemn me to a life of celibacy?'

Again she felt she could knock down any barriers between them because she didn't care enough. 'I don't think they'll mind you having sex, Simon – they just don't want you to marry again. They'll be suspicious that the woman is simply after your money.'

He looked peeved. 'Do you think I'm so very unattractive?'

She didn't even attempt to answer this one, merely bounced the question straight back to him with a facial expression and a shrug. *What do you think?*

She had driven herself in to the town and parked right outside Drapers' Hall. They finished their meal with plenty more friendly banter. Driving home Martha reflected that they were friends and would never be anything more than that. The chaste kiss he had given her on their parting defined the borders of their relationship. But now she realized she did like him. And this was the first time she had ever admitted it. In fact, it was an enormous step forwards. She smiled at herself, catching her eyes in the rear-view mirror and tempted to wink.

So now she bounced the very same question back to herself. *Do you think I'm so very unattractive?*

TWENTY-THREE

I t was mid-April before Martha held the inquests on the deaths of the three members of the Barton family. Predictably it was attended by the press and many others. Alex had told her privately that Jude was still being assessed by a mental health team who could not agree as to whether he was fit to plead.

'Personally I think he has a personality disorder,' he said. 'In which case he will manipulate the psychiatrists and they will never agree.'

There had been no more shared confidences but somehow Martha didn't think that Alex regretted the one time he had confided in her. If anything his manner seemed easier with her and he dropped in even more frequently, staying a little longer. She never asked after his wife but realized she didn't need to. The days he wore his haunted, unhappy expression were his wife's bad days; the others less so. She smiled and teased him a little. 'And what are you basing this diagnosis on, Alex?'

'He starts talking rubbish, fantasizing and saying odd things only when he remembers and when plenty of the right people are around. The rest of the time he's pretty normal. The officers at the remand centre all say that. He's clever, knows what to say to make people think he's crazy. But –' He held up his index finger. 'When I said to him that he could be consigned to Broadmoor for life it made him think. He isn't crazy, Martha, he's evil.'

'That makes the tragedy all the worse.'

Alex nodded.

In Martha's mind the verdict of the three deaths was never in any doubt – two homicides and one misadventure and once the witnesses, mainly Mark Randall, the pathologist, and fire personnel had given their evidence everyone in the room looked satisfied with the verdict.

Nigel Barton sat on the front row, shrunken and miserable, a young woman beside him – the secretary, presumably. Occasionally she touched his hand but he continued to stare at the floor, his shoulders bowed. Martha didn't think the relationship between these two would be a particularly happy one. Its foundations were set in too dark a place.

Three rows behind him DI Randall pointed out Monica Deverill flanked by two still very angry-looking men.

He leaned across. 'Her sons,' he said.

Martha had struggled to decide whether she should mention the roots of the fatal arson attack and resurrect the Shelton fire of the sixties. She and Alex had discussed this at length. In some ways it would be inappropriate yet in others the case made no sense at all if the fire at Shelton was left out. There were Monica Deverill's feelings to be considered. But the press were already making the connection between the fire at Sundorne and the Melverley Grange tragedy. Martha made her decision and summed up the evidence. 'Three family members died in one night in a house fire which was started deliberately. One of the people who died that night had been a fire officer who attended the fire at Shelton Hospital in 1968 which resulted in twenty-four people dying in a locked ward. I don't need to give you a full resumé of the story except to tell you that the two recent fires and the Shelton fire are linked.'

The woman Alex Randall had identified as Monica Deverill shifted uncomfortably in her seat.

Martha resumed her summing up. 'These deaths have some explanation in mental illness – initially a fire where people died because they had been incarcerated consequent of some abnormality in their psyche and more recently William Barton, an old man diagnosed with dementia, who reminisced about his brave role in the Shelton Hospital fire as a fire officer. William Barton was decorated for his consideration of the patients and his bravery on that night.' She paused. 'And now I want to make a point.' She looked around the room. 'Not to make a dogmatic statement but to provoke thought. Most of the people who were locked in Beech Ward on the night of February the twenty-fourth, 1968 would almost certainly be out in the community today.' She frowned. 'And perhaps, when you think of those events, in some ways they would have been safer.' She smiled. 'We like to believe we are more enlightened these days. But there is a tendency today to despise care in the community, the cynical amongst us wondering whether it is simply a cost-cutting exercise. As I see it the reason we are so scathing about care in the community is because when something goes wrong everyone knows about it, whereas in a mental institution it all takes place behind closed doors. Much of what happened was concealed. Well, now it is all out in the open.'

AUTHOR'S NOTE

On the twenty-fourth February, 1968 there was a major fire at Shelton Psychiatric Hospital on Beech Ward, a locked or closed ward for very disturbed females. Twenty-four people died and eleven were seriously injured. Due to overcrowding some beds had been placed 'top to tail' along the window wall. All patients sleeping in those beds died of asphyxia and carbon monoxide poisoning. The severely disturbed patients who were locked into single bedrooms survived because they slept on the floor, on mattresses for their own safety, behind thick wooden doors. There were forty-three female patients resident on Beech Ward the night of the fire.

Although the ward had open fires it was not believed that this was the cause, but a lighted cigarette smouldering in a chair for some time before igniting.

Patients were led to safety via the fire escape with difficulty as many were heavily sedated due to their mental state. Others were bedridden.

Several members of staff were subsequently awarded bravery medals. It appeared they were heroes.

Newspaper articles, however, painted a slightly different picture. A report in 1963 by the Shropshire Fire Service was clear that nurses should be trained in fire procedure but this was found to be lacking. It recognized a delay of ten minutes between the night nurse in charge first noticing smoke and then calling the fire brigade, although there were other factors beyond her control. The report also found the level of staffing at the hospital to be low. Locking patients into their ward was not unusual – although the 1959 Mental Health Act called for this to be avoided as much as possible.

Fire safety procedures at hospitals in the Midlands were reviewed after the Shelton fire. Hospitals today have learnt much about fire safety checks. The Shelton fire is a dreadful and tragic fact.

This story is pure fiction.